The Life She Dreams

A GRANITE SPRINGS NOVEL

Maggie Christensen

To my long-time friend, Jane,
who inspired me to start writing fiction.

Also by Maggie Christensen

Oregon Coast Series
The Sand Dollar
The Dreamcatcher
Madeline House

Sunshine Coast books
A Brahminy Sunrise
Champagne for Breakfast

Sydney Collection
Band of Gold
Broken Threads
Isobel's Promise
A Model Wife

Scottish Collection
The Good Sister
Isobel's Promise
A Single Woman

Granite Springs
The Life She Deserves
The Life She Chooses
The Life She Wants
The Life She Finds
The Life She Imagines
A Granite Springs Christmas
The Life She Creates
The Life She Regrets

Check out the last page of this book to see how to join my mailing list and get a free download of one of my books.

Prologue

It was a cold day, the sort of weather that made Liz Pender want to stay home and curl up with a cup of hot chocolate and a good book. But she couldn't do that. Her job as senior librarian in the elite girls' school in Canberra meant she had to brave the weather and front up to meet her students.

She sighed and dragged herself out of bed. She missed Dan so much. Maybe there would be an email from him today, or perhaps he'd manage to spare a moment to call her.

When she'd met the handsome Duntroon army cadet, Liz had been impressed by his uniform and confident manner. They married only a year later and after various moves around the country, settled here in Canberra when Dan accepted the role as training officer at the Australian Defence Force Academy.

It was a dream come true to return to her hometown, close to her parents and sister. Ailsa was married too now, to a teacher, and they had two boys. Liz couldn't wait till she and Dan started their own family. But, for now, she had to make do with her nephews and the girls she taught every day.

They'd only been in Canberra a short time, and Liz and Dan were talking about starting a family, when one of his friends from the academy returned from Afghanistan badly injured. It preyed on Dan's mind so much that he decided to seek deployment. Now he'd been gone for over six months with no end in sight.

She paused for a moment, her hand on the coffee maker, and gazed out the window at the grey Canberra sky. She remembered that day as if it was yesterday. They'd been sitting on the sofa enjoying a glass of red wine. Dan had put down his glass, his face becoming serious. He had taken both of Liz's hands in his, his thumbs circling the backs of her hands.

'I put in a request for a deployment. It's come through. Afghanistan,' he said, not quite meeting her eyes.

'But…' Liz's stomach started to churn.

'It's something I need to do, babe. I can't keep training these guys to go out there, while I stay safe here in Canberra. You'll be right, and I'll be back before you know it.'

It had been hard, but Liz supposed she'd known what she was taking on when she married a soldier. Dan's patriotism and loyalty were two of the qualities she'd admired in him. Those and his loving ways. Dan was a romantic at heart and often arrived home to surprise her with gifts of flowers or chocolates.

She missed him so much but tried to keep busy, hoping it would make the time go faster. She sighed and continued to make breakfast. The toast had just popped up and the coffee machine was gurgling and hissing when the doorbell rang.

Liz opened the door to see the uniformed man and woman at the door.

Her heart plummeted.

One

Marmaduke rubbed himself around Liz's ankles and meowed as if he knew today was important to her. She bent down to pick up the large ginger cat who was her sole companion and cuddled him tightly.

When she moved to Granite Springs almost twenty years ago, her only thought was to get away from Canberra, away from all the reminders of Dan and their life together there, from all the sympathy of well-meaning friends and colleagues and from the city that had come to symbolise all she'd lost.

It was exactly twenty years ago today that her life fell apart, when the two army officers arrived on her doorstep to give her the news. Dan's death, when the vehicle he was travelling in struck a landmine, put an end to all her dreams and forced her to reconsider her future.

Granite Springs hadn't been her first choice. Initially, when she decided to leave Canberra, it had been the south coast which had drawn her. Then her old friend, Judy, had invited her to visit, and Liz, worn out from trying to cope with her mountain of grief, arrived in Granite Springs for a weekend. Although Judy and her husband, Alec, lived on an acreage, it was the town itself with its wide streets, clean air and friendly inhabitants, that found a place in Liz's heart.

It was strange how Granite Springs wrapped itself around her. Without any hesitation, she decided to stay. At first, she found part-time work in the local library. Then, when Dan's death gratuity and the payout from his life insurance came through, she'd made the decision to fulfil one of her long-held dreams and open a bookshop.

3

Now she couldn't imagine living anywhere else.

Marmaduke meowed and wriggled in Liz's arms, interrupting her memories.

'All right, possum,' she said, setting him down before going into the tiny kitchen attached to the shop and filling a bowl of water for him. Although she had a comfortable home with a good-sized backyard, the cat preferred to be with her during the day. He behaved as if the bookshop was his own private territory and managed to charm her customers, especially the children.

The Reading Corner, located on a corner of Main Street in Granite Springs, was Liz's haven, her home away from home. It was where she and the large ginger cat spent their days, where Granite Springs' locals knew they'd find a friendly ear, and where a new generation of children discovered a love of books.

Having taken care of Marmaduke's needs, Liz made herself a cup of peppermint tea and began to unpack one of the boxes of books which had arrived the day before. This was one of her favourite tasks, the smell of the new books wafting up from their packing, the books themselves just waiting to be placed on shelves. She'd love to read every one of them, but there weren't enough hours in the day.

Liz tossed her hair across her shoulders, its red tints still bright despite her approaching fiftieth birthday. Where had the years gone? She grinned to herself, remembering how she and Dan had mocked their own parents as being old when they were only in their fifties.

As she was thinking of her parents, Liz's mobile rang, and she saw her mother's number. Dan's parents had passed away, but Liz's always remembered the anniversary of his death.

'How are you, dear?' Liz's mother's voice was filled with the usual concern.

Liz could picture her mother, her eyes reflecting the anxiety Liz knew the older woman felt for her, even after all this time. Sheila Browne might be in her seventies, but she had lost none of the vibrancy of her youth and always reached out to Liz on this day.

'I'm okay, Mum. How are you and Dad?' Liz's Dad had recently undergone a hip replacement and, when they'd last met, had been chafing at the bit, eager to get back to his usual routine. Always an active man, he didn't take kindly to being housebound.

'You know your dad.' Her mother huffed. 'He doesn't make for the best invalid. But he's able to get around more now and should soon be back to his old self. But what about you, dear. How are you feeling today? I know it's not easy for you.'

Liz sighed. She appreciated her mother calling, if only she'd stop going on about it.

'I'm good,' she said, then, 'Sorry I haven't been able to get to see you recently,' in an attempt to change the subject. She bit her lip, knowing she really had no excuse. But she still hated to visit Canberra with all its memories, preferring her parents visit her in Granite Springs.

'I know, darling. We'll be on the road as soon as. Do try to have a good day, won't you?'

'I will, Mum. Thanks.'

Liz ended the call and returned to opening boxes, tearing off the packing tape with more force than was necessary. Why did her mother's sympathetic words have the effect of annoying her? Maybe everything would annoy her today.

Liz knew she should make the effort to drive over to Canberra to see her parents, visit Dan's grave, maybe even catch up with a few old friends. But it was easier to remain here cocooned in Granite Springs, in her bookshop, with her cat.

She had finished her unpacking, served several customers, helped a young boy find the latest Treehouse book by Andy Griffiths, and was setting up a new window display when a familiar face walked in.

'Hi, Judy!'

'Liz. I knew it was Dan's anniversary and thought you might want some company.' She pulled Liz into a warm hug.

'Thanks, Judy.' Liz always felt humbled in her friend's company. Only a couple of years earlier, Judy had been diagnosed with breast cancer and there had been doubts about her recovery. But she'd remained positive through several rounds of chemotherapy and was now cancer free. The whole episode had made Liz grateful for her own good health, as well as being pleased for her friend's recovery.

'Can you take time for coffee? I'd love to have a chat. I have some news.' Her eyes twinkled indicating the news was good.

A quick check of the time showed Liz it was close to eleven. She'd been so busy all morning she hadn't taken a break. 'Sure,' she said, 'I'm not likely to get any customers before lunch now, and I can stick a note on the door. Give me a sec.'

She dashed into the back shop to freshen up her hair and lipstick, then, telling Marmaduke he was in charge till she got back, joined Judy again. 'I'm ready. Shall we go to The Bean Sprout?' she asked, naming their favourite coffee spot on the opposite side of Main Street and a few doors down.

'Now, what's the news? I can see you're bursting to tell me,' Liz asked when they'd been served with cappuccino for Liz and a flat white for Judy.

'We're having a baby!'

Liz's mouth dropped open. A baby? Judy was the same age as she was, and she and Alec hadn't been able to have children. It had been the one blot in an otherwise happy marriage, but they'd remained positive. Then, when Alec's nephew, Neil, decided to join them on the farm, it was almost as if he was their own son.

'Not me, stupid. Neil and Sally. And young Daisy's thrilled at the idea of being a big sister.'

'Remind me. Daisy's Neil's daughter, isn't she?' Liz had a vague recollection of Judy and Alec's nephew having been married to a woman who hated living in a country town and had fled back to the city, and there had been a child.

'That's right. She's ten now and quite a character. Neil and Sally are hoping to see more of her now her mother is remarried. I think there may be some issues there.' She tapped the side of her nose.

'Well, you must be pleased about the baby news,' Liz said, realising it was something she should have said right away. Even though Judy hadn't given birth to Neil or Sally, they were family. The only family Liz had were her parents, her sister and her two nephews. It wasn't the life she'd dreamt of when she and Dan married.

Judy didn't appear to notice her hesitation. 'Oh, we're tickled pink. It'll be so lovely to have a little one growing up on Wooleton. Alec and I had hoped...' For a second, her eyes clouded over. 'But this is the next best thing. We won't be the grandparents, of course, we'll just be Aunt Jude and Uncle Alec, but we'll have the joy of seeing the new bub every day.'

For a moment, Liz envied her friend, envied her happy marriage, her life on the family acreage called Wooleton, her ability to find the best in everything. Then she gave herself a mental shake. She might not be living the life she'd dreamt of, but she loved what she had, her bookshop, Marmaduke, her own home to which she could retreat and shut out the rest of the world. It was a lot more than many people had. She should be grateful and count her blessings.

'Finished, ladies?'

Liz looked up to see the café's owner standing by their table. Frank Beattie had lived in Granite Springs all his life, taking over the café when his father died. Usually cheerful, today Frank's forehead was creased in a frown.

'Is something the matter, Frank?' Liz asked.

'You mean you haven't heard?'

'Heard what?'

'The development plans for the other side of Main Street.'

Liz felt a chill run up her spine. The Reading Corner was on the other side of Main Street. What was Frank talking about?

Seeing her confusion, Frank drew up a chair and, looking around to check no one was listening, leant his elbows on the table. 'It came up at the council meeting last night. I heard it from Col Ford who heard it from Gordon Slater.'

Liz almost smiled, perhaps would have, if the topic of conversation had been different. Granite Springs might have grown in the last twenty years, but news still got around fast.

'Don't keep us in suspense,' Judy said, leaning forward.

'Well, it seems one of those big conglomerates wants to buy up a couple of blocks, redevelop them to build a supermarket and café/restaurant with flats above. It would spoil the look of the town and wouldn't do my business any good.'

'Which blocks?' Liz couldn't stifle the shiver of fear. She owned her shop. But she knew most of the neighbouring properties were owned by a large agricultural company and leased to the current tenants. She'd poured not only her money but her heart and soul into her book shop. She couldn't bear to lose it. But if the owner of the other shops was willing to sell to the developers, what choice would she have?

Two

'I don't know what to do, Dad.'

Sam Walker looked across his desk at the tall dark-haired man slumped in the chair opposite, the image of himself twenty years earlier. He didn't know what to say. He and his son weren't given to emotional outpourings. This was the first time Mitch had given Sam any indication his marriage wasn't happy. Brooke wouldn't have been Sam's first choice for his easy-going son, but he'd thought perhaps her managing ways might spur the lad into action.

It seemed it had. In the past six years, Mitch, who'd previously floated from job to job after his degree in IT, had secured a position with one of the top five accounting firms and was well on the way to a promotion.

'Thing is, Dad. She's thrown me out.' The young man dragged a hand through his already dishevelled hair. 'It was when I said I'd refused the promotion. She lost it, ranted and raved about the years she'd wasted on me. I thought she loved me,' he said, a note of disbelief in his voice.

'Have you spoken to your mum?'

'No way! She'd take Brooke's side. They've always got on well. Mum never understood me, not like you did.'

'Tell me again why you refused the promotion.'

Mitch let his hands drop between his knees and stared down at them. 'I don't really know. Suddenly it seemed as if it was all closing in on me. I didn't want to be there. It seemed as if all I'd done for the past six years was dance to someone else's tune. I wanted to do something for myself, something different. I told Brooke that, hoping she'd understand. But...' he shook his head, '...she blew up, said I wasn't the man she thought I was. Odd, because I wasn't working there when we met.'

'What about Abi?' Sam's granddaughter was almost six and the apple of his eye.

Mitch looked up, his eyes filling with tears. 'She won't let me see her.'

'Well, we can soon fix that.' Sam knew most courts would award Mitch visiting rights with his daughter at least. 'Where are you staying at the moment?' It was mid-week, a workday. Mitch should be in Canberra, in his office, not here in Granite Springs pouring out his heart to his father.

'I'm not... that is... I have my gear in the car. When Brooke told me it was over, she didn't want to waste her time on a no-hoper like me, I saw red. I resigned. I'm out of work and homeless, Dad. Maybe she was right about me. Maybe I am useless, and I needed someone like her to help me make something of myself.'

Sam sighed. He'd thought when his son grew up, his parenting days were over, but here he was, Mitch seeking his help again. 'Seems like you need somewhere to stay while you work out what to do next. How about I give you a key and you can bunk with me for the time being?'

'Thanks, Dad.' Mitch's face mirrored his relief. 'I'll get myself sorted out soon. I just need a bit of time.'

After Sam handed over his key and watched his son leave, he found it difficult to get back to work. When he'd moved here from Canberra the previous year, it had been in the firm belief his son was settled. After a career as a political journalist, Sam was burnt out. This position, as editor of The Granite Springs Advertiser had been a godsend. It had also enabled him to fulfil his dream to live on an acreage. He now possessed twenty acres on the outskirts of town, on the edge of broad acres, and was gradually learning how to manage them, planning to become one of the hobby farmers often ridiculed by the local farming community.

Unable to concentrate on the editorial for the next edition of the paper, Sam closed up his computer and told his assistant he was going for coffee. His one journalist, Jason, was out interviewing today and wouldn't be back till late, and Tim, the photographer who often doubled as another journalist, was with him.

Out in the fresh air, Sam drew in a deep breath. He was glad he'd made the move from the city. Here, he could breathe, there was space, fresh air, and the natives were friendly. He thought back to his first foray into the social life of the town, soon after he arrived. He'd been attracted to a woman he met at a dinner party, but while they enjoyed each other's company, the relationship had come to naught. Sam wasn't averse to meeting someone and knew that, at his age, it wasn't as easy as it had been in his twenties when he and Olga got together at uni. But it would be good to have someone to share his new life with.

Heading for The Bean Sprout Café, his favourite coffee spot, and not far from the office, he ordered his usual long black. Then he settled down by the window where he could watch the world go by and digest what Mitch had told him.

He also needed to consider what he'd heard at the council meeting the night before. To his surprise, there had been a heated discussion about a proposal to redevelop the opposite side of Main Street. Looking out at the existing buildings – the hairdressers, the newsagency, the pharmacy and the bookshop, which he had still to visit, Sam could sympathise with those who spoke out forcibly against the scheme.

'You were there?' Frank Beattie placed Sam's coffee on the table, leant back on his heels and folded his arms.

Sam knew what he was talking about. 'The council meeting. Yes. Caused a fair bit of debate. The new mayor seems to be in favour.'

'Gordon Slater would be in favour of anything that might line his pockets,' Frank said, his lips tightening. 'But I'm glad to hear there was some opposition. What was the outcome? I only heard about it third hand.'

'No decision as yet. It's been sent back to the planning committee.'

'Right.' Frank seemed to be trying to work something out. 'What's the Advertiser's view?'

Sam chuckled, glad to have his mind taken off his son. 'The Advertiser doesn't have a view. We provide fair and unbiased reporting of local events.'

'But you do have an opinion piece in your editorial.' It was Frank's turn to chuckle.

'You got me there.' That was exactly what Sam had been tussling with when Mitch appeared at his door.

'Well, if you need any help, don't hesitate to ask. I'd hate to see Granite Springs Main Street turn into a carbon copy of what's been happening in the cities. All the old neighbourhoods are disappearing, to be replaced by modern monstrosities.'

Sam smiled. It was easy to see where Frank's loyalties lay.

But once he was alone again, Sam's thoughts returned to his son. This was a turn up, quite unexpected. They hadn't seen as much of each other since Mitch and Brooke married. At first, it seemed she was thrilled to be related to the well-known Canberra journalist. But it soon became clear that his left-wing views didn't sit well with her friends, and invitations to dinner became few and far between. He and Mitch had met a few times for lunch or a drink after work, but those times had dropped off too.

When little Abi was born, Sam had made more of an effort, wanting to form a bond with his granddaughter. At first it worked, and Sam became a frequent visitor. But after a time, when it was clear his visits were unwelcome, and Brooke always seemed to have another engagement for the little girl, he'd all but given up. Brooke and Olga were good friends and Sam knew his ex had done her best to turn Brooke against him. Now, who knew when he'd see Abi again? At least Mitch had been almost grown when Sam's own marriage had broken down.

Now his son needed him again, but Sam didn't know what he could do this time. There were some things even a dad couldn't fix.

Three

It was over for another year. Liz closed the door behind her and gave a sigh of relief. Would she ever forget the sinking feeling she had when she saw the two uniforms on her doorstep? Just thinking about it made her run cold, and twenty years had passed since then.

Her parents had been wonderful. Her mother rushed to her side and fussed over her so much she wanted to scream. But it had been good of her. Liz fell apart, couldn't face going to work, couldn't face anything or anyone. For two weeks, she'd remained in bed hoping against hope it had been a mistake. Hoping Dan would suddenly appear as if nothing had happened, tell her it had been a dreadful blunder, and life would go on as it had before. But deep down, she knew that wasn't going to happen.

Then his remains had been brought back. She'd stood with her parents and other widows and bereaved families to watch the coffins covered in the Australian flag being unloaded from the plane. In a tiny part of her brain, she wondered exactly what was in Dan's coffin. If he'd been blown up by an incendiary device surely... She didn't want to go there. Instead, she imagined it was the Dan she knew, but pale and still, who lay in the coffin which bore his name.

Somehow, she survived the ordeal and the ensuing funeral, her parents and Dan's by her side, his mother weeping copiously. Liz had no tears. She'd shed them all in the weeks leading up to this event. Perhaps Kathleen Pender thought her heartless, but her own mother understood. She'd been there to see Liz's grief, to encourage her to get out of bed, to eat and drink, to keep alive when all she wanted was to die, too.

Then she received Judy's letter. It was almost lost amongst all the letters and cards of condolence, but it was exactly what Liz needed. While most friends and acquaintances were eager to express their sorrow at her loss, Judy understood. She knew Liz needed to get away. The weekend at Wooleton morphed into two weeks, at the end of which Liz had decided to stay and make this small country town home. Sometimes, she still dreamt of what her life might have been like if Dan hadn't died, but as the years passed, these times became fewer and fewer.

'And I have you now, too,' she said to the cat who rubbed himself against her ankles. Finding Marmaduke had been a serendipity, a bit like everything else that had happened to her in Granite Springs. He was one of a litter Judy and her husband had discovered in their barn. There had been no sign of the mother and the two ginger kittens were so gorgeous. Liz had fallen in love as soon as she saw Marmaduke, and an old woman from town gave a home to the other.

Liz had finished dinner and was treating herself to a glass of wine, Marmaduke purring happily at her feet, when her mobile rang.

She recognised the number. It belonged to Peta Beattie, a new friend who had arrived in Granite Springs just over a year ago and was now married to Frank Beattie who owned The Bean Sprout Café. 'Hi, Peta.'

'Liz. How are you? Frank said you were in the café today, and he told you about the development plans.' There was an awkward pause. 'You hadn't heard?'

'No.' And she'd tried to put it out of her mind, tried to ignore the feeling of despair at the thought of losing what she'd built here, tried to pretend it wasn't going to happen. 'I don't tend to keep abreast of council business.'

'But this could affect you.' Peta's voice rose. 'Frank thinks we should do something about it. Get together a protest group or something.'

'I know that!' Liz felt a spurt of anger. While the memory of what Frank had said still had the power to send a shiver down her spine, Liz almost laughed at the indignation in Peta's voice. They'd met soon after Peta came to town with her granddaughter in tow. Back then, she was shy and retiring, recovering from a trauma in Sydney, when she walked into The Reading Corner with her granddaughter. The little girl had fallen in love with Marmaduke and now, through an unusual set of circumstances, his brother Archie had become her pet.

Peta had gone through a lot, both before coming here, and in gaining the right to keep her granddaughter with her. Now, it seemed, she was ready to go in to bat for Liz's right to retain her shop.

'I still haven't got my head around it, Peta. I feel numb just thinking about it.' She tried to stifle her anger but couldn't subdue the sinking feeling in her stomach. 'Do you know where the planning proposal is up to?'

'Not really. But Frank says it's been sent back to some committee, so there's still time to stop it if we act soon enough.'

Liz sighed. It sounded as if it promised to be a long, drawn-out battle, one she had no desire to be part of. But she didn't want to lose her shop, and it was unlikely the developers would be willing to include a bookshop in their plans. Given the fate of many bookshops these days, it was unlikely. Liz had been lucky. She had a loyal group of customers and her regular storytelling for the littlies. Plus, the book clubs for the school age children were very popular and drew in lots of the young mums.

'What can we do, Peta?' Energised by another bolt of anger, Liz knew she was prepared to go into battle if it meant she could save The Reading Corner. It wasn't anything she'd anticipated happening. Since living in Granite Springs, she'd become accustomed to a quiet life, one without any ructions. But that could change in a flash. 'How can I get more information?' Her stomach churned at the thought of her livelihood disappearing with the stroke of a pen.

'Why don't you come to dinner tomorrow night? It'll just be us and probably my cousin Ann and her new man. He's pretty cluey with technology and could be useful. Lily would love to see you again, too. She's been badgering me to bring her to The Reading Corner.'

'She should join one of the book clubs,' Liz said without thinking, then wondered how long they'd be able to continue if this proposal went ahead. 'She loves books and I'm sure she'd enjoy discussing them.'

'Yes, she's talked about the clubs. But there never seems to be enough time. I don't know where time goes to. When I came to

Granite Springs, I thought it was a sleepy little country town. How wrong I was. There's always something happening. Now this. You will come, won't you?'

'Thanks, Peta. I'll be there.'

'We'll see you at seven.' Peta hung up.

Liz was left wondering exactly what she'd let herself in for, and what a few Granite Springs locals could do against a big developer. But it would be good to see Peta again, and Lily. She was a lovely child, bright as a button and an avid reader. Liz couldn't think why she hadn't already joined one of the book clubs. She and the Tait twins were thick as thieves. They'd never joined either, preferring more outdoor pursuits. Maybe that was the reason.

*

The next day passed in a flash. The shop was so busy, Liz barely had time to turn around, with no break to go out for coffee, and forced to eat her lunch in the back shop in a brief lull between customers.

All too soon it was time to close up and head for home. Once there, she had a quick shower and changed into a fresh pair of pants and sweater, ensured Marmaduke had plenty of food and water and set off for dinner with Peta and Frank.

'Good to see you,' Peta greeted her at the door. 'Come in. Ann and Chris are already here.'

'I brought this.' Liz handed Peta the bottle of wine she'd taken from her wine rack before leaving. 'And I have a little something for Lily.'

'Thanks. You shouldn't have. Lily!' Peta called over her shoulder. 'I think she's feeding Archie. She's been good about looking after him.'

'What is it, Grandma?' The girl appeared from behind Peta and smiled at Liz. 'Hello, Ms Pender. Mum said you were coming to dinner. How's Marmaduke?'

'He's very well, thank you. I have something for you.' She handed Lily one of The Reading Corner bags.

'Oooh! Is this…?' She opened the bag and pulled out a copy of Karen McManus' latest book, *The Cousins*. 'How did you know?' She beamed, clutching the book to her chest. 'I love her earlier books. Thank you, thank you!'

'I seem to remember you were waiting for this one. It came in an order this week.' Liz was thrilled with Lily's reaction. This was one of the things she loved about owning a bookshop – the pleasure she could bring to others. She couldn't bear to let it go. She was determined to get involved in whatever it was Frank intended.

'You're too good to her,' Peta said, leading Liz into the living room where the three others were already seated with glasses of wine. 'You know Ann, and this is Chris.'

Liz smiled at Ann who was one of her frequent customers and looked at the man by her side. She'd heard how Peta's cousin had been reunited with an old flame and about the Dr Chris Thomas who'd set up a subsidiary of his world-renowned IT business in Granite Springs Technology Park. But this was the first time she'd met him. 'Nice to meet you, Chris.'

'Likewise. Ann tells me you own the lovely bookshop on Main Street. I can't think why I haven't been in there yet. Young Lily is clearly a fan.'

Lily beamed. She was still clutching the book as if afraid to let it go.

'Why don't you put the book by your bed, Lily,' Peta suggested. 'Then you can start it in your reading time.'

'Okay, Grandma.' Lily ran off, and everyone smiled after her.

Before Liz could say anything, Frank had risen to pour her a glass of wine, and Ann patted the space beside her on the sofa.

'Frank's been telling us about what went on at the council meeting last night. It must be a worry for you,' Chris said, his brow furrowing. 'I imagine it's difficult enough for independent bookshops these days without the developers moving in.'

'Yes.' Liz put a hand on her stomach as if it would stop the churning she experienced every time she thought about the development proposal. 'But I'm not the only one who'll be affected. There are four other shops. We're all in the same boat.'

Chris raised an eyebrow in Frank's direction. 'Have you spoken to them, Frank?'

'Not yet.' Frank was still standing. 'Liz is the only one who owns her shop. Being on the corner, it managed to escape the group who bought the others. I guess we should include them, though. Liz is right.'

Liz squirmed in her seat. It wasn't much, but she was glad to have something to contribute.

They sat down to dinner, but their minds weren't on the food and, by the time the meal was over, a plan had been devised to organise a town meeting. The protest group was underway.

Four

When Sam arrived home, he found Mitch lying on the sofa in front of a blaring television, his iPad in one hand, a can of beer in the other – exactly as he'd been the previous evening, and the one before that. His blood boiled. When he offered his son accommodation, it had been in the expectation he'd make himself useful around the place, not that he'd laze around like this. He was beginning to get some insight into why Brooke had thrown him out.

'Hi, Dad.' Mitch pulled his attention away from the screen for a moment, before focussing on it again. Sam walked across the room and turned the television off. The silence was bliss. 'What have you been doing all day?'

'Oh, this and that. There's not much to do here, is there?' Mitch gazed disparagingly around as if seeking some form of entertainment.

Sam silently counted to ten, reminding himself Mitch was suffering. His marriage was in tatters. He should allow him a bit of slack. His day hadn't gone the way he expected either. He was still struggling with his editorial about the last council meeting. As he'd told Frank Beattie, The Advertiser didn't take sides. But it was difficult to give a fair representation of the discussion without appearing to favour one side or the other.

It was tempting to join Mitch on the sofa with a beer. But someone had to be the adult here. 'Hungry?' he asked.

'Mmm.' The thought of food seemed to be enough to distract Mitch from whatever he was doing on his device. 'There's not much in the fridge.'

Damn! Sam had forgotten to pick up the few basics on the list he'd prepared that morning, and the steak he'd intended to barbecue for dinner was still in the freezer. Mitch was right. The fridge was a sorry sight. Sam still hadn't got used to living out of town, to being more than a few steps from the local supermarket. 'Why don't we go into town for a meal? The local RSL does a mean steak, and we need to have a chat about what you intend to do with yourself.'

'Sounds ominous, Dad. Hope you're not going to play the heavy father,' Mitch chuckled.

Sam winced. He'd never played the heavy dad when Mitch lived at home. But he'd never needed to. The younger Mitch had been a lively, intelligent young man, keen to do well and make his parents proud. What had happened to that young man? Surely some remnant of him remained inside this layabout who was wasting his days away?

'This is more like it.' Mitch looked around the ex-serviceman's club with approval. 'Come here a lot, Dad?'

'A bit,' Sam admitted, not wanting to reveal to his son, just how mundane his life was. Not that he thought of it that way. After the drama of Canberra politics, it was exactly what he needed. And he was gradually learning how to get his acreage into shape and figuring out what he wanted to do with it. Recently, he'd met a retired solicitor who now had a herd of alpacas, and who told him about a neighbour of his who kept goats. He wasn't sure either of those options were for him, but it was interesting to speculate. Meanwhile, he'd leased out part of the property to a neighbouring farmer for agistment and now around forty sheep were grazing in the paddock.

He was standing at the bar ordering drinks while Mitch found them a table, when he felt a hand on his shoulder. 'Sam, don't often see you here, but then I'm not often here myself.' Col Ford gave a hearty laugh. 'What brings you into town? My excuse is that Jo is on duty at The Riverside and I decided to give myself a break from it.'

'I'm here with my son.' It was almost as if Sam had thought Col into existence – Col and his alpacas. 'Why don't you join us?' Sam knew Col's company would preclude any in-depth discussion with Mitch about his future, but that could wait. Nothing would have changed by tomorrow, or the next day. Of that, he was sure. Mitch wasn't going anywhere soon.

'If you're sure.'

'I am.'

The two men carried their drinks across to where Mitch was seated, his eyes on his iPhone. A niggle of irritation rose in Sam. Couldn't Mitch sit for a few minutes without fiddling with one device or another? It seemed to have become an obsession with him. Sam remembered how Mitch had been like that in his teens, usually playing games on them. He thought he'd outgrown that phase. Perhaps the trouble with Brooke had made him regress.

'Mitch, this is Col Ford. Col, my son, Mitch.'

The two men shook hands.

Mitch picked up his beer. 'Thanks, Dad.' He resumed checking his phone, much to Sam's annoyance.

Sam and Col began to discuss the weather and Col's alpacas, while Mitch remained lost in his own little world.

Then, 'A rum do at the council the other night.' Col took a sip of his beer. 'Wasn't there myself, but I heard all about it. You'd have been there, I expect.' He gazed at Sam enquiringly.

'For my sins,' Sam muttered. He couldn't seem to avoid the topic.

'What happened?' Suddenly Mitch seemed to take an interest in the conversation.

'There was a debate about a development proposal,' Sam said shortly. He had no wish to discuss it.

'Really? I thought this dead-end town didn't do development.'

'Far from it,' Col said. 'My wife's son is at the forefront of some very large developments on the outskirts of town and has recently opened a technology park. None of these have done anything to despoil the beauty of the centre of town. This one would.' He frowned. 'You really should join us, Sam.'

'Join you?'

'Frank Beattie is getting a group together to protest the development. They're hoping to hold up the planning process long enough to ruin the whole thing. It would be a bonus to have The Advertiser behind us.'

'Frank's already approached me. I'll tell you what I told him. The Advertiser isn't about taking sides on this or on anything else controversial. We're non-political.'

'It doesn't sound like a political issue to me, Dad.'

Sam's eyes flickered to Mitch. Why did he have to decide to join in on this part of their conversation?

'It's local politics.'

'Sorry you feel that way.' Col picked up his glass. 'If you change your mind…' He took a swallow of beer.

Sam knew he wouldn't. When he'd taken his present position, he'd made himself a vow to keep out of politics, local and national. He'd had enough of the backbiting that always ensued. All he wanted was a quiet life, and he'd been managing that pretty well. Until this blew up – and Mitch arrived on his doorstep.

But Mitch hadn't finished. 'A technology park. Sounds interesting. What companies have set up there?'

'Not a lot as yet,' Col replied. 'And they're mostly small local ones. The only one you might have heard of is CAT. It's owned by a local man who started it up in Canada. He now has a subsidiary in Granite Springs and…'

'CAT? Here?'

There was a spark of interest in Mitch's voice that made Sam stare at his son in astonishment. He was planning to interview Chris Thomas. He knew who he was. He was the man who'd supplanted him in Ann Baird's affections, but he'd soon recovered from her rejection. He'd interviewed Thomas' daughter after a motorbike accident, but still had to meet the man himself.

Mitch turned to Sam eagerly. 'They're the tops, Dad. I can't believe they'd choose a place like Granite Springs over Sydney or Melbourne – even Canberra.'

'We're not quite a backwater,' Col said, amused. 'I think Dr Thomas was impressed by Danny's initiative – he's the guy behind the development – and his daughter – Chris's – is studying at our university. His partner lives here, too. So, you see, it's not so strange.'

'But…' Mitch fell silent.

No more was said about it. They ordered their meals and Mitch didn't speak as Sam and Col discussed the forthcoming country music festival. This was something Sam was happy to promote. It was the first year Granite Springs had chosen to host the festival and there was a lot of excitement about it in the town. Col's neighbour, local university professor and director of the Granite Springs Choristers, Owen Larsen, was the leading light behind the event. Sam was keen to meet him properly.

'Come to lunch on Sunday,' Col said as they rose to leave. 'I'll invite Owen and Fran over and you can have a chinwag. You, too, Mitch,' he said, shaking the young man's hand and clapping him on the shoulder. 'Maybe we can persuade Danny and family to come too. They'd be closer to your vintage than we are. I'm sure you'd prefer some younger company.'

'Thanks.' Mitch brightened.

On the way home, Mitch seemed to come out of the mood he'd been in since he arrived and started asking Sam questions about the technology park and about Chris Thomas. Sam was surprised at his interest, but thought anything that could gain Mitch's attention was worth pursuing. And he had studied IT.

It wasn't till later, when Mitch had gone to bed, and Sam was sitting rolling a glass of brandy between his hands and gazing out into the darkness that it occurred to him he still hadn't decided what to put in his editorial.

Five

Saturday was Liz's favourite day of the week. It was the day when The Reading Corner was busiest, the day when she ran one of the two book clubs for teenagers, the day when she knew this shop had been a good decision.

But this morning, there was a niggle at the back of her mind, spoiling her mood. She couldn't help thinking of her dinner with Peta and Frank. The whole development business was a big worry. She'd tried to put it out of her mind but it was always there, waiting to pounce when she least expected it.

She sighed as she sat sipping her ginger tea and watching a couple of galahs pecking at something on the grass in her backyard. Marmaduke was standing in front of the French doors, alert for any sign he could escape and scare them off. 'What can I do, Marmaduke?' she asked, as if the cat would have the answer. She'd always avoided protest movements, even when she was at uni, and all her friends were protesting about one thing or another. It seemed to be a popular student pastime. But, until now, Liz had never been tempted to become involved, always believing it was best to stay out of such events.

This one was different. Her livelihood was at stake. The bookshop meant everything to her. What would she do if it disappeared? This time she had to take action, be part of whatever it was Frank had in mind.

She drained her cup and stood up. Marmaduke, sensing her movement, left his post at the window to rub himself against her ankles, his familiar presence comforting her. 'And what would I do without you?' she asked, leaning down to scratch his ears. He purred loudly in reply.

It was a typical Saturday morning. Once Liz had set up the corner for the book club, and a new display on the table at the front of the shop, she was inundated with customers, barely having time to draw breath. There was no time to consider any protest group or the future of The Reading Corner.

'Did you see yesterday's editorial in The Advertiser?' Judy had snuck in when Liz wasn't looking. She was accompanied by Neil's wife, Sally, and a young girl Liz assumed was Neil's daughter. 'That's Neil's Daisy,' Judy said, seeing Liz's eyes follow the girl who had discovered Marmaduke lying on his favourite bean bag in the children's corner. He'd avoided it during the book club but returned to his favourite spot as soon as the book club members left. 'She's with Neil and Sally for the September school holidays. It'll be a wrench when she has to go back to her mum again.'

'She looks lovely. Seems to have taken to Marmaduke. All the kids do.' Liz hadn't yet read the local paper the day before. From Judy's expression, she assumed it had something to do with this damned development. She didn't seem to be able to get away from it.

'You haven't read it?' Judy took a copy of the paper from her capacious bag and handed it to Liz. It was open at the editorial. 'Doesn't say much, but he must have been at the meeting. What are you going to do?'

'Oh, Judy! I can't stop thinking about it.' She couldn't keep the apprehension out of her voice. 'I had dinner with Frank and Peta. I'm going to join this protest group he's setting up. Peta's cousin and her new partner are getting involved too, and I don't know who else.'

'I'm sorry, Liz. I've never heard you sound like this. I can understand how upset you must be. Is there anything…?'

A couple of women entering the shop, accompanied by a group of boisterous children, put paid to any further conversation, and Liz was kept busy helping them find what they were looking for and ensuring they didn't annoy Marmaduke. While he loved being admired and stroked by the shop's young customers, he didn't take kindly to being fussed over by large groups of them.

Judy drifted off, to return when the women and children had left with their purchases. 'Come out to lunch tomorrow,' she said, as Liz was wrapping books for Sally and Daisy. 'We can have a proper chat then.'

Liz agreed. Sunday was her one day off. When she opened the bookshop, she'd intended to be open seven days. But she had soon discovered Granite Springs was a community which observed the sabbath and considered Sunday to be a day of rest, a day when the main street was deserted. She also found she needed at least one day in the week in which she could relax.

*

Next morning Liz awoke to the sound of church bells. She lay there for a few moments enjoying that she didn't need to rise straight away. Then the sound of Marmaduke mewling and the thud of him leaping from his spot on the bed to the floor reminded her he needed to be fed. For him, Sunday was like any other day, and his days started early.

'Okay, puss, I'm coming.' She threw on her robe and opened the door to be greeted by a loud purr, telling her the cat had got what he wanted. Yawning, Liz headed for the kitchen where she filled his food and water bowls. Then, deciding there was no point in going back to bed, she filled the coffee maker and pulled the muesli container from the pantry and a carton of yoghurt from the fridge.

*

Driving out to Wooleton, Liz began to sing along to the radio. This was familiar territory. It was where she had her first glimpse of country life. And, while she'd chosen to live in town, she always enjoyed visiting with Judy and Alec.

It was quiet once she'd turned off the main road until a car flew past and threw up a cloud of red dust. She grimaced. People living out here should pay attention to other road users, she thought in annoyance. But her irritation was soon forgotten as she drove up the long driveway lined with gum trees to reach the homestead, an old sprawling building set on a rise overlooking the property.

'It's so peaceful here,' she said to Judy who came out to greet her with a hug. 'I always pinch myself when I visit. It's as if we're in the middle of nowhere. It's difficult to imagine Granite Springs is only a few kilometres away.' She sniffed the air, redolent with the scent of the lemon gum which towered over them.

'We like it too,' Judy said smugly, then looked up as Alec wandered over to join them, two sheepdogs at his heels. Liz couldn't help feeling a twinge of envy. Judy had been through a lot, but she did have a husband who loved her and she lived in this beautiful spot. Liz wondered what it would be like to live on a family property, to be part of the generations who'd worked the land. It must be so rewarding.

'Just got a call from Ken. They're running late,' Alec said.

Liz looked at him, enquiringly.

'Oh, didn't I say? Ken and Lyn are coming to lunch, too. They recently got back from their travels, the Caribbean I think it was.' Judy chuckled. 'They're not wasting any time. Lyn had a list of all the places she wants to see, and it turns out my brother-in-law had a few on his list, too. Now he's semi-retired, they're off every few months. I can't keep up.'

Liz was saved from replying by the arrival of Neil and Sally accompanied by Daisy.

'It's the lady from the bookshop! I've started reading my new book already,' Daisy said proudly, 'and Sally's making me a special book bag for my library books for when school starts. I wish...'

'None of that,' Neil said, picking her up and twirling her around. 'You know your mum would miss you if you stayed with Sal and me.' He dropped a kiss on her head before putting her down again.

'But...' she looked at him, then at Sally. 'I want to be here for the new baby. I'm going to have a little sister,' she informed Liz.

'Or brother,' Sally laughed. 'We don't know yet which it will be. But you'll see him or her when you come to visit, Daisy.'

Daisy pouted.

Liz climbed up to the veranda with the others and was enjoying a gin with lime and soda when Alec's brother Ken and his wife, Lyn, appeared, both tanned from their recent holiday which turned out to have been to Guadeloupe in the Caribbean. They were full of stories about their trip, keeping everyone entertained and slightly envious.

It wasn't until the steaks had been eaten, and all the adults were on their second glasses of wine that Judy asked Ken, 'What have you heard about the proposed development on Main Street?'

Liz pricked up her ears. She'd known the subject would come up, and she was interested to hear from Ken. He'd owned a major real estate business in town for years and been a member of the council. Although semi-retired, she knew he kept a finger on the pulse of everything that happened in town.

'Danny filled me in,' Ken said. 'Seems it's a mob from the city who have their eye on the block. He says his dad's all for it.'

'We all know what Gordon Slater's like,' Neil said. 'Sorry, Sal. I know he's your father, but he always has his eye on the main chance. Your bookshop is there, isn't it?' he asked Liz.

'It is and I have no intention of selling.' Liz hadn't realised how forcibly she'd spoken until she saw the others look at her in surprise.

'So, you'll be joining this group that's forming to oppose it?' Ken asked. 'I hear the other shopkeepers are eager to get involved and…'

'I certainly will.' Liz pressed her lips together, her anger rising again at the all too real prospect of what could happen. She'd anticipated it would come up in the conversation, but she hadn't expected Ken Thompson to be the one to bring it up.

Judy stared at her in surprise. 'But… if the owner of the other shops decided to sell, how can you not? I mean… your shop is part of the block. They can't knock down the rest and leave the corner intact.'

Liz felt dizzy. This was the thought that had been keeping her awake the past few nights, the picture of her precious shop being ravaged by a demolition team. 'I'd rather not talk about it,' she said stiffly. It was as if, by refusing to discuss it, it would go away. She didn't want to think about it, not here.

'Sorry.' Judy put a hand on Liz's arm. 'It's only that we care for you. We're concerned. I know how much the shop means to you.'

'Thanks.' Liz smiled at her friend, but she doubted Judy did know. She had her family. The shop was all Liz had. She didn't count her parents and her sister. They lived in Canberra. Her life was here. Without the shop, what would she do?

'You need something else in your life.' Judy was talking to her quietly, the others now engaged in a conversation about some issue with the sheep. 'What you need is a man. I'd be lost without Alec and I always thought it a pity you never met anyone. You've been alone for a long time. I wonder...'

'No!' Liz couldn't believe what Judy was suggesting. No one could ever replace Dan.

Six

Sam stretched out in bed listening to the cackling of kookaburras on Sunday morning. It was a sound he'd become used to in the months he'd lived here. But, more than the birds, it was the silence that had drawn him to this spot of paradise. Set on the edge of broad acres there wasn't another house in sight. His nearest neighbours owned the sheep property called Wooleton, and the two homes on the property were a distant speck on the horizon.

He'd met Alec Thompson a couple of times, the most recent when he'd agreed to provide agistment for some of his sheep. Sam had no problem agreeing to the farmer's request, knowing it would keep the grass down till he decided what to do with his mere twenty acres. It seemed a lot to him, more accustomed to a city block in Canberra, but he had the distinct impression the sheep farmer thought it was a joke.

He sniffed the aroma of coffee teasing his nostrils. Was Mitch awake and up already? This would be a first. He swung his legs out of bed and slowly made his way to the kitchen. The house was ten years old having been built by a couple who, like him, wanted to escape the busy city life. Sadly, the husband had died suddenly, leaving the wife feeling lonely and afraid out here on her own. Their misfortune had been a stroke of luck for Sam who had jumped at the opportunity to make a dream come true.

'Hi, son.' Sam rubbed a hand over the top of his son's head, ruffling the hair, so like his own. Sam's was still thick, but these days its dark colour was fading to silver wings above his ears. 'You're up early.'

'I thought about what you said.' Mitch looked rueful. 'Decided to pull my finger out and earn my keep.'

So, the pep talk he'd had with his son last night had paid off, for now at least. Sam wasn't optimistic enough to believe this new leaf would last, but determined to enjoy it while it did.

'I've made a start on breakfast.' Mitch pointed to the bowl of beaten eggs and the slices of bacon lying on the benchtop. 'Now you're up, I'll get it going. I used to enjoy making Sunday breakfast for Brooke before…' He fell silent. 'I miss her, Dad, her and Abi. I was a fool. I realise that now. But it all got too much for me. She didn't understand.' He kicked the leg of the table.

Sam winced, but he was pleased Mitch was starting to come to his senses. Maybe he wasn't such a lost cause after all. 'What brought this on?'

'I couldn't sleep last night. I lay awake thinking.'

'Mmm.' Sam poured himself a coffee and took a long drink. Boy, it felt good. There was nothing like a strong cup of coffee to set you up for the day.

'This technology park. I'd like to know more about it. Did you say you planned to interview this Thomas guy, Dad? Could I tag along? I'd really like to meet him.'

'Whoa! I don't know about that.' While pleased Mitch appeared to be thinking more positively, Sam didn't like the idea of him tagging along when he interviewed the owner of CAT. He hadn't spoken to the guy yet, though they'd been in touch when Sam set up an interview with Chris Thomas' daughter the year before, and Thomas was the man Ann Baird had chosen over him. It still rankled, but only a little. He and Ann had never had time to form any sort of relationship. He'd been new in town, looking for a friend. Now she and Thomas were a couple, she'd suggested inviting him to dinner, but so far it hadn't eventuated, perhaps for the best.

'This is good, son.' Sam took another mouthful of the bacon and scrambled eggs Mitch had prepared and washed it down with a swallow of coffee. Maybe having Mitch stay wouldn't be such a bad thing after all. But it would be better if he and Brooke could resolve their differences. That wouldn't happen unless Mitch found some other position, and he was expressing an interest in CAT. 'I'll let you know when I have an interview set up with Chris Thomas,' he said, taking a last bite of toast. 'But you'll have to promise not to interfere.'

'Thanks, Dad. I promise.' Mitch made the two-finger cub scout salute, forcibly reminding Sam of the small Mitch wearing his blue cub scout uniform and yellow neckerchief. It didn't seem so long ago, yet so much had happened since then. Sam's eyes pricked.

'You all right, Dad?'

'Fine, son. Thanks for a great breakfast. I have some work I need to finish before we head off to lunch. I'll be in my office if you need me.' But Mitch was already busy on his phone. Some things never changed. Sighing, Sam cleared the dirty plates, rinsed them and loaded the dishwasher before heading to his office to finish an article he'd begun the night before.

*

Sam was driving along the dirt track heading for the main road when he was surprised to pass a car he didn't recognise. It was unusual to meet anyone other than the Thompson family on this stretch of road. He caught a glimpse of a cloud of red hair before the car vanished in a swirl of dust, probably more of his making than hers. He registered the driver was a woman, but not much else. She must be visiting Wooleton.

'Where is this place we're having lunch, Dad? We seem to be travelling towards the town.'

'We are. Col and his wife live on an acreage too, but theirs is on the other side of Granite Springs. It's mostly twenty-acre blocks out where they are. They were soldier settlements after the first World War. My place is different. It was carved off from one of the sheep properties later, probably in a year when the farmer needed the money more than the pasture. That's why we're out of sight of any other houses.'

'Mmm.' Mitch settled back, his eyes closed to the beautiful scenery.

'Can you rouse yourself to open the gate?' Sam had decided not to interrupt his son's nap, but now they were at the entrance to Yarran, as Col and Jo's property was called, it was time for him to wake up.

'What?' Mitch opened his eyes and gazed blearily around. 'Are we there?'

'This is where Col and his wife live. You'll need to get out to open the gate, then close and fasten it after I've driven through,' Sam explained. He tried to stem his impatience, remembering all of this was new to Mitchell who'd never been outside the city till now.

'There's nothing here. It's like where you live.' Mitch slid back into the passenger seat and Sam drove towards the low-set house surrounded by a wide veranda. It wasn't unlike Sam's own home, but seemed more settled into the landscape. 'What are those weird animals?' He pointed to several cream and brown creatures with long necks grazing in the paddock.

'Alpacas. I guess you've never seen them before.'

Mitch shook his head, staring around him. 'They're not like sheep.'

Sam chuckled. He'd never make a country man out of his son.

Col came out to greet them as they approached the house, an old Golden Labrador waddling at his heels. 'Glad you made it,' he said, as Sam and Mitch stepped out of the car. 'Hi, Mitch. Good to see you again.' He shook Sam's hand, then held his out to Mitch. The dog was sniffing around their ankles. 'This is Scout,' Col said. 'He's getting on, but still has a lot of life in him. He's actually Jo's dog but seems to have a liking for men.' He chuckled. 'Come in and meet her.'

Col had just poured them all beers, and they were sitting on the veranda when they saw a couple walking up the lane.

'Here are Owen and Fran now,' Col said.

The pair made their way across the paddock and approached the house. The woman looked smart, and Sam recognised the man from his brief foray with the choir the previous year. He was wearing ripped jeans and had straggly greying hair tied back from his face.

Owen joined the men while his wife disappeared into the kitchen. But it wasn't long before the women joined them, and the barbecue was fired up.

'So,' Owen said, once the steaks and salads had all been consumed and they were enjoying coffee, 'Col tells me you're interested in the music festival, Sam.'

'I am. I'm pleased to have met you properly at last. I haven't been in Granite Springs very long and I'm still finding my way around. I've heard a lot about how you've set the place on fire, first at the university, then with the choir. And now there's this music festival.'

'I haven't really done anything much,' Owen said.

'Of course you have,' Fran said, patting her husband's knee. 'He's modest, too,' she said to Sam, looking at her husband with such affection Sam was forced to avert his eyes. What would he give to have someone look at him like that?

He fell into a reverie in which he was sitting on his own veranda, a woman whose face was indistinct was sitting opposite. She had a glass of wine in one hand, the other was lying on his thigh and…

'Dad?'

He was pulled back to the present by Mitch's voice. 'Sorry, son. I blanked out for a moment. What did I miss?'

'Owen was telling us about the festival. It sounds cool. Not what I'd have expected to find here in Granite Springs.'

'Granite Springs might surprise you,' Jo laughed. 'People come here expecting a sleepy country town, but there's more to the place than meets the eye. I think Owen has discovered that. Maybe you have too, already?' She fixed Sam with her eyes. 'I know you haven't been here long, but as editor of the Granite Springs Advertiser, I'd be willing to make a guess you're privy to everything going on here.'

'Mostly, though some things seem to escape my notice.'

'Not much, I'll bet.' It was Mitch who spoke. 'Dad's always been one to have his ear to the ground. Why, when he was in Canberra…'

'That's enough, son.' Sam had no intention of having his journalistic exploits bandied around with his new friends. He checked his watch. 'We should be going and letting you good folks get on. I'd guess you have things you need to do with your animals.'

'You're right,' Owen said. 'I need to check those goats of mine haven't broken the pipe to their water trough again. I think they only do it to spite me. It's been good to meet you, Sam. That interview you want. Why don't you drop into my office at the university? It will be easier for you than driving across town again and I'm there every day. If you call Fran, she can let you know when I'm free.'

'Thanks.' Sam could see it was Fran who kept Owen organised. But even this short meeting had shown him the other man wasn't as disorganised as he pretended to be. He wouldn't be a professor at the local university if he was, nor would he have gained his reputation with the local chorister group. Then, there was the music festival he was organising…

'And remember the choristers meet on Tuesday evening. You should join us. Maybe you too, Mitch.' Owen turned to face the younger man. 'We could do with a couple more bass voices. Seven o'clock in the music room at the university. It's on the edge of the campus. Anyone can tell you where it is.'

Sam nodded, but made no promises. He did enjoy music and had a good singing voice but wasn't sure if he wanted to join the choir. The two sessions he'd attended the previous year had been leading to what he thought might be a relationship with Ann Baird. But that had come to naught. And he didn't think it would appeal to Mitch.

He slid a sideways glance at his son as they drove home. 'What did you think? Not too much of a boring lunch? It's a pity Jo's son didn't make it.'

'Yeah. It wasn't too bad, Dad. They're nice people. Owen is a character. That choir of his might be a laugh.'

'Hmm.' Sam wasn't so sure. But anything that could spark some interest in Mitch was to be fostered. Maybe he'd go after all. What harm could it do?

Seven

Liz looked at the clock and bit her lip. She'd promised Peta she'd be at the meeting tonight but was having second thoughts. Although the proposal still preyed on her mind causing her sleepless nights, she was beginning to wonder what good it would do. If this big conglomerate from the city was hellbent on buying up the line of shops to which The Reading Corner was attached, how could a group of Granite Springs locals stop them?

But, she sighed, she couldn't sit home and do nothing. That was why she'd rushed home from work, heated up an instant meal, fed Marmaduke and was now changing into a pair of black wool pants which were tighter than they should be – she needed to lose those few extra kilos. It was why she was planning to spend a perfectly good Monday evening sitting in the hall of Granite Springs High School listening to Frank Beattie go on and on about how they were going to win this fight.

She had nothing against Frank. He was one of the good guys. His heart was in the right place. But it wasn't *his* livelihood that was being threatened, though the proposed new café/restaurant would no doubt cost him business. He wasn't doing this for any selfish reason. He had the good of the community at heart – *her* good, as it turned out.

She thought back to the discussion at Judy's the day before, to what Ken Thomson had said about the development plans. If someone didn't take a stand, they would go through and Liz would lose her shop, lose all she'd worked for. According to Ken, Frank was providing a community service in getting this group together.

Telling herself she was going to keep her own anger in check, listen, see who else was there, hear what they had to say, she had settled Marmaduke – who wasn't happy she was leaving him alone – and was about to go out the door when her mobile rang.

Liz checked the screen, hoping to ignore the call, when she saw her mother's number. Her first thought was for her dad. Her stomach clenched.

'Mum?' Liz dropped her bag onto the floor and pressed one hand on the doorjamb for support, worried it was bad news. Sensing her concern, Marmaduke silently moved from the corner of the sofa, where he'd been curled up in disgust at being abandoned, to join her, weaving in and out between her legs. 'Is it... How's Dad?' Her breath caught in her throat.

'The old fraud's a lot better. That's why I'm calling. He wants us to make the trip to see you next weekend. But *I* thought... why don't you come here instead? We'd love to see you. It seems like ages since you came to Canberra, and the wattle's still in bloom. You know how you always used to love to see it.' Her voice trailed off, no doubt remembering it had been twenty years since Liz enjoyed a spring in Canberra, twenty years since she turned her back on the capital, on the city of her birth, twenty years since Dan died.

How could her mother have forgotten the yellow of the wattle forcibly reminded her of the day of Dan's funeral when their bright blooms seemed to mock her, their symbol of renewal highlighting all she'd lost? She didn't have time for this right now.

'I'm on my way out, Mum. Glad to hear Dad is on the mend. Can I ring you back?' She was already running late. She wasn't sure she wanted to go to the meeting, not sure what it could achieve, but she didn't want to agree to go to Canberra either, and, at this very moment the meeting seemed the lesser evil.

'Well, if you don't have time to speak, but I expect to hear from you tomorrow, and Dad's really looking forward to seeing you. I'm sure Ailsa and the boys would love to see you, too.' The words hit her like a blow. Her mum knew how much Liz loved her nephews. There was more than a hint of reproof in her mother's voice, one Liz was used to hearing. She sighed. She couldn't win. She knew she'd end up agreeing, driving over to Canberra on Saturday after a busy day at the shop, being bombarded by memories as she drove through avenues of the golden blooms. But it would be good to see her parents again, especially her dad for whom she had a soft spot. He was less demanding than her mother and he'd had a bad trot healthwise. It would be good to see her sister and her boys, too. Liz didn't see them often enough. Ailsa rarely had time to make the trip to Granite Springs and the boys were growing up and were in danger of forgetting their Aunt Liz if she wasn't careful.

*

Liz pushed open the door to the school hall, surprised to see it already almost full. The large room rang with the sound of voices and, looking around, she recognised many of her customers. Her stomach churned as she made her way to the front to take the seat next to Peta. She'd been feeling like this on and off all day and wondered if she was about to have a panic attack. She took a deep breath and tried to appear calm.

The room grew hushed as Frank Beattie called the meeting to order and explained the purpose of the evening. There was a swell of muttering as those who hadn't read the report of the council meeting in The Advertiser realised what they were up against. Though, Liz thought, even if they had read the editorial, they might still be in the dark. The editor had been very sparing in his comments, as if he had no real opinion on the matter.

As Frank continued to expound the evils of the proposed development, Liz let her mind wander. She checked the room, seeing her neighbouring shopkeepers seated close by along with Ann and Chris. There was no sign of the paper's editor who Frank was now criticising as mealy-mouthed. Liz had never met the man and would only have recognised him from the photo at the top of his column in the paper.

Frank seemed to think he should be prepared to take a stand, to support the protest. Liz supposed it might help to have The Advertiser come out against the proposal, but even so, what influence would a couple of articles in a regional newspaper have on a group of city developers?

Suddenly alert, Liz heard Frank say, 'Liz Pender is one of the shopkeepers whose life will be irrevocably changed if this goes ahead. She chose to come to Granite Springs close to twenty years ago and has made this her home. I'm sure many of you here owe your love of reading to The Reading Corner, the bookshop she opened which has continued to flourish and cater for new generations of readers.'

Liz shrank in her seat. He was making her sound ancient. She saw various people craning their necks to see if she was here. She turned and smiled awkwardly as several recognised her with a smile and nod, wishing Frank hadn't singled her out.

But she wasn't to be the only one in Frank's sights. He continued to identify each of the affected shops, naming them and their owners. Unlike Liz, several stood up at the mention of their name, to be loudly applauded by the audience.

When Frank finally sat down to Liz's relief, his place was taken by Danny Slater. Liz was familiar with the younger man who she knew to be the son of Jo Ford and Gordon Slater, the recently appointed mayor of Granite Springs. She knew Danny was himself involved in various new developments which had attracted a degree of censure from some diehards in the community, not least the technology park on the outskirts of town. His own real estate business had been merged with Ken Thompson's a year or so earlier to become a major force in Granite Springs real estate sales and developments.

Liz wondered if he was going to present the opposing view. But once he began to speak, it was clearly not the case. She gave a sigh of relief. Like Frank, he abhorred what he called the ransacking of Main Street for commercial purposes. Danny spoke of the history of the township, the importance of preserving the historic buildings, then proceeded to itemise the process which the planning committee would follow and how the group could attempt to influence their decision. It was a well-planned and thought-out speech which attracted loud applause. Liz wondered what his father would say when he heard about it, as he would. News travelled fast in Granite Springs and, even if the editor wasn't present, she thought she'd seen one of The Advertiser's reporters standing at the side of the hall.

The meeting finally wound up with calls for support and plans to lobby council members, especially those on the planning committee.

Although fired up as a result of listening to both Frank and Danny, Liz was about to slip away quietly, when she felt a hand on her shoulder.

'Glad you came?'

She turned to see Peta's smiling face.

'It was interesting,' Liz said, but she was eager to leave and get home. In her view, the evening hadn't achieved much. What had it gained, apart from stirring up the community? She would have been better staying at home with Marmaduke and a good book. Words, regardless of how harsh they were, weren't going to stop this. But what would? They could hardly chain themselves to their shops or lie down in front of the bulldozers.

'A few of us are going to Pavarotti's for a glass of wine and dessert. Join us?'

Liz was torn. She thought longingly of the ARC copy of the latest Fiona Mackintosh which had arrived in the mail that morning and was sitting by her favourite armchair. Her armchair and book beckoned. But she knew if she refused, Peta would be hurt, Frank, too. And she wanted to be part of this, curious as to what Frank planned to do next.

'That sounds lovely,' she said, not entirely lying. Pavarotti's was one of her favourite places in Granite Springs. The family-owned restaurant was an institution in the town and Liz's mouth watered at the thought of one of their cannoli accompanied by a glass of prosecco.

An hour later, she was sure it had been the right decision. Those at the restaurant included not only Peta and Frank, but Danny Slater and most of the other affected shop owners, all strident in their desire to see the development proposal fail. It was a noisy group, their vociferous arguments about what steps to take taking precedence over Liz's pleasure of her late-night treat. And it made the likelihood of the development seem to come closer.

'What about you, Liz?' her neighbouring shopkeeper asked. 'You've been very quiet. Don't you have anything to add?'

Liz looked at Tom Price who leased the pharmacy, had done for years. He must be close to retirement. What was he getting so het up about? Surely he'd be eligible for some compensation to help fund his declining years? Then she realised the others were all staring at her, waiting for her response.

'I...' she began. 'I'm not sure what we can do, other than picket the town hall or confront the developers.' There was a stunned silence. 'But I appreciate what you're doing, Frank, and I hope it has some impact.' She stopped abruptly, knowing the others felt she'd let them down. 'I saw Tim from The Advertiser was at the meeting,' she added. 'Maybe we can hope for a supportive article. That might have some impact and...' She paused, trying to gather her thoughts. 'It would be good if we could get more publicity, perhaps interest one of the news channels.' She fell silent seeing their doubtful expressions. Perhaps they'd been hoping she'd suggest something more radical.

'He asked for a picture of me with Danny,' Frank offered. 'But I'm not sure how much he'll be allowed to report. When I spoke to Sam Walker, he assured me The Advertiser wasn't in the business of taking sides on what he viewed as local politics.'

There was a murmur of dissent.

Soon afterwards, everyone rose to go. Liz said farewell to Peta and thanked Frank for his efforts. As she drove home, her mind went back to the meeting, to the swell of support it had engendered. Perhaps she'd been wrong to dismiss their reaction as only words, perhaps it would work. She hoped with all her heart that it would and wondered what more she could do to help. No one was going to take her shop from her if she could help it. There must be a way of getting more publicity. Surely the local paper was the place to start?

Eight

Sam looked at the photos lying on his desk. Tim had ignored his instructions to stay away from the community meeting. He had not only attended, but produced a report including photos of the targeted line of shops, one of Frank Beattie with Danny Slater which would anger the mayor, plus candid snaps of the shopkeepers taken at the meeting.

'What do you think, boss?' Tim's eager face appeared in the doorway. 'Make a good centre-page feature for Friday's paper. I know you told me to stay away but it's local interest. We should let people know. I can work up a good piece on it, include some of the history of the street.'

Sam shuffled the photos around. Tim was right. It would make good copy. But he stood by what he'd told Frank Beattie. He didn't do politics and he wasn't about to change his mind. But… He picked up a pen and tapped the desk. The history approach was a good idea.

'I can't let you use those,' he said, pointing to the photos of Frank and Danny and the candid shots of the shopkeepers. But the one of the shops is good, and I like the idea of reminding people of the history of the place. I bet some of those guys have been in the same shop for years. Maybe a feature on the history of Main Street, and not restricted to this particular line of shops. I seem to have heard other family businesses like The Bean Sprout and Pavarotti's have been there for generations, too. Perhaps a series of features?'

'You got it, Sam.'

'But easy on the development. Okay?'

Tim nodded and sauntered off, whistling, while Sam silently congratulated himself on managing to keep his employee happy while avoiding compromising his principles.

Satisfied with his decision, he picked up the phone to call the university, where he spoke to Fran Larsen and set up an interview with Owen for two days hence. He was about to end the call when Fran said, 'We'll see you at the choir tonight?'

Sam had completely forgotten about the choir. He was about to make excuses, plead another engagement when he remembered Mitch had expressed some interest, and changed his mind. 'Seven, I think Owen said. Looking forward to it.'

'See you there. You may enjoy it more than you think.'

Sam hung up with Fran's chuckle ringing in his ears. How did she know?

*

To Sam's surprise, Mitch was eager to discover what the Granite Springs Choristers were all about. Though he did suspect his son's keenness stemmed from curiosity rather than any real desire to join the choir. But they did manage to engage in conversation on the trip to the university campus, with Mitch expounding his theories of why country people seemed to be involved in so many social activities.

'I've been checking out past copies of The Advertiser, Dad,' he said, as they drove along. 'Picnic races, St Patrick's Day Parade, Christmas lights, show day, balls. It's never-ending. What I think is…'

'We're here,' Sam said, glad to be able to interrupt Mitch before he said something he might regret. Now he was living here, Sam considered himself to be one of the country people his son was describing. Since he'd moved to Granite Springs, Sam had attended the picnic races and the St Patrick's Day parade – the latter with Ann before he discovered her heart lay elsewhere – and he would be attending his first Granite Springs show in two weeks' time. He'd heard so much about the annual event and as editor of the local paper, he'd be expected to attend. He'd even been invited to judge one of the events, though what he knew about pumpkin scones could be written on the head of a pin.

'There are Owen and his wife.' Mitch pointed to a couple leaving the car park as Sam drove in. 'We can follow them.'

When he saw the large group of choristers, Sam almost turned tail and left, remembering his previous visits. But, surprisingly, Mitch urged him forward. 'This might be fun,' he whispered.

Sam gave him a look of surprise, not sure if he was serious, but Mitch had a straight face.

'Good to see you,' Fran greeted them. 'Owen wasn't sure you'd turn up. You probably know some of the people here.' She waved a hand in the general direction of the groups of men and women which were forming into the semblance of a choir with lots of muttering and laughing. They were certainly a cheerful bunch.

Owen appeared, shook Sam's hand, clapped Mitch on the shoulder and handed them some sheets of music. 'Welcome, take your places over there with the basses. We'll be starting shortly. We're practicing for our Christmas concert. We always do The Messiah. But we'll begin the evening with a few fun pieces to get everyone in the mood.'

Sam and Mitch did as they were bid, the men on either side of them giving them welcoming smiles.

Owen called the group to order, tapping his baton on a lectern. 'We have a couple of new members this evening,' he said, pointing to Sam and Mitch with the baton. 'Many of you will already be familiar with the face at the top of The Advertiser's editorial. Sam Walker has decided to grace us with his presence, along with his son, Mitch. Welcome to the Granite Springs Choristers.'

Sam blushed. He hadn't expected to be singled out like this. Last time, he'd managed to sneak in unobserved. But he'd already realised it was impossible to predict Owen Larsen's actions.

*

Standing with the contraltos, sandwiched between Kay Kerr and Donna, who worked in the library, Liz swivelled to see the newcomers. So, that was Sam Walker. He was better looking in real life than in the photo in the paper – tall, his dark hair showing silver streaks above his ears, and broad shoulders. Her glance moved to his son, standing beside him. Sam must have looked just like him when he was younger, a fine figure of a man.

What was she thinking? She wasn't interested in a man, any man. Especially not this one who refused to take their side and support them in the issue before the council.

The evening followed its usual pattern, and all Liz's thoughts and energy were focussed on the task as their voices soared in the glorious renditions of the familiar harmonies. Lost in the pleasure of the music, it was a disappointment when Owen called them to a halt.

'That'll be all for tonight,' he said. 'You've done well. But we still have a way to go before we can be satisfied with our performance. Next week, I have a treat for you. George Turnbull has agreed to come along to check up on us.'

There was a general muttering and cheer at the mention of the previous conductor of the group. George had retired a few years earlier and handed over to Owen who was new to the town. Owen took a different approach to the choir, but he and George had developed a good relationship, and the older man still enjoyed being invited along to give his opinion on their progress.

Normally, after choir practice, Liz would stand around chatting with a few of the others. She'd belonged to the choir for years and made some good friends among the choristers. But tonight, she had something else in mind. She saw Sam Walker have a few words with Owen, then linger in the doorway waiting for the younger man he was with.

Even from this distance she could see Sam Walker was an attractive man – his bearing, the broad shoulders, his profile.

Stifling the tremor in her stomach that threatened to derail her determination, Liz took a deep breath and walked towards him.

Nine

Sam watched as the curvaceous redhead walked determinedly towards him. There was something vaguely familiar about her, but he couldn't figure out exactly what it was, perhaps the hair? There weren't many women in Granite Springs with hair the colour of autumn leaves.

Steady on, he warned himself. It wasn't like him to be so poetic. He assumed what he hoped was a bland expression. Maybe it wasn't him she was headed for. But it was. She stopped right in front of him. And she wasn't smiling.

'You're Sam Walker.' Her voice matched her appearance, low and husky, like burnt toffee.

'Guilty as charged.' He laughed and held up both hands in submission.

'I'm Liz Pender.' She paused as if expecting him to recognise the name.

He did. She was the woman who owned the bookshop – The Reading Corner – the one which was in the line of shops that… Was that where he recognised her from? He tried to recollect the candid shots from the meeting Tim had given him, the ones that still lay in an untidy bundle on his desk.

'From the bookshop. Right?'

'Right. I didn't see you at the community meeting last night,' she accused. She didn't point a finger at him but might as well have, given her tone.

'You're right. I wasn't there.' He was beginning to be amused. Why hadn't he met her before now? Why hadn't he visited her bookshop?

She was... not exactly the sort of woman he expected to meet in Granite Springs. A host of thoughts flitted through his mind, most of them X-rated. She was the sort of woman he wanted to curl up with in front of a warm fire with a glass of champagne or good red wine.

She drew herself up to her full height which, while she was tall for a woman, was still a full head shorter than him. 'Don't you think you should have been there? As editor of our local paper? It was a community meeting.' She seemed to run out of steam, perhaps confused by the amused twinkle in his eyes. It was a long time since he'd locked horns with such a fiery woman, and he was enjoying it. It seemed her temper matched her red hair. He wondered...

'No. I believe one of my journalists was in attendance.' *Albeit against my express orders.* 'He took some photographs. There was a good one of you.' He waited for her reaction which came sooner than he expected.

'What? I didn't see... When did he photograph me?' She seemed displeased, angry even, if it was possible for her to become more irate than she'd been already.

'He took some candid shots of the audience.' *No need to tell her the shots were only of the shopkeepers. He'd keep that gem for later.*

'But...' She flushed. A delightful pink suffused her face.

Sam took pity on her. 'It won't be published. Tim wanted to do a double page feature on the meeting, but I put the kybosh on it. Instead, we're going to do a series of background articles on the town, particularly Main Street, examining the history of the shops and their owners – all the shops, not just those in danger of being demolished.'

'Oh!' For a moment she seemed to be taken aback. Then, 'But you will report on the meeting.'

'No.'

'Why not?'

Sam crossed his arms and rocked back on his heels. He was enjoying watching the colour come and go on her face, a lovely face, perfect creamy skin, the changing expression in her eyes, deep brown eyes, and that hair... 'The Granite Springs Advertiser is non-political.'

'But...'

'Ready, Dad?' Sam turned to see Mitch at his side.

'This is my son, Mitch. Mitch, meet Liz Pender. She owns The Reading Corner on Main Street.'

'Hi. We should go, Dad.' Now he had finished talking with whoever he'd been talking to, Mitch was impatient to leave.

'Don't let me keep you.' Liz's voice was icy.

'I've enjoyed meeting you. We must talk again. I meant what I said about the series of articles. Good evening.'

Leaving Liz staring after him – he could feel her eyes on his back – Sam followed Mitch out of the room and headed for the car park. When he reached his car, he cursed, realising he'd forgotten to say farewell to Owen and Fran. That blasted woman had completely distracted him.

Ten

The hide of the man! How could she ever have thought him attractive? Liz watched Sam Walker and his son leave. He walked as if he owned the place, as if he hadn't a care in the world. She'd met his sort before, in Canberra, when she was with Dan. They acted as if the world owed them a living.

Liz fumed all the way home, where she fumbled with her key and dropped it, before managing to open her front door. As she entered the living room, Marmaduke stretched and rose from the corner of the sofa to greet her. She dropped her bag and picked him up, cuddling him and rubbing her nose in his soft fur. 'I need to forget about the nasty man,' she said to the cat. 'Sam Walker's not worth bothering about. I don't know why I let him get under my skin.'

Marmaduke wriggled out of her grasp with a cry and padded into the kitchen to stand over his food bowl. He gave a pitiful meow.

'You've already had your dinner,' Liz told him, but she opened the bag of cat food and poured a small amount into the empty bowl. Then she took a carton of milk from the fridge. What she needed to soothe her, was a mug of hot chocolate with – she fossicked on the top shelf of the fridge – yes, there was still some cake left. She took out the piece of strawberry flan. It was left over from a cake one of her long-term customers had given her in appreciation of her efforts to find her an out-of-print copy of a favourite book.

Back in the living room, sitting by the fire with Marmaduke curled up in her lap, everything looked brighter. Liz was able to examine her conversation with Sam Walker dispassionately as she forked up bite-sized pieces of the flan. *She really should go on a diet.* She pulled in her stomach. *But she did love giving in to her sweet tooth.* And Dan had loved what he called her cuddly womanly figure.

But Dan wasn't here anymore. And the past twenty years had seen her gain more than a few kilos as she indulged her passion for desserts and cakes like this one. She licked the crumbs from her lips and took a sip of the warm milky drink. In a corner of her mind, she wondered what Sam Walker had thought of her.

Stop right there, she told herself, shocked by where her thoughts were going. What did she care about the opinion of the boorish editor of The Granite Springs Advertiser? No, that was wrong, unfair, not boorish. But what? What was it about the man that had annoyed her so much?

Liz let the scene in the music room replay behind her eyes. His face, his eyes, the way they crinkled up and twinkled with… amusement. He'd been amused. He'd been laughing at her!

But, she allowed, while he was adamant he wasn't going to take sides on the development proposal – and she had to admire his apolitical stance – he had committed to this feature on Main Street, albeit with a historical focus.

She thought about what he'd said, his objection to supporting the group she now considered herself part of. To some point, she agreed. She'd had enough of politics during her years in Canberra. Growing up in the country's capital, she'd learned very early that politics could be a nasty game. Then, when Dan died, it had been hard to accept the statements made by politicians which appeared to glorify what Dan and others like him had been doing. So many had lost their lives like Dan, and many more would never recover from their experiences. She sometimes wondered what her husband would have been like if he had survived and returned to her. Would he have been the same cheerful, loving man she'd farewelled, or a husk of the man she'd married, condemned to a life filled with nightmares and depression?

Who was Sam Walker, she wondered? What was there in his past to make him believe so strongly in his views? Because, despite his obvious amusement at baiting her, he clearly held firm views which made him determined to remain apolitical. She thought and thought but could come to no conclusion. Then she castigated herself. Why was she spending so much time thinking about him? What was it about Sam Walker that had got under her skin?

*

The week flew past, the bookshop busier than ever with many coming in to ask Liz about what was going to happen. They hated to think of the town losing this valuable asset as well as the newsagent and pharmacy who were her neighbours.

By the time Sunday came around, Liz was exhausted. She was glad she hadn't agreed to go to Canberra till the following weekend. All she wanted to do was relax, but she discovered she couldn't do that either. She was too worked up about what might happen in the council planning committee and, if she was honest with herself, with the memory of Sam Walker at the choir on Tuesday. She couldn't help wondering if last week had been a one-off, or if he intended to become a permanent member.

It shouldn't matter to her one way or another. But it did. His face – with its sardonic expression – had infiltrated her dreams leading her to awaken feeling annoyed and… something else she couldn't identify.

Unable to relax, Liz did what she'd always done when she had time on her hands, she baked. This Sunday, she chose to make a batch of the pumpkin scones Dan had loved, hoping this reminder of her husband would force Sam Walker's image out of her head.

Distracted by both her thoughts and Marmaduke as she measured out the familiar ingredients, she almost made a mistake in the quantities, catching herself just in time from adding more sugar than required. How could she have been so stupid? She needed to concentrate on the task at hand.

The scones were about ready to come out of the oven, their delicious aroma wafting out from the kitchen, when there was a loud knock at the door and she heard a little voice say, 'Do you think she's home, Grandma?'

Liz threw open the door. Peta and Lily were exactly the distraction she needed, and they could help eat the batch of scones which was too much for her to handle on her own. She wasn't sure what she'd planned to do with the excess, freeze them perhaps.

'Sorry to disturb you on your day off, Liz,' Peta apologised. 'Lily wanted to show you a story she's written and she couldn't wait till tomorrow after school.'

'A story? How wonderful. I'd love to read it. And I've just made a batch of pumpkin scones and need someone to help me eat them.'

'Pumpkin scones, yum.' Lily rushed inside to where Marmaduke was grooming himself in a sunny corner of the living room. 'Hello, Marmaduke. Archie sends his love.' She crouched down beside the cat and began to stroke him, triggering loud purrs.

Leaving Lily and Marmaduke together, Liz led Peta into the kitchen. 'Tea or coffee?'

'Tea, please. Herbal if you have it.'

Liz took the scones out of the oven, put on the electric jug and took two lemon grass and ginger teabags out of the cupboard. She thought this would go best with the scones. Then she filled a glass with milk for Lily.

'Ms Pender.' Lily sidled into the room, a collection of A4 sheets in her hand.

'I think you could call me Liz now, don't you?'

Lily gave a shy smile.

'Why don't we wait till your grandma's and my tea is ready, then I'll read your story?'

'Okay.' Lily took a seat, but her impatience showed in the set of her head and her pursed lips.

Liz set out the scones and a dish of butter, served up the tea, then took a seat.

Lily thrust the sheets of paper at her.

'Don't rush Liz,' Peta said. 'Let us have our tea first.' She took a bite from her scone. 'This is delicious, Liz.' She wiped the crumbs from her lip.

'It's okay, Peta. I'm ready.' She took the dogeared sheets from Lily.

'It's about...' Lily began eagerly.

'Let me find out for myself.' Liz began to read, every so often taking a sip of tea or a bite of scone without raising her eyes from her reading.

The other two sat in silence, apart from when the swinging of Lily's legs made contact with the leg of the table. This was followed by a low, 'Sorry' from the girl.

Finally, Liz came to the end. 'This is very good, Lily.' She meant it. The story was exceptional for a girl of Lily's age. She had captured the fantasy genre which was popular with her age group and had taken it a stage further to develop an intricate story.

Lily beamed and squirmed in her seat. 'There's a short story competition at school. It's mostly for the older classes. The best ones will be on display at the library. Do you think I should enter? Is it good enough? The twins said it was, but I thought they were being kind.' She bit her lip.

Liz had a vague recollection of Donna from the library telling her about the competition. She knew who the twins were. Lottie and Livvy Tait were Jo Ford's grandchildren, and they and Lily had become bosom pals from the moment Lily arrived in Granite Springs.

'Of course I do. I think you have a good chance of winning.' She handed the sheets back to Lily.

Lily blushed and took a gulp of milk, leaving a white rim around her mouth.

'Thanks, Liz. I told Lily it was really good, but she was determined to get your opinion. Satisfied now, sweetie?'

Lily nodded.

Marmaduke, who'd followed Lily into the kitchen, chose that moment to leap up onto her lap.

'He's so like Archie,' Peta said, referring to their cat who was from the same litter as Marmaduke. They'd given a home to him when his former owner could no longer care for him.

Now the story had been read, the conversation revolved around the goings on in Granite Springs – the proposed development, the new technology park, the upcoming Granite Springs Show, and the country music festival planned for November.

'I don't know how I ever imagined living in the country would be relaxing,' Peta said. 'There's always something happening, something to look forward to. I'm glad you came to the meeting on Monday. We need everyone to get involved.'

Liz blushed. 'I spoke to the editor of The Advertiser at choir on Tuesday. He's an arrogant prick. Said the paper was apolitical.' She recalled his expression, his amusement – and her annoyance. 'I'd love to know what his background is.'

'I believe he was a political journalist before he came here. Burnt out, Frank suspects.'

'Oh!' Did that make it better – excuse him? Probably not.

'But good-looking don't you think?' Peta tilted her head to one side.

'If you like that sort of thing.' Liz remembered her first impression of the man; the faded dark hair, the silver wings above his ears, the broad shoulders, the way his eyes crinkled, the way his lips curled up as if enjoying a private joke. The image she'd been trying to dismiss ever since Tuesday.

'Many would.' Peta gave Liz a penetrating look, then looked away.

'He did say he intended to publish a series of feature articles about the history of Main Street and its shops. Frank will be pleased.'

'He will. I'll let him know. The Bean Sprout isn't the only shop that's been a family business for generations. Maybe we can use this series in our fight with the council.'

'Maybe.' Liz was doubtful.

'We should go and let you get on. Frank will be wondering where we've got to. Ready to go home, Lily?' Peta rose and gave Liz a hug. 'It'll all work out. You'll see. Maybe you should pay Magda a visit.' She winked at Liz.

Liz rolled her eyes. She had no time for such nonsense.

Magda Turnbull was the local fortune teller. Actually, she was a masseuse running her business from home on an acreage outside town. But she was also known to read tealeaves and to offer sometimes unwarranted advice and predictions of the future.

'I felt that way, too. But she was spot on when she told me about a silver lining and wedding bells. I could never have imagined Frank and I…' She smiled and gazed into space.

'I have no intention of marrying again.'

'Oh, I didn't necessarily mean marriage. I was thinking about your shop and the development. But…' she gave Liz a speculative look, 'is it such a ridiculous idea? How long has it been?'

'Twenty years. And I'll never forget Dan.'

'Of course you won't, but that doesn't mean you need to stay alone for the rest of your life.'

'Oh! You and Judy!'

'Judy? Did she suggest seeing Magda, too?'

'No, she thinks I need a man in my life. That's her answer to all my woes. As if…' Liz wished Peta would leave. The turn the conversation had taken made her feel uncomfortable.

At the door, Peta gave Liz another hug. 'Thanks for doing this for Lily. And thanks for the tea and scones. You know, they really are very good. Have you thought of entering them into the scone section at the show?'

'Me? You must be joking.'

But after Peta and Lily had left, Peta's words stuck in Liz's mind. She went back to the kitchen and took a bite from one of the remaining scones, savouring the pumpkin flavour, the spices she always added giving it extra bite. Maybe it wasn't such a bad idea. But as for her comments about Sam Walker… Liz wished her married friends would leave her alone. She was quite happy as she was. She didn't need a man to complete her.

Eleven

The campus looked different in daylight. It was a hive of activity. There were students everywhere, standing in groups, moving around and sitting on the grass. Sam found a parking spot and followed Fran's directions to the building labelled School of Music and Drama. It was a modern building unlike some of the others he passed on the way, and today the entrance was buzzing with groups of students, many carrying instrument cases.

'Welcome to the Mad House,' a young man said to him as he pushed open the door. Sam chuckled. He'd already heard the students' nickname for Owen's workplace and thought it fitting.

He climbed the stairs to see Fran through an open door. She was busy at her computer. He knocked gently on the door.

Fran looked up, a smile of welcome on her face. 'Hello, Sam. You found us. Come in. I'll let Owen know you're here.'

Sam entered the tidy office, to hear Owen's voice coming from an inner sanctum. Then the man himself appeared. To Sam's surprise, he looked exactly as he had at the barbecue. He was wearing a disreputable pair of tattered jeans, an equally old pair of trainers and his shirt was hanging out of his waistband. His long grey hair, pulled back in a band, looked as if he'd been running his fingers through it all morning. As Sam watched, he pulled off the band and retied his hair back into the semblance of a bun.

'Come in, come in. You'll have coffee? Fran…'

'Thanks.' Sam nodded.

Smiling, Fran walked towards a Nespresso machine in one corner of the office, while Owen swept a pile of papers from a chair and gestured Sam to sit down. This was going to be an interesting interview.

When she'd made and served the coffee, Fran soundlessly retreated, closing the door behind her.

'Don't know what I'd do without her.' Owen shook his head. 'But you didn't come here to talk about Fran, PA and wife extraordinaire. You want to know about the country music festival.'

'Do you mind if I record this?' Sam took out his phone.

'No worries. By the way, good to see you at the choir again last night. Your son didn't make it?'

'No. Not Mitch's cup of tea. It was a good night. Good to see George Turnbull there. He's a character.' While Sam had enjoyed the music and the camaraderie, Mitch had considered the other members too old for him. 'More your vintage, Dad' had been his opinion.

'Saw you talking with Liz Pender last week. Good woman. You could do worse.'

Sam gulped. *Had Owen read his mind?*

'The festival.' Owen changed the subject without further ado. 'It's a first for Granite Springs, the first of what could become an annual event.' He rubbed his hands together before picking up his mug and taking a sip of coffee. 'It's still a way off. November. But it's coming along nicely. I still have a few contacts in the music business.'

'Can I ask you a bit about that?' Sam had done his homework and also remembered hearing about Owen Larsen and the band he'd played in back in the day. They'd been popular for a time, then had disbanded and were never heard of again.

'It was a long time ago.' Owen waved a hand in the air. 'Before marriage and parenthood got to me. I still play, but more for pleasure these days, and do a bit of composing to keep my hand in,' he said modestly.

'I'd like to include something about it in the article, if I may.'

'Do your worst. There won't be many around who still remember me. It was a student thing. We all moved on.' He gazed reflectively up at the ceiling. 'Those were the days. But enough about me. I've managed to get Trent Bridges for the festival,' he said, naming a well-known country music singer. 'He should appeal to the older section of the community, and Cecy Wright will get the younger generation along. She was runner-up at the Tamworth Music Festival last year – a good voice, she'll go far.'

Sam was impressed. Owen was correct when he said he had contacts in the business.

'Then, of course, there are the local lads. Some of my former and current students. And we're planning a contest of sorts to attract new talent. Should be a good weekend.' He grinned. 'You might think me disorganised,' he grinned again at Sam's expression, 'but where music or drama is concerned, I'm in my element. It's just the day-to-day stuff I can't hack.' He dragged a hand through his hair, ruining the bun he'd carefully fashioned. 'That's where Fran comes in. She keeps me on the straight and narrow.' He chuckled. 'Women! We can't live without them.'

Sam wasn't sure he'd agree. He was managing to live perfectly well without a woman in his life. Though he would like the companionship a woman would bring. Who was he kidding? He'd like the whole enchilada. A picture of Liz Pender, her auburn hair flowing across her shoulders, her brown eyes looking into his, floated before his eyes, to be quickly supressed.

'Sounds like it's going to be an amazing event. Where will it be held?'

'In the showground. It's the perfect venue. All we need is to pray for good weather and we'll be set. Tickets are already selling online, and I understand we're getting a good number of sales from out-of-towners including some from interstate. Then there are the locals, of course. But the visitors should be good for the community, bring in some money to local hotels and businesses. The flow-on effect, I've been told it's called.'

'Right.' Sam knew he had almost enough to flesh out into a good article. 'One more thing, would I be able to speak with a couple of the students who'll be involved?'

'Sure thing. I'll get Fran to check with them and pass on their details. Is that all?'

'I think so. If I need anything else, can I contact you?'

'Sure. I'm always here, though I may be in class. But Fran will he here. She has my diary.'

The two shook hands and Sam left. As he made his way downstairs past more groups of chattering students, he found himself impressed by Owen. Now he'd met him in three different settings, but the man didn't change. Unlike some university professors he'd met – and he'd met a few in his Canberra days – Owen lacked any of the pretensions of many of his peers. At heart, he hadn't travelled far from the student who played in a band. He was an aging hippie who just happened to have been appointed to a professorship. The students must love him. But despite this, he was about to set in motion what promised to be a very successful music festival, one which was sure to put Granite Springs on the map.

*

Sam spent the rest of the day outlining the article and researching Trent Bridges and Cecy Wright. Maybe he could get quotes from them to include, and he'd contact their agents for photos. He needed to have Tim take some of Owen and his students too. He'd check it out with Fran when they next spoke.

Back home, he found Mitch busy on the computer. At least that was better than his iPad or iPhone. He peeked over his shoulder, seeing what he was looking at before his son quickly exited the website.

'Doing some research on CAT?' he asked. 'I thought you were familiar with Thomas' company.'

Mitch swung round to face Sam. 'I was. I am. I was checking what the website says about his Australian operation, why he chose Granite Springs, and what he's doing here. When are you interviewing him?' There was an enthusiasm in his eyes, Sam hadn't seen for some time.

'Not for a couple of weeks. You still want to come with me?'

'Maybe… or maybe I'll try to contact him myself.' Mitch grinned. 'You were right, Dad. It's time I pulled my finger out and started thinking about my future. I do aim to do something with my life, show Abi she can be proud of me – Brooke, too. I just have to find the right opening. I contacted Brooke, and she's agreed I can see Abi. I'm going over to Canberra on Saturday week to take her out for the day.'

'Saturday week? You'll miss the Granite Springs Show.' Sam really wouldn't mind missing it himself, but as editor of the local paper he was bound to make an appearance – and he had to judge the pumpkin scones. He sighed at the thought.

'Oh, I'm devastated.' Mitch rolled his eyes. 'But Abi might enjoy it. I wonder if I can persuade Brooke to let me bring her back here.'

'What a good idea.' Suddenly Sam warmed to the idea of the show if it meant he might get the chance to see his granddaughter. 'There are bound to be lots of animal exhibits, maybe even some rides.' He remembered attending a few country shows when he was a child. His mother's family came from country Victoria and he'd often visited them there. That's what had given him the desire to live on a property of his own. Sadly, neither his parents nor grandparents were still alive.

'Thanks, Dad.' Mitch beamed, making Sam realise how infrequently he'd had cause to praise his son recently. He vowed to find ways to do it more often. We all like to get a positive response from time to time, and Mitch did seem to be making more of an effort. Maybe he wasn't such a lost cause, after all.

Twelve

Liz turned the sign on the shop door to closed with a sigh of relief. It had been another busy Saturday, with the thought of the trip to Canberra eating away at the back of her mind. Now, she had to rush home to feed Marmaduke before heading along the highway, every kilometre of which would take her closer to those memories she wanted to forget.

All of her memories of Canberra weren't bad. She'd enjoyed growing up there. It was where she'd met Dan and they'd had some good years when they returned. But, somehow, the memories of those dreadful days after the news of Dan's death had managed to wipe out all the good ones. Liz knew it was all in her mind and strove to change the pattern, but it was no use. She couldn't erase the sinking feeling she got every time she entered the avenue of trees on the outskirts of the city.

In an attempt to put herself into a more positive frame of mind, Liz tuned into a music channel and sang along to the familiar melodies as she drove along.

It was already dark when she arrived at the family home and turned into the familiar driveway. As soon as she drew up, the front door opened sending a beam of light across the front patio.

'We heard the car,' her mum said, coming out to greet Liz and enveloping her in a warm hug. 'Your dad's been on edge all day in case something happened to prevent you coming.'

'Well, I'm here now. I left as soon as I could.' Liz stifled the urge to make a sharp comment. Her parents knew she ran a bookshop, but often refused to acknowledge she had obligations to her customers. 'How is Dad?'

'Improving. He's a bad patient. I'll be glad when he's back to normal, though the doctors say...'

Liz didn't hear what the doctors said as her father's voice, as strong as ever, called out, 'Is that our Lizzie? Come in and give your old dad a cuddle.'

Smiling, Liz went into the living room, where her father was ensconced in what had always been his favourite armchair. The only sign of his recent surgery was the fact he didn't rise to greet her, and the walking stick by his side.

'So, you finally managed to leave that shop of yours to visit us,' he said, when their greetings were over.

'I'm sorry I couldn't make it here sooner.' Liz didn't know why, but her parents always made her feel the need to apologise. 'But now I'm here, you must tell me everything that's been happening. I'm glad to see you looking so well.'

'Hmph. No thanks to those doctors. They seem to think...'

'Now, now, Doug. They do their best. You just need to be patient.' Liz's mother patted his arm. 'Liz doesn't want to hear all your complaints. Dinner's ready to eat. We thought you'd be here earlier,' she said to Liz.

The dining room hadn't changed. The long table set with her mother's second-best set of cutlery and china reminded Liz of all the meals she'd eaten here while growing up, then the eventful dinner at which she'd introduced Dan to her parents. He'd set out to charm them, and they'd immediately fallen in love with the handsome officer cadet and with his cheeky grin.

Liz blinked to dismiss the image which dredged up from her subconscious and stop herself from tearing up. Her parents wouldn't understand how much the memories hurt her.

'So, anything happening in that sleepy town of yours?' her dad asked jokingly, when the coronation chicken – her mother's favourite stand-by – had been eaten, and her father had given her a blow-by-blow description of his time in hospital.

Liz knew both her parents thought her mad to have hidden herself away in Granite Springs for so long. They'd tried to be understanding when she first moved there, recognising she needed a break. But, as the years went on and she made her life in the small country town, they'd become less accepting of her way of life. Now they were simply bewildered she chose to remain there instead of returning to Canberra.

'Oh, the usual,' she said, deciding not to mention the development proposal. They would only worry and redouble their efforts to have her return. She racked her brains for something to offer them instead. Then she had a brainwave. 'It's the Granite Springs Show next weekend, and I've decided to enter my pumpkin scones in the baking section.'

'That's my girl.' Her father thumped the table with his fist. 'You show them. Are you going to use Flo's recipe?' he asked, referring to the wife of a former premier of Queensland, famous for her pumpkin scones.

'No, Dad. I actually have a recipe of my own. I took a few different ones and added my own touches. It has more spices than most. I don't expect to win anything, but a friend made the suggestion, and I thought why not?'

'Why not, indeed,' her mother said. 'You always liked to bake when you were younger. At one time I thought you might study cooking or nutrition but...' She pursed her lips.

Liz knew her mother had never been completely happy with her career choice – even less with her decision to open a shop. Sheila Browne still held the opinion the best career for a woman was as a wife and mother, tending to ignore the fact her daughter had been a wife but was now a widow. She'd like nothing more than to hear Liz had met someone and planned to remarry. It wasn't going to happen.

The conversation staggered along till Liz yawned. 'I think I'll turn in. I've had a busy week.'

'You don't need to...' her mother began, only to button her lips at a glare from her husband. 'Ailsa's coming to lunch tomorrow. She's looking forward to seeing you.'

'I'm looking forward to seeing her, too. The boys? Bob?'

'Oh, Nathan and Patrick have their own lives now.' She sniffed her disapproval. 'They don't have time for us old folks. And Bob – I'm not sure. We haven't seen a lot of him recently.'

Liz wondered at the brusque tone in her mother's voice. Bob had always been prickly, but he and Ailsa seemed to rub along all right. Liz always regarded theirs as another happy marriage. She remembered how the four of them had double-dated for a while, before she and Dan took to sloping off by themselves. That was a long time ago. Their two boys were in their twenties now, older than Liz's children would have been if she and Dan...

Don't go there.

Once in her room, Liz felt able to breathe again. The bedroom now bore little resemblance to the one she'd grown up in. When she and Dan married, her mother took the opportunity to remodel it, leaving no sign of her teenage years. Probably a good thing, Liz thought as she slipped under the covers, but it now felt more like a hotel room than home. Despite her reluctance, she was glad she'd come. Her parents were both looking older. Her father's surgery had taken a lot out of both of them, giving their faces lines that hadn't been there before. She had to remember they were both close to eighty. As she closed her eyes, she vowed to be kinder to them in future.

*

After a sound night's sleep, Liz felt more able to face her mother over breakfast.

'You'll come to church with me, Liz?' her mother asked as they were enjoying a second cup of tea. 'Or will you stay home with Dad?'

Liz was surprised at her request. Surely her mother knew she hadn't been to church since Dan's funeral. She hadn't been able to speak to the god who'd let her soulmate die. 'No, I think I'll go visit Dan's grave,' she said, only just making the decision. It was a long time since she'd been there. In the absence of an Australian War Cemetery, Dan had been buried in the Gungahlin Cemetery, in a family plot purchased by his parents. Liz had been too distraught to take any part in organising his funeral.

It was a tranquil setting, beautifully landscaped with a lake which attracted many bird species, but it always made Liz shiver. Like most places in the Australian Capital Territory, it was only a short drive away, and she reached the gates of the cemetery before she was mentally or emotionally prepared. Taking a deep breath, she drove in.

'Why did you have to die?' Liz stood at the grave, all that was left of the husband she'd loved more than life itself, and read the quote from the army ode which Dan's parents had inscribed on the stone – *They shall not grow old as we grow old.* How she hated that. It was the reason she avoided RSL clubs too, with their daily two minutes silence and recitation of the ode. She hated the army and everything to do with it. It was the army that had taken Dan from her. But it was accurate. Dan would never grow old. In her imagination he would forever be the handsome young thirty-year-old who'd left one morning, never to return.

Liz let the tears trickle down her cheeks as she thought of all she'd lost. She closed her eyes, picturing the young man whose remains lay there. It was almost as if she could feel his presence, his arms around her, his breath on her cheeks. She had a strong sense he was trying to tell her something.

A bird gave a loud call.

Her eyes flew open. What was she thinking? Dan wasn't here. Why had she come? Was it only an excuse to get away from her parents? Slowly, she retraced her steps. But she couldn't dismiss the feeling that somehow Dan had been reaching out to her, telling her… She shook her head.

*

Lunch was a cheerful affair. Liz's mother had pulled out all the stops and cooked her standard Sunday lunch of roast leg of lamb accompanied by roast veggies, followed by apple pie with cream.

Bob hadn't appeared and, when lunch was over and the washing up done, Liz's sister drew her out onto the veranda to let their parents take a well-earned rest.

'Remember how we used to sneak out here for a sly smoke?' Ailsa leant against a veranda post. 'Those were the days.'

'Mmm. How are the boys?' There had been little mention of them over lunch.

'They're good. Now they both have their own places, they only drop in when they need a good meal or want some laundry done. But they're doing well. Pat has a girlfriend. We've met her. I think this one may come to something, but we're not holding our breath. And Nate, well, he's Nate. He'll never change. He's still the cheeky larrikin he was at seven, only now he's taller than both Bob and me. I can't see him ever settling down.'

'And Bob?' Liz wasn't sure she should ask. 'He didn't come with you today.'

'Obviously. He had work to do.' She hesitated, then, 'Hell, Liz, it's always work these days. He doesn't have much time for anything else, not me, not the boys.' Her voice broke and she turned away to gaze across the yard.

Liz rose from the sunlounge and put a hand on her sister's shoulder. 'I'm sorry, sis.'

Ailsa shook it off and turned to face her. 'It'll be right. We'll be right. We have to be,' she said, drawing in a shaky breath. She forced a smile to her lips. 'But what about you? No man in sight?'

'Ailsa!'

'Liz, it's been twenty years. Surely that's long enough to grieve? I hate to think of you on your own. Isn't there anyone in that small town of yours – some handsome farmer?'

Liz almost burst out laughing. But how dare her sister try to pair her off, especially when it seemed her own marriage might be in trouble. 'Leave it. I'm happy as I am with…'

'I know, I know, your bookshop and your cat. But neither of those will keep you warm at night. I knew Dan, too, remember. He wouldn't want you to…'

'How would you know what Dan would want?' Liz felt her anger rise. How dare Ailsa? But for some reason, Liz remembered the moment at Dan's graveside when she thought he was trying to tell her something. Could Ailsa be right?

'Anyway, there's no one,' she said belatedly, ignoring the image forcing itself into her subconscious, the image of an amused expression on the face of the editor of The Granite Springs Advertiser.

Thirteen

Liz was glad she'd gone to Canberra. It had been good to see her mum and dad again – and Ailsa, though her sister's comments about Bob were a worry. She made a mental note to quiz her about it next time they spoke. And it had been good to visit Dan's grave. But the niggling feeling he wanted to tell her something refused to go away.

She picked up the photo which sat by her bedside, the photo of the smiling young man she'd married. It was a favourite of hers, taken on a holiday in Queensland. He was sitting on the beach, the wind ruffling his hair, his eyes squinting in the sunlight. She remembered the day vividly. They'd spent the whole day on the beach, swimming and lying in the sun. Then they'd had dinner at the surf club before returning to their hotel where they'd drunk champagne on the balcony before going to bed.

Dan looked so young in the photo. He *was* young. She'd been young, too. Liz caught sight of herself in the mirror and grimaced. Where had the years gone?

She kissed the photo and replaced it on the bedside table, before turning back to the mirror to comb her hair and renew her lipstick. Then, telling Marmaduke to be good, she went out to the car.

She drove towards The Bean Sprout Café where tonight's meeting of the protest group's committee was to be held. It hadn't taken much effort on Frank's part to persuade Liz to become part of the inner group, and tonight was to be their first meeting in the back room of the café.

Once they had all settled with coffee, Frank revisited what they knew so far. 'It seems we might have a bit of time up our sleeves,' he finished. 'The planning committee only meets once a month.'

'That's right,' Danny said. 'I managed to speak with Dad without letting him know my views on the matter. He thinks because I'm involved in development, I must be in favour of any developments in the town, regardless of their impact on the community. I have done a bit of research,' he added, pulling out his iPad. 'I did wonder if we could have the shops designated as being of historical significance. They are pretty old.'

Liz leant forward. Was this going to be their answer? How wonderful if it could all be easily resolved.

'I asked Roy to check it out for me as he's been here longer than the rest of us. Roy?'

'No good.' Roy shook his head.

Liz's heart plummeted.

'It wouldn't work. Age alone isn't enough. They would have to meet at least two of the set criteria and as far as I could work out, they don't.'

There was a collective groan.

'Well,' Liz said. 'It seems we need to get more publicity. The community meeting was a good start. But if The Advertiser won't do it for us, we need to do it ourselves.' She looked around the group. 'I suggest we get leaflets and posters made. We can have them placed in all shops that agree – not only those under threat.'

'And in the library, the schools, the university, the hospital, the art gallery – everywhere people go,' Frank said, warming to the idea.

This energised the group, with others making suggestions. By the time the meeting wound up, Liz was feeling more positive. But Sam Walker's refusal to help them still rankled. What was it with the man? Couldn't he see how important this was to the community? How could he allow his stupid dislike of politics to get in the way of helping save the shops?

*

Next evening at the choir, there he was again. Liz felt her anger threaten to boil over at the sight of Sam Walker's figure standing among the basses. His son didn't appear to be with him tonight, but *he* was there large as life and twice as annoying.

Once the music started, Liz was able to forget his presence, but when Owen called a halt to the rehearsal, she could see him out of the corner of her eye. She was chatting with Donna about the writing competition Lily had entered and could see him talking to Owen, then... Oh, no! He was walking in their direction. It looked as if he was heading straight for them. Liz deliberately turned her back towards him, farewelled Donna and walked off. She had no intention of speaking to him again, not tonight, not ever.

Fourteen

The day of the Granite Springs Show dawned. A glorious spring day. Sam whistled as he prepared a breakfast of bacon and eggs with his usual mug of coffee. Mitch had left for Canberra the previous evening. He'd managed to persuade Brooke to allow him to bring Abi to the show as long as he promised to have her home before her bedtime, and had arranged to spend Friday night with an old friend. He was excited at the thought of seeing his daughter again. Sam thought he was also excited about going back to Canberra, but he could be wrong.

Mitch had set up a meeting at the CAT office with Chris Thomas during the week. He'd returned with a smile on his face, but refused to say anything about what had transpired, merely saying it was early days.

It was a long time since Sam had attended a country show, but he had fond memories of wandering around the exhibits with his grandfather. He remembered loving the lines of cages containing all the different breeds of hens and being lifted up to sit on the seat of a tractor. He must have been pretty young at the time. Then there had been the dog trials with dogs called Pink and Brown. And the fairy floss. How he'd loved the fairy floss.

And this time, he was to be a judge. What did he know about pumpkin scones? But he supposed it couldn't be too difficult. He suspected they'd all taste much the same.

Driving through town, he was surprised to see the streets empty, before realising everything was closed for Show Day. Everyone would be at the showground. He slowed as he passed the bookshop on the corner of Main Street. He still hadn't made time for a visit. Remembering the feisty redhead, he wondered if she'd be at the show along with the rest of the Granite Springs community. Maybe he'd bump into her there.

The showground was a hive of activity when Sam pulled into the parking area. His phone pinged with a text just as he stopped the car.

We're here, Dad. Meet you by the baby animal display. M.

Sam smiled. Of course, Abi would have wanted to see the baby animals first. He made his way through the throng of excited people – children running everywhere and farming families who had come in from outlying properties for a day out.

Finally, Sam found the tent with the sign he was looking for. Inside, sandwiched between two groups of other parents and children, he spied Mitch and Abi. The little girl was totally engrossed in patting a pet lamb, her face beaming.

'Look, Grandpa,' she said, when she caught sight of Sam. 'He likes me.' She giggled as the little creature's tongue explored her fingers.

Sam spent the next hour with Mitch and Abi inspecting all the animal tents, before he heard the call for judges for the cooking competitions to make their way to the cooking pavilion.

'That's me,' he said ruefully, loath to leave his little family. It was fun to see the pleasure Abi was having, and how her eyes lit up at the sight of the stick of pink fairy floss, so big it almost hid her face.

'Meet us for lunch, Dad. We're heading off to see the dog trials now.'

'Come too, Grandpa,' Abi pleaded, her voice muffled from the sugary confection which Sam was sure Brooke would disapprove of.

'Sorry, sweetie. I can't. But I'll see you again soon.' He ruffled her dark curls, so like her dad's, before hurrying off.

When he reached the pavilion, filled with tables containing a multitude of cakes of all shapes and sizes, he was greeted by an officious-looking woman carrying a clipboard. 'Sam Walker,' she said, making a mark on her board and handing him an A4 sheet of paper. 'These are the criteria. You should have presented yourself here earlier.' Her voice held a note of reproof. 'You'll find the scones in the back left-hand corner. The pumpkin ones are clearly marked. You need to assess them on these criteria and cut only a small bite from each for tasting. Can you do that?' She looked at him as if doubting his ability.

'I think I can manage.' Sam tried to hide his amusement. It was only a cooking competition. It wasn't going to be the end of the world if he made a mistake. He was beginning to wish he hadn't accepted the invitation.

The tent was empty apart from the other judges, most of whom seemed to be taking their roles more seriously than Sam. He made his way to where the pumpkin scones were displayed. There were six exhibits, each of five scones. To Sam's uneducated eyes they all looked exactly the same. He studied the sheet of paper he'd been given: *Scones should be approximately five centimetres in diameter; well risen, straight sides, thin golden crust top and bottom, no flour base; fine, moist texture, good crumb, good flavour and according to type.* He could do this.

Sam glanced around at the other judges, all of whom were intent on their task. Stifling the urge to laugh, he began to examine the scones laid out before him according to the set criteria, then, using the knife and plate provided, he cut off a small piece from each. He could find no difference in taste between the first five bites, leading him to think he might have to draw a straw to pick the winner. But as he bit into the final scone, he tasted something different. There was a hint of… he closed his eyes and chewed carefully… ginger, and something else he couldn't identify. Whatever it was, it set this scone apart from the others. This would be the one to receive the blue first prize ribbon. As for second and third, he closed his eyes again and picked them at random.

Relieved to have done his duty, he returned his results to the woman with the clipboard who still stood guard at the entrance to the tent and went on his way.

Sam's stomach told him it was lunchtime, the small bites of scone only succeeding in giving him an appetite. He followed the lines of people now heading for the lunch tent where he'd promised to meet Mitch. Inside, he saw Mitch and Abi. Abi was sipping what looked like flavoured milk through a straw and Mitch was guarding a plate containing two meat pies and two packets of sandwiches. He was holding two cans of beer.

'Just in time, Dad. The pies are getting cold and the beer's getting warm.'

'Thanks, son.' Sam slid into the seat opposite Mitch. 'How were the dog trials?'

It was Abi who answered, 'The dogs are so clever, Grandpa. They knew what to do. They got all the sheep together. They even jumped up and ran on their backs.' She giggled. 'It was funny.'

'How were the scones?' Mitch chuckled.

Sam didn't blame him. The whole idea of him judging scones was a joke. 'They were okay. I was given the criteria, so…' He scratched his head, realising he'd ignored most of them and had gone solely on taste. 'Anyway, it's done now.' And next time – if there was a next time – he'd be ready with an excuse.

'You can write it up in your paper.'

'Ha ha.' Though it might not be a bad idea to get the winner to share her recipe – or did those who entered their cooking prefer to keep their recipes secret? He was a complete novice in such matters.

'Where are we going now?' Abi had finished her milk and demolished two of the sandwiches. 'Can I go for a donkey ride and on the chairoplanes and…'

'One thing at a time, Abi.' Mitch gave Sam a rueful grin. 'We passed the funfair section on the way here and I promised Abi we'd go back after lunch. If you want to do something else, we can meet up again later.'

'No, I'll come with you. I just need to…' Sam searched his pockets for his phone. He wanted to check Tim was here as promised to report on the day. The local community would never forgive him if *The Advertiser* didn't provide full coverage. But where was his phone?

He thought back. He'd had it in the cookery pavilion when… He remembered putting it down on the table when he cut the tiny sections from the scones, then… Had he left it there? 'I think I must have left my phone back with the pumpkin scones,' he said. 'I'll catch up with you later.'

The crowds seemed even thicker than before as Sam pushed his way through. Once inside the tent, it was quieter, but still busier than during the judging. Now people were oohing and aahing over the prize-winning entries. There seemed to be an argument going on at the back of the tent where…

'I can't believe it,' the grey-haired matron was saying, her voice loud with anger. 'My pumpkin scone recipe always takes out first prize. There must have been some mistake, or some bribery going on. Who was the judge this year?'

Sam wished he could disappear. He could see his phone still lying there. All he needed to do was reach out and pick it up. But before he could, there was a flash of red, and he heard a vaguely familiar voice.

'Look, Liz. These are yours aren't they, the ones with the blue ribbon? You've won first prize.'

Fifteen

Liz looked to where Judy was pointing. Sure enough, there, sitting in front of her plate of scones, was a blue ribbon proclaiming her the winner.

'It's not fair! She must have bribed the judge.' A solid country woman Liz had never seen before was shouting so loudly everyone had turned to look. Her companion tried to shush her.

Liz raised her eyebrows at Judy.

'That's Maud Corbett,' Judy whispered. 'She's won first for her pumpkin scones for as long as I can remember. I'm really glad you pipped her at the post this year. She's unbearable but a stalwart member of the Country Women's Association. Was president three years running.'

'Maybe there *has* been a mistake,' Liz whispered back. 'Maybe...'

At that moment, a hand reached out to grab something on the table close to Liz's scones.

'It was you!' the woman screamed. 'What did she offer you?'

'I'm sorry?' Sam Walker, to whom the hand belonged, slid the phone into his pocket, while Liz and Judy watched on in surprise.

What was Sam Walker doing here and what was he apologising for?

'I'm afraid I was the one who judged the scones this year and, in my opinion, those were the winners.'

Sam Walker had judged her scones, had awarded her first prize?

'Come away.' Judy pulled Liz away from the argument which looked as if it might continue as Sam tried to defend his decision, and Maud

Corbett's friend tried to silence her. There was already quite a crowd of people listening to the altercation.

'I didn't offer him anything, Judy. I barely know the man. I've spoken to him once and not in the friendliest of terms. I don't even like him.' Liz thought back to the conversation at the choir and the way she'd ignored him at the following rehearsals. It was lucky the entries were judged blind. There was no way he'd have awarded her first prize if he'd known they were hers. 'I didn't even know he'd be judging them.' *Or I might not have entered the blasted competition.*

'Don't be silly. I know Sam Walker, or rather, Alec does. We have some sheep on his land. He's straight as a die. No way he'd be swayed by anything. He must really think your scones were the best.' There was a twinkle in her eye, making Liz wonder what her friend was thinking. She dragged Liz out of the tent. 'Best we stay out of Maud's orbit. She can be vicious when she takes a dislike to someone. I don't envy Sam.'

'What about me?' Liz wailed. 'They are *my* scones.'

Judy chuckled. 'This may just be the highlight of my day. I've wanted to see her taken down a peg for years. I don't think anyone else has been game to overlook her entries. She's only ever won by default.'

'But how did the other judges know?' Liz asked, when they were some distance from the tent.

'No one knows. But we've all suspected she put some distinguishing mark on her plate to let the usual judge know which ones they were.'

Liz allowed herself to be steered towards the luncheon pavilion where Sally was waiting for them, having declared herself too tired to go with them to check out the results of the scone competition. Alec and Neil were at the sheepdog trials. They didn't have an entry themselves this year but, for them, it was an unmissable event. They'd all planned to meet here for lunch.

'Guess what?' Judy enthused when they joined Sally, who had stocked up with packets of sandwiches ready for their arrival. 'Liz's scones won her section.'

'Well done! You must give me your recipe – unless it's secret.' Sally grinned and shifted in her chair.

'No secret. I add ginger, cinnamon and nutmeg and a dash of lemonade. I don't know what all the fuss is about,' Liz said, taking a seat, while Judy went off to get three cups of tea. 'No sign of Alec and Neil?'

'Oh, they'll be ages yet.' Sally dismissed the men. 'Once they start talking sheep, they're on another planet. But I've got used to it.' She gave an affectionate smile. 'I knew what I was getting into when I married Neil. I love being a farmer's wife. And this one will probably be another farmer.' She patted her still flat stomach.

Liz smiled politely. She glanced around to see where Judy had got to and saw her talking to an elderly couple. *It wasn't who she thought it was, was it?*

'Look who I bumped into.' Judy placed the three cups of tea she was juggling on the table and turned to the couple behind her.

'Liz, Sally, you've met Magda and George Turnbull, haven't you?'

Liz nodded. She knew George. He'd been director of the Granite Springs Choristers for years until Owen Larsen took over, and she'd seen Magda around, though they'd never met. She wasn't one of the many women who swore by her massages, or who, like Peta, believed her prophecies of the future.

'I don't think I have,' Sally said. 'But I've heard of you both, of course. I think everyone knows your story. It's like a fairy tale.'

Magda chortled, while George looked down at his feet, embarrassed.

'You'll be young Neil's wife,' Magda said, peering at Sally. 'That's a fine boy you're carrying. He'll be a big help to you in years to come, him and his sister.'

Sally's mouth fell open. 'You mean...'

'It'll be a boy? Yes. I can see him as clear as day.'

Liz squirmed. This was too much. She'd heard all about Magda over the years. Of course she had. And Peta had told her about what she'd said to her. But she'd been under the impression the so-called predictions were couched in vague terms, in ways that those hearing them could take one way or another. Predicting the gender of an unborn child was something else.

As if sensing Liz's thoughts, Magda turned to fix her with a penetrating gaze. 'You've known sorrow,' she said. 'But you mustn't allow it to ruin your life. There's a silver lining waiting for you. You just need to be willing to hold out your hand. Happiness is yours for the taking, and when and where you least expect it. It won't all be smooth sailing, but it'll come right in the end.'

Liz stared at her. She was supposed to believe a string of platitudes from this old white-haired woman? But a shiver went up her spine. She had the same feeling she'd had standing at Dan's grave, that he was with her, trying to tell her something. It was as if time stood still. As if everyone around her disappeared and she and Dan were wrapped in a silken cloud.

She realised Judy had spoken to her. 'Sorry, Judy. What did you say?' When she looked up, Magda and George had disappeared, and Judy was gazing at her in concern. Had she imagined what just happened?

'I asked if you wanted your tea. It's getting cold. You went very quiet, as if you were in a trance.'

'I'm fine.' She picked up her tea and took a sip, then slit open a pack of sandwiches. 'Magda Turnbull, she was here, wasn't she?'

Judy's forehead creased.

'She was and she told me I'm having a boy. Neil will be pleased.' Sally grinned.

'How could she know?' Liz didn't want to pour cold water on Sally's delight but couldn't help herself.

'Who knows?' It was Judy who replied. 'She's never been wrong yet. Some say if she'd been born five hundred years ago, she'd have been burned as a witch.'

'Not in Australia,' Liz said, striving for accuracy, but she knew what Judy meant. The old woman had an other-worldly air about her. Liz now knew what people meant when they spoke about Magda – and she didn't like it.

Sixteen

For the next few days, Sam couldn't stop thinking about the fracas in the show tent. He felt he'd been an innocent pawn in the attempt to turn the scales on the woman who'd been so angry with him. It was only later he'd discovered the choice of him as judge had been a deliberate ploy to foil the charade which had been going on for years, years in which the same woman – a local called Maud Corbett – had won that specific competition.

'I'm sorry,' one of the senior committee members told him later, full of apologies. 'It was the only way we could be sure it was a fair contest. Maud has been around for so long she knows everyone. The others were too afraid to let another contestant win. You were perfect. You deserve a medal.' He laughed. 'I wish I'd been there to see her face.'

Sam didn't share his amusement at the time. But, when he learned the identity of the owner of the scones he'd awarded the blue ribbon to, he did enjoy a quiet chuckle. Liz Pender. He'd never have guessed.

He wished he'd seen *her* face when she realised she was the winner. Her scones were delicious, and now he had even more reason to want to meet her again. He vowed to drop into her bookshop as soon as he could find time.

But it wouldn't be today. Today he was to interview Chris Thomas and he was looking forward to it. Thomas sounded a man much like himself. From what Sam had heard and read about him, it appeared he'd grown up here in Granite Springs before heading off to the States, then Canada where he made his fortune and an international reputation. What puzzled Sam was why he'd returned and why he'd set up this subsidiary office in Granite Springs rather than in a major city. Hopefully this interview would clear it up.

Then there was Mitch's connection with the guy. When Sam asked him if he'd like to accompany him to the meeting, he'd refused, only saying all would be revealed in due course. But Mitch had certainly seemed more cheerful recently, and his reunion with Abi on the weekend had done him the world of good.

Driving out to the technology park, Sam rehearsed the questions he wanted to ask. He suspected this interview would be unlike the one with Owen Larsen a couple of weeks earlier. The article on the music festival had gone down well, with a good number of letters to the paper praising the initiative and The Advertiser's coverage of it. Sam made a mental note to make sure they did a thorough report on the actual festival.

The entrance to the technology park was impressive, more reminiscent of a village than an industrial site. Danny Slater had managed to retain trees and much of the surrounding bush, giving the place the same sort of ambiance as the university campus – without the students. And there was the usual cacophony of local bird life.

There were several cars parked outside the building featuring the logo CAT in large blue letters. It was a low whitewashed building with large glass windows which radiated a welcoming effect.

Inside, it had the same warm feeling, perhaps due to décor which was cleverly done and reminded Sam of the bush outside.

A familiar face greeted him. 'Hello, Sam. Good to see you again. I'll take you through to Chris.'

Sam followed Ann Baird, any awkwardness he might have felt at seeing her again dispelled by her friendly manner. He hadn't known she was now working here with Chris, but it shouldn't have come as a surprise.

A tall man with fading chestnut hair rose to greet Sam as he entered an inner office. He held out a hand. 'Chris Thomas. Welcome to CAT, Granite Springs.'

So, this was the man who'd ousted him in Ann's affections?

'Good to be here. Thanks for seeing me. It's quite a setup you have here.' On his way in to meet Chris, Sam had noticed a large open office with several workstations, and what looked like a group of students being shown around.

'It's coming along.' Chris was smiling with what Sam took to be satisfaction. 'But we still have a way to go. Thanks, Annie,' he said, as Ann brought in two coffees.

'Now, where would you like to start?' Chris asked, when they were both seated at a low table which appeared to have been hewn out of a tree trunk. 'Red cedar,' he said, seeing the direction of Sam's glance. 'It grows closer to the coast, but Peta of *Forrest Interiors* who did the interior design is a clever woman. She knew exactly what would work here.' He stroked the polished surface.

'It's beautiful.' Sam cleared his throat. 'I understand you grew up here and only returned recently. You're well-known internationally, but it seems a bit odd that you've chosen to come back to Granite Springs.'

'Ah! There's a bit of a story there. I guess you could say I was highjacked by the women in my life – my daughter and my partner, Ann, who I understand you know.' He gave Sam a penetrating look. 'But that's not completely accurate. It was my daughter's accident that brought me back – you know about that. Then I discovered this technology park, and circumstances were such that it seemed like a good idea. I suppose you want to know the details?'

'Yes please. I'm also curious to know your motivation to set up CAT in the first place.'

'Right. Well, it was like this…'

It must have been an hour later – and Ann had popped in to replenish their coffee and provide a plate of biscuits – when Chris finally stopped speaking. It was an amazing story, how a young man from Granite Springs had become a world-renowned expert. And he was so modest about his achievements.

'And do you intend to remain here or return to Canada?' Sam asked.

'The million-dollar question.' Chris leant back in his chair and steepled his hands. 'And I don't have the answer. Obviously, the main office will always be Vancouver, and I do need to put in an appearance there from time to time. Annie and I are popping over in a month's time to touch base. But I have a good second-in-command over there, though not here, not yet. But I'm optimistic.' He chuckled. 'I take it Mitch hasn't said anything to you yet?'

'Mitch?' *What did his son have to do with it?*

'Mitch Walker's your son, isn't he?'

'He is.' *And he'd come here to see Chris.*

'We had a good yarn. He's working on a few things for me. I may be able to use him, and if it works out, then…' He smiled, his mouth curling up in delight. 'I may have found the person I'm looking for.'

'But…' Did this mean if Mitch found work at CAT he'd be staying in Granite Springs, or more accurately, with Sam?

'I guess you two need to talk.'

Chris was right. Just wait till he saw Mitch. How could he have kept this from him? His son was more of a dark horse than he'd given him credit for. But Brooke and Abi were in Canberra. Sam had thought… He shook his head. He'd thought Mitch wanted to get his marriage back together again.

*

Sam couldn't wait to get home, but first he had to go back to the office. He couldn't just drop everything to find out what Mitch was up to.

'There's to be another community meeting of this protest group, boss. Do you want one of us to cover it?' Jason popped his head through Sam's door, interrupting his train of thought.

'I don't think so. The Advertiser can't be seen to be taking sides on this matter. Is there nothing else going on?' Damn the protest mob, as Sam had begun to think of them. He'd seen enough protests in his time as a political correspondent covering countries where they really knew how to protest. What was this tinpot protest against a development proposal in a small country town compared to those major insurrections?

'I guess so.' Jason melted away, leaving Sam to remember the fiery woman who'd accosted him at the choir. He'd tried to speak with her the following week but hadn't succeeded. He suspected she was deliberately avoiding him. And it had been *her* pumpkin scones he'd judged at the show. They'd been damn good. She was a beauty, too. And he wasn't accustomed to being ignored by the fairer sex. Why, only last year… but that hadn't ended well, either. Maybe he was losing his touch.

Not that he'd ever been much of a ladies' man. He and Olga had married young, divorced when she couldn't take his frequent absences overseas any longer. Since then, there had been a few women, but nothing serious. He'd been too wrapped up in the job to think of anything long term. But now, here in Granite Springs, it was a different matter. And Liz Pender intrigued him.

*

Mitch was on his computer when Sam arrived home, and there was a delicious aroma filling the kitchen.

'Good day?' Sam asked, before opening the fridge to remove a can of beer and holding it up to Mitch.

'Thanks, Dad.'

Sam tossed him the can, taking out another for himself and snapping it open.

'Pretty good. You?' Mitch took a slug of beer. 'You were meeting with Chris Thomas today, weren't you?'

'That's right.' Sam pulled out a chair, turned it around and sat astride it. 'He mentioned you.'

'Thought he might.' Mitch looked smug. 'I wanted you to hear it from him.'

'He didn't say much, told me to talk with you. So, what gives?'

Mitch swung his chair round to face Sam. 'I went to see him. I told you I did.'

Sam nodded and took a swig of beer.

'Well, I gave him a copy of my CV and told him what I'd been doing in Canberra. I also mentioned a few things I've been working on outside of work, more along the lines of the sort of stuff CAT does. He was interested. I was hoping…' Mitch looked down. 'I thought maybe he could use some of my skills, the ones I'd taught myself when I was bored out of my mind. He seemed to be impressed. But he was also interested in the project management stuff I'd been involved in. Dad, I think he might be going to offer me a job.'

This was what Chris Thomas had hinted at. But what did it mean for Mitch, and for Sam?

He was about to ask, had opened his mouth to speak, when Mitch forestalled him. 'I know what you're going to say, Dad. What about Brooke and Abi? I'd really love to work with CAT. It'd be like a dream come true. But I do want to try again with Brooke. I miss her and Abi. It was so good to see her on the weekend. She's growing up so fast.'

'So, what about Brooke and Abi?'

'That's it. I need to persuade Brooke to move here, to Granite Springs.'

'Have you spoken to her about it?'

'Not yet.' Mitch sighed. 'When I took Abi back on Saturday, she... she was in a bit of a mood. It wasn't a good time.' He bit his lip. 'I just need to find the right time.'

'Have you really thought this through, son? Brooke is a city girl. She might find it difficult to adjust to life in a small town, away from her family, her friends, the big stores.' Brooke was a habitual shopper.

'I know, Dad, but...' he gave Sam a piteous look, '...it'd be such a great opportunity.'

'When do you plan to tell her?'

'I thought I'd go back to Canberra next weekend. Abi's going to a birthday party, so Brooke and I can have the chance to talk. We have a few things to sort out anyway. I left in such a rush.' He gave a wry grin. 'Didn't have much choice. But if she sees I'm trying, that this could lead to better things, don't you think...?'

Sam drew a hand through his hair. 'I'm the wrong person to ask. Look at your mum and me, and I haven't found anyone since who's willing to put up with me.' An exaggeration, but it served his purpose.

'I thought, if she agrees, we could all stay here for a bit, till we can find a place of our own.'

Sam's heart plummeted. Having Mitch stay was one thing. He was his son, and he hadn't really had any choice. But Brooke and Abi? Abi was a dear girl, but Sam wasn't used to having a child around all the time, and Brooke... He and his daughter-in-law had never been close. She had developed a closer relationship with his ex and Sam always felt the two discussed him when they got together, listing his shortcomings and working out in what ways Mitch and he were alike.

'Let's just see what happens,' he said. 'Now, what is that delicious cooking smell?'

After a tasty dinner of a spicy curry which reminded Sam of his student days in a share house in Canberra, Mitch sloped off to bed, leaving Sam to ponder on their conversation. While he was delighted Mitch had found something he wanted to do, and that Chris Thomas appeared to be impressed with his son's capabilities, the ramifications of Mitch moving to Granite Springs on a permanent basis were huge.

The potential arrival of Brooke and Abi would be a disruption to the peaceful life he'd established here. But, if they didn't agree to join Mitch, where would it leave his son? Either way, life wasn't going to remain the same.

Seventeen

Liz settled Marmaduke on the sofa, ensured his bowl was filled to the brim and gave him a cuddle. It was good of Judy to invite her out to Wooleton for lunch again. She didn't need an excuse but had said she wanted to celebrate her blue ribbon from the show, so Liz had baked another batch of scones which were now sitting in a Tupperware container on the back seat of her car.

The show had only been a week ago, but it seemed like much longer. It had been a busy week, not only in the bookshop, though there had been a flurry of customers eager to congratulate her on her winning scones. Liz hadn't thought it such a big deal, showing how little she knew of the women of Granite Springs, despite having lived here for twenty years.

Liz's evenings had been busy, too. Now she'd decided to come on board with Frank's committee, she discovered there was a lot of preparatory stuff to do in order to make their submission to the planning committee, which still hadn't met.

On Tuesday, The Advertiser had begun its feature on Main Street, starting with a spread on The Bean Sprout Café which delighted Frank who'd been able to pull out old family photos and tell anyone who asked – and a lot who didn't – how his parents had fled Italy after the war to seek refuge right here. It was news to many that not everyone in Italy had supported the fascists, and the article had resulted in extra trade for the café.

But, to Liz's disappointment, Sam Walker had stuck to his guns and there had been no mention of the development proposal, or the threat to the other side of Main Street. She had to admire the man's principles. There weren't many like him these days. But surely it wouldn't have hurt to take a stand on something so crucial to the town's future?

She couldn't forgive him for that, so, despite his having judged her pumpkin scones to be the best in the show, she'd avoided him again at the choir on Tuesday evening, managing to walk away when it seemed he might be moving in her direction.

But, if she had managed to avoid the man himself, she hadn't managed to dismiss him from her thoughts. As she drove out to Judy's, she wondered how a man like Sam Walker came to end up in Granite Springs.

When she drove up to the Wooleton homestead, Liz was surprised to see an unfamiliar car already parked there. Judy hadn't said anything about another guest or guests. Her eyes flitted over the dark red Range Rover, wondering who owned the beast. She had a vague recollection of seeing it somewhere. Perhaps it belonged to a neighbouring farmer.

'Here she is.' Judy's voice greeted Liz as she climbed the steps to the wide veranda, the container of scones in one hand. 'You know Sam Walker, of course, Liz, don't you?'

Liz stared at the man who now rose to greet her, hand outstretched, his face filled with amusement.

'The lady with the scones,' he said.

'I... I brought some for you,' she said to Judy, glaring at her friend as she handed over the container, and smiling to Judy's husband, Alec, who was sitting near Sam.

Judy's eyes twinkled as if she could read her mind.

Liz studied Sam Walker surreptitiously, noting the silver flecks which dotted the dark hair, the flicker of amusement in his eyes that never seemed to be far away. While she was angry with Judy for setting this up – sure Alec had nothing to do with it – there was something about Sam Walker that aroused her curiosity about this man who seemed to keep popping up in her life.

Looking at his outstretched hand, the old woman's words came back to her and she almost refused to shake it. But good manners prevailed. 'Hello again,' she said, her mouth suddenly dry as she took his hand, then sank into one of the cane chairs which dotted the veranda.

'We have sheep on agistment at Sam's place,' Alec said, unintentionally coming to her rescue. 'Over yonder.' He pointed into the distance. 'And Judy tells me it was him who did the judging at the show. Set the ladies of the CWA talking, you did,' he said to Sam with a chuckle.

'I think that was the aim of it.' Sam gave a wry grin. 'I'll be more careful next time I'm invited to judge anything in Granite Springs. But they were the best scones, the tastiest.' He smiled at Liz.

Liz felt her legs go weak. Then gave herself a mental shake. He had charm all right. She supposed it was his background in politics. He'd need to have been able to winkle information out of those hard-headed Canberra bods. But he needn't think he could charm her.

'You look as if you could do with a drink, Liz.' Alec reached for a bottle of wine which was sitting in an ice bucket on a side table, and Liz realised the others already had glasses.

'Thanks.' She accepted the glass of white wine and took a welcome sip, listening as Alec and Sam discussed the lack of rainfall and the options Sam had for his twenty acres.

'Can I help?' Liz asked, when Judy rose, muttering about lunch. Without waiting for a reply, she followed her friend into the kitchen.

'I know what you're up to,' she said, as soon as they were out of earshot of the two men. 'How dare you!'

'I don't know what you're talking about.' Judy chuckled. 'Alec wanted to have a chat with Sam, and I thought it would be a good idea to invite him to lunch. I didn't expect you to get your knickers in a knot just because an eligible single man joins us for lunch.'

'You… you…' Liz was lost for words. She took a deep breath, then a sip from the wine she'd carried in with her. 'I told you I didn't need a man in my life.'

'I know what you told me.' Judy took Liz's hand. 'But you have to admit, he's pretty hot.' She grinned. 'If I wasn't married to Alec, he could put his Blundstones under my bed any time.'

'Judy!' Liz pretended to be infuriated, but Judy's words conjured up the image not only of the shiny brown boots Sam Walker was wearing, sitting neatly under her bed, but the man himself *á poil*. She blushed. 'Sorry, Dan,' she muttered under her breath. She hadn't thought of another man that way in twenty years.

'Apart from anything else, he's refusing to support us in opposing the development.' Liz took a sip of wine, stifling the annoyance she always felt at Sam Walker's refusal to help them. 'Now, what needs to be done?'

'Nothing really. I only have to take a quiche and salad out of the fridge. Methinks you protest too much, Liz. What is it about Sam that has you in such a lather?'

Liz twirled her glass and tried to come up with an answer, some logical reason for her antipathy to the man. But she couldn't think of a reason Judy would accept, other than his refusal to allow The Advertiser to support the protest group. 'You don't understand,' she said at last. 'He's so… so…' She raised both hands, almost spilling the remains of her wine in the process. 'It's the way he seems to find everything amusing,' she said at last, knowing how weak she sounded.

'Oh, if that's all.' Judy grinned as she opened the fridge.

'Oh!' Liz wanted to stamp her feet, just as she would have when they were both eight years old and quarrelling over something in the school playground. But she wasn't a child any longer and couldn't indulge in a tantrum, however much she wanted to.

'How's lunch coming along?' Alec popped his head into the kitchen followed by Sam wearing the amused expression that made Liz want to throw something at him.

'Be nice,' Judy mouthed silently to Liz, before saying, 'Ready in a tick. Could you set the table on the veranda, Liz?'

'Another beer, Sam?' Alec reached past Judy to extract two cans from the open fridge.

Liz set down her glass and, taking four sets of cutlery from the drawer, went onto the veranda. It was peaceful out there with only the sound of the birds and the occasional snuffling of the farm dogs. She slowly managed to regain her equilibrium and forget Judy's comments – and her own reaction.

She had just finished setting the table when she sensed a presence behind her. Turning quickly, she almost bumped into Sam Walker's broad chest. 'Oh!' She put a hand out to steady herself and found she was fighting for breath.

'We seem to have got off on the wrong foot,' he said, with that infernal grin of his. 'I'm not really a monster.'

Liz could feel the blush rise to her cheeks. It took all her strength to stop her hands rising to them, too. This was one of the curses of her pale skin. She knew exactly how it would look. She forced herself to meet his eyes, knowing what she'd see there. But, instead of the amused grin she considered to be patronising and arrogant, she saw only concern and… interest.

'I don't think you're a monster,' she mumbled in embarrassment. She was a guest in her friend's home. He was a guest, too. She owed it to Judy and Alec to be polite, to 'be nice' as Judy had requested, or had it been more of a demand?

'I realise you don't agree with my editorial views, but can we bury the hatchet and be friends?'

Liz looked into his eyes again, expecting to see the arrogance she believed would be there, but seeing instead a pleading expression which reminded her of Marmaduke when he wanted something from her. She weakened. 'Maybe, but…' She was prevented from continuing by Alec's appearance.

Lunch progressed smoothly, with Liz discovering very little more about Sam Walker than she already knew.

'I guess I got burnt out,' he said ruefully. 'When this job came along, it was a godsend. I grabbed it with both hands. It's why I don't want to get involved in local politics,' he said to Liz. 'I'm aiming for a peaceful life. I want The Granite Springs Advertiser to be impartial. I'm not about getting involved in contentious issues.'

'But…' Liz began, then bit her lip as Judy gave her a gentle kick under the table. 'Your article about The Bean Sprout Café was good,' she said instead.

'Thanks. I was pleased with it, too. I suspect there's a lot more history to discover in the town. I'd like to interview you about The Reading Corner.'

'Oh!' Liz hadn't expected that. 'I haven't been there long enough for it to be interesting, not like the Beattie family.'

'You've been there for almost twenty years,' Judy said. 'That counts for something.'

'It certainly does.' Sam smiled across the table at Liz.

To her annoyance, she felt her resolution falter under his gaze.

'Perhaps we could set a time?'

Liz felt trapped. She didn't want to set up an interview with Sam Walker. But both Judy and Alec were looking at her expectantly. It would be churlish to refuse. 'Perhaps,' she said, hoping it would be the end of it for now. She could always pull out later.

'I know you'll be busy during business hours. How about I shout you a drink at *The Springs*? We can chat then. Are you free on Wednesday? Seven o'clock?'

Eighteen

Sam wondered how Mitch was getting on. He'd gone to Canberra for the weekend to talk with Brooke. He'd been pretty tight-lipped about it, but it was Sam's impression his son wanted to mend fences with his wife. Now there was a new job in the offing – assuming all went well with Chris Thomas – he had hopes Brooke might change her mind.

But that had been three days ago. It was now Monday evening and there was still no sign of him. Sam fingered his mobile phone. Should he call, text? But he slid it back into his pocket. Mitch was a grown man. It was his life. He wouldn't thank his dad for interfering.

After a meal of steak and potatoes with a side of cauliflower, Sam settled in front of the television. But even the reruns of his favourite British detective show didn't hold his attention and he decided to have an early night.

After tossing and turning for what seemed like for ever, he finally fell into a restless sleep, only to be rudely awakened in what seemed to be the middle of the night, by a set of headlights shining in through his bedroom window.

Mitch was back.

Deciding now wasn't the time to confront his son, Sam turned over and tried to get back to sleep, vowing to talk with Mitch in the morning.

Six o'clock came too soon for Sam, but the cackle of kookaburras wakened him at the usual time, causing him to remember Mitch's late arrival the previous night. Refreshed after a cool shower, Sam dressed and popped his head into his son's room.

Mitch was still dead to the world. He must have been exhausted when he arrived home because, although his shoes were lying on the floor, he hadn't taken time to undress and was stretched out across the bed, covered only by a blanket. There was a distinct smell of alcohol in the room.

Sam smiled and closed the door again. Any discussion would have to wait till the evening. He sighed. He'd planned on going to the choir again, to seeing Liz Pender there, to perhaps managing to have a proper conversation with her before they met the following evening. She was an interesting woman. She intrigued him. And he was looking forward to getting to know her better.

Tuesday was one of their publication days at the paper, so he was kept busy for most of it, but did manage to do some research on The Reading Corner in preparation for his meeting with its owner. To his surprise, there wasn't a lot of information apart from records of author talks, book clubs and various competitions for children. He did discover the shop had been empty for several years before Liz bought it and turned it into a bookshop. That in itself was interesting. The neighbouring shops had been bought over some time after her purchase, meaning she was the only sole owner.

He wondered what would happen if she held out while the others caved into the developer, before deciding it was none of his business. He wasn't going to get involved in local politics, not even for Liz Pender.

*

As a result of his lack of sleep, Sam was feeling weary when he drove home that evening. He'd tried to call Mitch during the day without success, and assumed the younger man was either still in bed or otherwise occupied and didn't want to talk to him. Too exhausted to contemplate cooking, and unsure Mitch would have prepared anything to eat, he picked up a couple of dishes from the local Chinese restaurant before leaving town.

'Dad!' Mitch greeted Sam as he walked in. 'I got back late.'

'I heard you. You were fast asleep when I left this morning.'

'Yeah.' Mitch dragged a hand through his hair. 'I… I had a few drinks with a mate before I left Canberra. Lucky I didn't meet a breathalyser on the highway.' He yawned.

'When did you get up?'

'I don't know… About four?' He yawned again.

'I brought some Chinese takeaway. Hungry?'

'Mmm.'

Deciding to ignore Mitch for now, Sam set about unpacking the food and placing it in the oven to warm while he set the table and poured himself a glass of wine.

When the meal was ready, the aromatic aroma filling the kitchen, Mitch roused himself to take a can of beer from the fridge. 'Hair of the dog,' he said.

Sam grunted, waiting till the meal was over before asking, 'How did it go with Brooke?'

'Not good.' Mitch shook his head. 'At first, she didn't want to talk with me at all, but Abi was pleased to see me, so she let me into the house. I told her about CAT, about how Chris Thomas seems to be impressed by me, the job he's offering. But it cut no ice with her. She's adamant, Dad. It's Canberra or nothing. I can't face going back to what I was doing before. But I want my family. I want Brooke and Abi. I don't know what to do.'

Mitch looked so despondent. It reminded Sam of when his son was small and missed out on getting into the footie team. Back then, he wanted Sam to fix things for him, to make it right. But Mitch was no longer a child. He was thirty years old. This was something Mitch had to work out for himself. 'Do you still love her, son?'

Mitch gave Sam a dazed look. 'Of course, I do, Dad. Her and Abi. But this job with CAT. I never imagined something like this would come my way. If only Brooke…' He shook his head.

'Well, there's nothing to be done about it right now. Seems to me what you need is a good night's sleep. Maybe things will look brighter in the morning.'

'Hmm.' But Mitch rose from the table and ambled off to bed.

Left by himself, Sam wondered how he could help. He didn't want to interfere in his son's marriage – he hadn't made such a good fist of his own – but maybe if Brooke could be persuaded to at least visit Granite Springs, meet some others of her own age. He thought of Neil and Sally. Alec Thomson's nephew and his wife. Alec's wife, Judy, seemed like a sensible woman. Maybe she'd have some ideas.

Nineteen

What had possessed her to agree? But, with Sam Walker's eyes on her, Judy and Alec smiling their approval, how could she have refused?

Now she was obligated to meet him at *The Springs* for an interview. At least she hadn't had to face him at choir the previous evening. She'd kept an eye on the door until Owen called them to order, but there had been no sign of Sam Walker. Nevertheless, the prospect of him arriving had spoiled her customary enjoyment of the music. Damn the man! How was it he had this effect on her?

Despite her reluctance to meet Sam, Liz had spent the day, between customers, working out what to wear. But now the time had come, she decided the black wide-legged pants and thigh-length multicoloured tunic top she'd worn all day would have to do. She checked herself in the mirror, seeing a middle-aged woman of forty-nine who had more curves than she'd had at twenty-nine, or even thirty-nine. Living alone meant she often snacked instead of cooking a proper meal, and those snacks all added up to extra kilos. She twisted this way and that, but no matter which way she looked at herself, there was no hiding the extra layers of fat the years had added.

What was she worrying about? This wasn't a date. It was an interview, an opportunity to promote the bookshop and perhaps, if she was clever, to promote the case against the development.

The community meeting on Monday had gone well with a larger crowd showing up than had at the first meeting. The posters and leaflets had done their work, though she'd been disappointed no one from The Advertiser had attended. Now she had agreed to join the committee she was committed to their cause. The group comprised Frank, Peta, Peta's cousin Ann, Ann's partner, Chris, two of the other affected shopkeepers and the realter, Danny Slater.

Liz felt like she imagined the early suffragettes felt when they chained themselves to the railings outside Buckingham Palace. What the committee had done, was to prepare a submission for the planning committee, one which outlined the background of their argument and requested a halt to the process. Frank had presented it to the meeting and received an enthusiastic response.

Liz gazed around when she entered *The Springs* foyer. The motel was relatively new and set on the outskirts of town. Liz hadn't visited it before, though she'd heard all about it from her friend, Peta, who'd been responsible for the décor. She smiled at the sight of the Australian bush motifs which were Peta's hallmark.

Sam Walker rose to greet her, his outstretched hand again reminding her of Magda Turnbull's prediction before she dismissed the memory. It was a lot of rubbish. Everyone shook hands when greeting. Why did Sam Walker's perfectly ordinary gesture call up the old woman's words? Hold out her hand for happiness indeed – the woman was mad or suffering from dementia. Liz almost snorted and covered it with a cough.

'Did you say something?'

'No. Sorry. I was admiring the décor. I haven't been here before.' Liz gazed around again, hoping he wasn't a mind reader and the blush which rose to her cheeks would quickly subside.

'We can sit over here.' Sam led her to a corner booth. 'I often interview people here. It's relatively quiet and they find it easier to relax. What can I get you to drink? Wine?'

'White, thanks.' Liz watched him make his way to the bar. Relax? She was so tense she thought she'd snap. Maybe a glass of wine would help.

'Thanks.' Liz accepted the wine, her fingers slipping on the moist glass. She took a sip.

'Have you lived in Granite Springs for long?' Sam leant back in his seat and took a drink of his wine. It seemed he wasn't in a hurry to start the interview.

'Long enough.'

'And how long is that?' There was his amused expression again.

'Twenty years.' Liz looked down at her hands, her laced fingers, her answer taking her back to that first visit to Judy and Alec's property, to the peace she'd found there, to her decision this was where she wanted to spend the rest of her life.

'And you came from?'

'Canberra,' she said shortly. She knew what he was doing. Soften them up, then move in for the kill. Though it wasn't an apt metaphor. There was no kill. He only wanted to know about the bookshop, didn't he?

'Twenty years ago…' Sam gazed into space, '…I would have been in Afghanistan back then. Not something I want to remember.'

The hairs on the back of Liz's neck rose. Afghanistan. When Dan was there. When he… She swallowed. She wanted to ask him but didn't want to tell him about Dan. It was too personal, too private. 'It must have been difficult,' she said.

'Yeah. It had its moments.' He took another drink then shook his head. 'But I was only a journalist. The poor bastards who were fighting were the ones who deserved your sympathy.'

Liz thought she was going to be sick. 'I… you'll have to excuse me.' She stumbled away from the booth, her eyes searching for a sign to the ladies. Finally finding it, she pushed open the door.

Grasping the edge of the basin with both hands, Liz dry-retched then took several deep breaths before looking into the mirror. To her surprise, her face showed no sign of the shock she was feeling. She cupped her hand under the tap and took a welcome sip of water. Then she walked back to join Sam.

'Is everything all right? Was it something I said?' She noticed he'd renewed their drinks while she was gone.

'Yes, thanks. No. Sorry.' She returned to her seat.

'So, you're a Canberran, too?'

'Born and bred.' This was a more comfortable conversation.

'It's a good city, but things are more laid back here in Granite Springs.'

'What brought *you* here?' Liz was curious as to why the top rate journalist had chosen to leave the limelight for a small country town newspaper. 'Why Granite Springs?'

'Got sick of the high life.' He chuckled. 'No, to be honest, as I think I said, I was burnt out. After years in war zones, followed by the political climate of Canberra, I was in need of a quieter life – and I found it. That's why...'

'Why you choose to stay out of local politics?' Liz asked, neatly, she thought, bringing up the issue *she* wanted to talk about. 'I didn't see The Advertiser represented at the community meeting on Monday.'

'Let's not go there. We're here to talk about The Reading Corner.'

'But if the development goes ahead, there will be no Reading Corner. It will become part of a commercial retail hub or some such thing.'

'Perhaps. All the more reason to put it on the map now, while there's still time.' He tilted his head to one side, making Liz wonder exactly what he was thinking.

'Do you mean you think these articles about Main Street are your way of... of supporting us?' Her eyes widened.

'I didn't say that.' He still looked amused, but this time his expression didn't annoy Liz. She was beginning to realise there was more to Sam Walker than met the eye. He was an experienced journalist, maybe this was his way. 'There's more than one way to skin a cat,' he said with a grin, reinforcing her theory.

'Do you mind if we record our conversation?' he asked, taking out his phone and placing it on the table, a sign the interview proper was about to begin.

The next hour passed swiftly as Sam gently and cleverly encouraged Liz to talk about how she made her dream of owning her own bookshop into a reality. Liz was surprised when he finally turned off the recording and said, 'I think that covers it. I should have enough for the article. Do you mind if I send Tim along to take some photos?'

'Not at all. We're done?' She looked at the empty wineglasses, at the room behind them which was now filling up with late-night drinkers.

'We are.' Sam slipped his phone into his pocket. 'Unless you'd like another glass of wine?' He raised one eyebrow.

'Thanks, but I don't think so. Two is my limit.'

'It wasn't too painful, was it – the interview? You seemed pretty tense when you arrived, then you dashed off like that. I hope I didn't touch any nerves.'

'No, quite painless.' Liz smiled. The interview had actually gone much better than she'd expected. Sam had a way with him, a way of gently drawing a person out. She found she'd been much more forthcoming than she'd intended about herself and her goals and dreams. The only thing she hadn't mentioned was her marriage and Dan's death. Both of those were far too personal to share with someone like Sam Walker, even if she was beginning to revise her opinion of him.

'Can we do this again?'

Liz looked up, startled. 'But I thought…'

Sam chuckled. 'Not another interview. I've enjoyed your company. I'd like to get to know you better. I think we could have a lot in common. I'd like to invite you to dinner.'

'Oh!' Liz didn't know what to say. If anyone had suggested to her, before tonight, that she'd even consider accepting his invitation, she'd have told them they were mad. But, now she'd spent time with him, Sam Walker had ceased to annoy her. She even suspected she might enjoy his company – and she might even be able to change his mind about The Advertiser's policy.

'No need to decide now,' he said. 'Take time to think about it. But you have to agree I'm not the ogre you seemed to imagine I was. How about I call you?' His lips twisted into a smile and his eyes crinkled in a most attractive way.

'Not an ogre at all,' she said, smiling back at him.

Twenty

Pleased with the outcome of his interview with Liz the evening before, Sam wasted no time before speaking with Tim on Thursday morning to arrange for the photographs to go along with the article he had already started to write. He'd decided to accompany Tim to the bookshop to give him an excuse to see Liz again.

While the interview had gone well, Sam felt there was more to Liz than she'd been willing to reveal. He still didn't know why she'd chosen to leave Canberra. She must have been in her twenties at the time, and it was unusual for someone of that age to leave the city for a country town. It was different for someone of his age who was weary of the city and all it stood for, who was seeking a measure of peace in his life.

She hadn't refused his invitation to dinner, but she hadn't accepted it either, and he hadn't wanted to push it. It might be better to lead her into it gently, to accompany Tim to the bookshop and ask her again when he was there. He wanted to see where she worked, the shop she'd set up. What he really wanted to know was what had driven her to come to Granite Springs in the first place, what she was running away from. Because, in his opinion she must have been running away from something or someone. Was there someone in Canberra she wanted to flee from or was she, like Mitch, running from a job she hated?

Thinking of Mitch reminded Sam of his decision to talk with Judy Thompson. He picked up his phone.

*

Three o'clock saw Sam crossing Main Street to The Bean Sprout Café. He could see Judy already seated by the window. Luckily for him, she already had plans to come into town for shopping and was happy to meet him for coffee. 'I'll be ready for a break by three,' she said, 'if that works for you.'

'Thanks,' he said, as Frank slid a cup of black coffee towards him.

Judy was already enjoying a flat white. 'What's this about, Sam? You sounded worried on the phone. How can I help?'

'I don't know you can, Judy. But I thought… It's Mitch.' He took a sip of coffee.

'Is he all right?'

'Yes and no. As I may have told you and Alec, he arrived in Granite Springs unexpectedly. His wife and daughter are still in Canberra.'

'The lovely little girl who was with you at the show? I remember when Daisy was her age – Neil's daughter from his first marriage. Has your son's marriage broken up?'

Sam hadn't known Neil had been married before, a daughter, too. He hadn't seen any sign of her on the farm so she must live with her mother. He hoped Mitch and Brooke could patch things up. He'd hate his granddaughter to miss out on having her father with her.

'Not exactly, but I'm afraid it's on the cards.' He briefly outlined the situation finishing with, 'I'm not sure if you can help, Judy, but you were the only person I could think of. Can you suggest any way we can tempt Brooke to come to Granite Springs, and how we can persuade her to move here? It would mean so much to Mitch, might even save his marriage.'

'Wow! You expect a lot from me. Maybe you should be asking Magda Turnbull.'

'Who?'

'Sorry. My little joke. She's a local woman who's well known for making accurate predictions about the future. We all think she's a bit of a witch, and it sounds like you need a bit of magic to change your daughter-in-law's mind.'

'You're not wrong.' Sam slumped in his seat. Maybe this hadn't been such a good idea. What had he expected Judy to say?

'But let me think. Your Mitch and his wife would be around the same age as Neil and Sally?'

'He's thirty. Brooke, too.'

'Mmm. Well, Sally came here from the city and she loves it. But she had a reason to come here. I guess Brooke would have, too.' She picked up her cup and clasped it in both hands. 'I wonder… would it be possible to persuade her to come for a visit? Sometimes Granite Springs takes a hold of people.' She chuckled. 'It happened to my friend, Liz. When her husband died, she needed a break, wanted to get out of Canberra. She never left.'

Sam felt a tightness in his chest. Liz Pender was a widow. But that didn't explain her apparent antipathy towards him – though he did sense it was lessening. He wanted to know more. How did her husband die? Was it in an accident? But he didn't want Judy to become aware of his interest. 'You've known her a long time?' he asked instead.

'Liz? Since primary school. We both grew up in Canberra.' She laughed. 'I guess you could say Granite Springs trapped me, too. Though Alec and I met at uni. He didn't plan to become a farmer. He was going to be a city lawyer. We had our life all mapped out, then…' She sighed. 'But it wasn't to be. The old man wanted him to come back to the farm and, like a good son, he did. We've been here ever since and haven't regretted it. But my story doesn't help your son. Sorry.'

'But you've given me an idea. I'll suggest to Mitch he invite Brooke and Abi to visit.' Even if it meant a difficult time for Sam.

'Let me know when you do. We'll put on a barbecue, get Neil and Sally along. Maybe even…' She paused a moment. 'It's not common knowledge, but they're working on Daisy's mum to let her move here to live with her dad. Tina's remarried and Neil gets the impression her new husband's not too keen on having Daisy around. Together with the fact Daisy is begging to be here for the baby's birth, he may manage to swing it.'

Sam didn't see how that could help.

'If she's here when your granddaughter comes to visit.'

'Oh!' It might make a difference, at least where Abi was concerned, but Sam thought it would take more to sway Brooke. 'Thanks Judy. I'll talk with Mitch. You've given me food for thought.'

But as he drove home, he wasn't thinking about what Judy suggested to help Mitch. He was wondering about Liz Pender, how devastated she must have been at the death of her husband. Twenty years ago, he'd have been a young man, in the prime of his life. Aware of the warmth he'd already experienced from the Granite Springs community, he wasn't surprised Liz had found a haven here. It made him more eager than ever to know her better.

Twenty-one

Liz dressed more carefully than usual on Friday morning, knowing the photographer from The Advertiser would be coming to the bookshop. She didn't know Tim Clark well, but Granite Springs was a small enough town for her to have come across him a few times. He was a pleasant young man and an excellent photographer.

She examined herself in the mirror, hoping the matching green pants and tunic were as slimming as Eve Tait had assured her in the boutique. At least she knew the colour suited her – Dan had always loved her in green – though she doubted the paper would print a coloured shot.

Marmaduke must have sensed something was up. He'd been fussing around her ankles ever since his breakfast, meowing and purring and generally getting in the way.

Maybe you'll have your photo taken, too,' she said to him, picking him up and popping him into his cat basket.

As a batch of satisfied customers walked out, chatting among themselves, Liz saw Tim Clark taking shots outside. Then, the door opened to not only Tim, but...

'I didn't expect to see you today,' she said to Sam Walker, trying to subdue a fluttering in her stomach at the sight of his now familiar smile.

'I decided it was time I visited your bookshop,' he said, his gaze moving around to examine the shelves and displays, finally settling on Marmaduke who was curled up in his favourite spot, on a beanbag in the children's corner. 'A cat, too.'

'Marmaduke.' *What was Sam doing here?* It was more than idle curiosity. She knew Tim was perfectly capable of taking photos without his editor breathing down his neck.

'Nice place you have here. Mind if I browse while Tim does his thing?'

'Not at all.' *What else could she say?*

Tim set up the lighting he'd brought along and fussed around taking shots of Liz, Marmaduke, the shelves of books, a couple of delighted customers and even a few of Sam with his nose in a book.

'I think I'm done,' he said at last. 'Thanks. I can let you have copies if you like.'

'Thanks, Tim. I would, very much.'

'Be seeing you.'

Tim left, the noise of the door slamming shut behind him seeming to bring Sam out of the book he'd been perusing intently. He wandered over to where Liz was standing behind the counter and placed the book down. 'I'll take this one.'

He was still standing there when Liz had completed the transaction. He coughed. 'I've been meaning to call,' he said. 'But I'm here now. Are you free for dinner tonight? Pavarotti's serve excellent pasta.' He smiled.

'They do.'

'So, is it a date?'

Liz realised she hadn't answered his question. While she was free tonight, she did think it a bit presumptuous of him to invite her on such short notice. She hesitated.

'I know it's short notice, but… I booked a table in the hope you'd be free.' He smiled again, but it wasn't the amused smile that irritated her. It was the winning smile of a little boy who'd been naughty but hoped for forgiveness.

Despite herself, Liz found she was smiling back. 'That sounds lovely.' She did like Pavarotti's, another family business. 'You'll be doing a feature on them, too, I expect.'

'Definitely. I've already spoken with the current family members. Fascinating background, not unlike the Beattie family, but the Pavarottis decided to retain their Italian name.'

*

The restaurant was crowded. As soon as she entered, Liz saw Sam raise his hand from a table against the far wall. 'I'm meeting…' She gestured to Sam in response to the waiter who greeted her and weaved her way across to where he was seated.

'Hi there, you're looking lovely tonight.'

'Thanks.' Liz quickly took a seat. She had dressed carefully, aware this was her first date in twenty years, but the compliment unnerved her. She glanced down at the patterned wrap dress she'd chosen from her meagre wardrobe. She wasn't in the habit of going out to dinner.

'I took the liberty of ordering a bottle of pinot noir,' Sam picked up the bottle, 'but if you'd prefer something else…'

'No, that'll be fine.' Liz watched as he poured her a glass.

'I've been here a few times,' he said, glancing around. 'I've never tasted such good gnocchi.'

'It's one of their specialties, but my favourite is the spaghetti marinara.'

'You'll have that tonight?'

'Yes, please.'

'With garlic bread?'

'Lovely.' *And there go another few kilos*, she thought, but she did love the food here and the unleavened garlic bread was to die for.

'Thanks for coming tonight,' Sam said when they'd ordered. 'I wasn't sure you'd agree. After our initial conversation, I had the impression you considered me the enemy. But meeting you again at Wooleton gave me hope.'

'Well, I was pretty upset you refused to support us in objecting to the development proposal. I still am. I don't understand…'

'I thought I made my position clear.'

'Perhaps you did. But The Reading Corner is my livelihood. You can't expect me to accept your objections without a fight.' Liz tried to stem the anger which began to swamp her again. The guy was buying her dinner. She'd agreed to meet him. This wasn't the time or place to get into another argument. 'But you're entitled to your views. Let's not talk about it tonight. You said you have a background in political journalism. That must have been interesting.'

The ensuing conversation continued through their meal with Sam entertaining Liz with his accounts of the seedier side of politics. It wasn't till they were enjoying coffee that he said, 'But it was all pretty mild after my years as a war correspondent.'

Liz felt a chill run up her spine. *How could she have forgotten that part of his background?*

Sam didn't appear to notice anything amiss. He continued, 'I don't know how those army guys stuck it. It was hell on earth. We were only journalists, but…'

'Where did you say you reported from?' she asked, nervously fingering the stem of her glass, remembering how last time he'd mentioned Afghanistan. A perverse part of her wanted to hear him say it again.

'You name it, we were there.' He began to enumerate, counting off the locations on his fingers. 'East Timor, Iraq, and, of course, Afghanistan. Are you all right?'

Liz could feel the blood drain from her face. Her fingers tightened on her glass, threatening to break it. 'My husband was killed in Afghanistan,' she said, her voice barely a whisper.

*

Sam saw the lovely woman sitting opposite suddenly turn white. She looked as if she'd been struck by lightning. Her husband! How could he have known? He hadn't even known he was Army. But now it all made sense – why she'd left Canberra and buried herself away here, why she appeared to be guarding a secret, why she was so difficult to get to know. Sam had come across a few army widows in his years in Canberra and most were shell-shocked. They tended to react in one of two ways. Some chose to paint the town red as a way of coping with their grief while others, like Liz, hid it away. But one thing they had in common – they never forgot. How could he compete with a dead hero?

He realised he hadn't responded to her revelation. 'I'm so sorry. I didn't know. Do you… do you want to talk about it?'

He cursed himself. Of course, she didn't want to talk about it. It would be like rubbing salt into a wound. 'Sorry, of course you don't. What was I thinking of?'

Liz shook her head and took a sip of wine. Her hand trembled as she raised the glass to her mouth.

Damn! He'd managed to ruin the evening. He should have kept his big mouth shut. But how could he have known? He knew she came from Canberra and she was a widow. Not every widow in Canberra was a result of conflict caused by enemy action.

'I guess you'd like to go home.'

Liz nodded. She was clearly trying to stem her tears.

They left the restaurant together to stand awkwardly outside. Any ideas Sam might have had of prolonging the evening had vanished. He only hoped he hadn't ruined any chance of a relationship with Liz.

'I'm sorry I upset you,' he said again, touching her lightly on the arm.

'Not your fault,' she said with a weak smile. 'You weren't to know Dan died there. I left Canberra because I couldn't stand to be reminded of what happened to him, of the whole Army thing. He was in a truck and was blown up by an incendiary device. I was told it happened a lot.' She raised her eyes to meet his.

Sam saw they were filled with tears. He'd reported on several instances of what happened to her husband. It wasn't a pleasant death, but no death in conflict was. He'd been glad to leave it all behind and join the ranks of the Canberra press gallery.

'I'm sorry to fall apart like this. I didn't expect…'

He patted her arm in an attempt to comfort her, but knew it was useless. 'No need to be sorry,' he said.

'Thanks for dinner. It was lovely. I really enjoyed tonight until…'

'Maybe we can do it again,' Sam suggested, holding his breath. 'I promise to steer away from anything upsetting.'

'Thanks, I'd like that, and I promise not to fall apart on you again.'

Twenty-two

Liz didn't get much sleep. The searing pain of the memory of Dan's death hit her every time she closed her eyes. Eventually, she gave up, went to the kitchen and made herself a mug of hot chocolate. Marmaduke joined her, leaping onto her lap to curl up and knead her with his paws. They sat like that till the sun came up, filling the sky with a rosy glow, and the kookaburras began their morning chorus.

'Time to get moving,' she told the cat and rose, dislodging him from her lap. Marmaduke landed on the floor with a yowl, then made his way to his food bowl and stood over it expectantly.

'Don't ever change,' she told him, filling his bowl and making sure he had enough water. Then she turned on the coffee maker. After her sleepless night, she'd need at least one cup to get her going and see her through the day.

Liz had just arrived at the bookshop when her phone pinged with a message.

Good morning. Hope you're feeling better this morning. I really enjoyed last night. Sorry I brought up sad memories for you. Can I make up by cooking you dinner tonight? I promise not to raise any contentious subjects. My place at seven? I'm on an acreage two k along the lane from Wooleton. Sam

Liz smiled. Two nights running? Judy would say he was keen, but Liz thought he only wanted to make up for his blunder. She didn't reply immediately, but his invitation sat at the back of her mind all morning as she served customers and kept an eye on the book clubs

– and Marmaduke, who seemed to be particularly frisky today. She wouldn't tell Judy or Peta, who would be sure to make something of it, too. It was only dinner, a chance for him to rectify what he saw as his mistake. And he had been good company. She waited till the shop was empty and texted back.

Thanks. See you at seven. Liz

After several cups of coffee throughout the day, Liz was wired when she closed the shop to drive home. A shower helped refresh her as she dressed for the evening, choosing the pants and tunic she'd worn for the photographer. As she applied her makeup, Liz wondered what Sam's place would be like. She'd been surprised at Wooleton to learn he lived on an acreage. He seemed more of a city type. But what did she know?

The drive through town and out to where Sam Walker lived was a familiar one. It had been her first introduction to Granite Springs all those years ago. Back then, she'd been an emotional wreck and this small part of Australia helped her find a way forward. She'd be forever grateful to Judy for inviting her to visit.

As she turned off the main road onto the dirt track leading to Wooleton, Liz was again plunged into that sense of peace and wellbeing she always experienced here. She opened the car window and breathed in the air which always seemed fresher, letting in the loud sound of the cockatoos and cockatiels both of which loved to perch in the tall eucalypts.

This time, she drove past the Wooleton sign above the impressive entrance to the property and along the lane as Sam had indicated. This part of the track showed it hadn't been used as frequently as the part between the road and Wooleton. As she went farther and farther from the main thoroughfare, it seemed to Liz she was travelling into no man's land. It was still light, almost dusk, Liz's favourite time of day after the early morning.

Finally, she saw a gate and a small building standing alone in the paddock. Once through the gate, she could see what she knew must be Alec's sheep grazing on the patches of remaining grass.

The house was smaller than the one at Wooleton but, like it, was surrounded by a wide veranda, though this one had no steps. The entire house and veranda, plus a stretch of patchy lawn and what appeared to be an unkempt vegetable garden were bordered by a wire fence presumably to keep the sheep out. Liz pulled up and stopped.

Sam must have heard the car or been looking out for her. Liz had barely time to open the car door before he appeared on the veranda, a wide grin on his face. 'Welcome! Glad you found your way.'

'This is lovely!' Liz couldn't hide her pleasure. While she admired Judy and Alec's home, being an old homestead it was too large for her liking. But this house, nestled as it was in a dip in the valley, was perfect.

'I like it, too.' Sam beamed. 'Come in and see the rest. I'm afraid the house itself is very much a male domain. There's just me – and my son at the moment.' A frown crossed his brow making Liz wonder what the problem was.

'I didn't know your son was living with you.'

'It's temporary, at least I hope it is.' He drew a hand through his hair. 'He's grown, married, but his wife… it's difficult.'

'Ah!' Liz thought she understood. Marital problems. She thought of Ailsa, hoping her sister could work through whatever was happening with her and Bob.

'He's not here now. Went to Canberra for the weekend to see if he can sort something out.'

From the expression on his face, Sam hoped it would be the case.

Given Sam's comments, Liz wasn't sure what to expect, but when she walked in, it was to a large family kitchen, against one wall of which was an Aga. In the centre of the room was a large, scrubbed wood table. She immediately felt at home.

'Take a seat.' Sam indicated the table around which were several ladder-backed chairs.

Liz sat down.

Sam took two glasses from a high cupboard. 'Red or white? I'm roasting a chicken.'

Only then, did Liz notice the aroma of roast chicken permeating the kitchen. 'White please,' she said.

'You don't get lonely out here – when your son's not with you?' she asked, once the wine was poured and they'd taken their glasses out to the veranda.

'Lonely? Never. I love the peace. I sometimes wish I didn't need to go into town at all.'

Liz could understand what he meant. If she lived here, she'd never want to leave either. But she was surprised Sam felt the same way.

They sat in silence enjoying the ambiance of the place, listening to the distant sound of birds and the rustling noise made by those sheep who'd ventured closer to the fence surrounding the house. Liz felt so comfortable here. She took a deep breath. 'Tell me what it was like, in Afghanistan.' She hadn't known she was going to ask this until she actually said the words.

Sam gave her a shocked look, no doubt remembering how she fell apart in the restaurant. 'Are you sure you want to know?' he asked.

'Not really. But it's been preying on my mind since last night. I'm sorry I let it affect me the way it did. I've never spoken about Afghanistan to anyone who was there. None of Dan's friends wanted to talk about it. I didn't either. But now...' She glanced up at him, noting how his lips had tightened.

'Well, if you're sure...' Sam took a gulp of wine, placed his glass down, leant his elbows on the table and clasped his hands. His eyes took on a glazed expression. 'Hell doesn't begin to describe it. I was in the background, so I don't know what the poor blokes who were on the front line went through – army guys like your husband. It was hot, incredibly hot, and dusty. The dust got everywhere, in your clothes, your hair, your nose, your eyes. The poor sods never knew when they'd cop a bullet. They were dicing with death every minute of every day.' He shook his head. 'I saw so many returning soldiers who were so messed up, they wished they'd never come back.'

Liz took a gulp of wine, gripping the stem of her glass so tightly it was on the point of snapping. Why had she asked? It was because she really wanted to know, to try to picture what life had been like for Dan in the days and weeks before his death.

Sam, who had been staring into space, brought his gaze back to Liz. 'Sorry, you probably didn't need to hear all that.'

'No, I did. Thanks.' Liz dropped her eyes to hide her shock. She'd known it must have been bad, but this... *Oh Dan!* she thought. *How could you bear it? And why did you have to go?* It was the question she'd asked so often over the years, imagining a different scenario, one in which Dan chose to remain in Canberra with her, in which they had two children and a normal happy family life. She sighed.

'You okay?' Sam placed his hand on her arm, his touch helping dispel the images his words had conjured up.

'I think so.' Liz wasn't sure. The picture Sam painted was so much worse than anything she could have envisioned. And she had the feeling he hadn't told her everything.

'I think dinner should be ready. Will you be all right if I go inside?'

'I'll come with you.' The sun had gone down, and suddenly, what had been a peaceful scene now seemed to be filled with menace, as if a terrorist with a gun might suddenly appear from nowhere and… Liz shivered.

Once inside, Liz felt better. The warmth of the room she'd felt earlier enveloped her, and she almost laughed at her foolishness. But the feeling had been real. 'Can I do anything to help?' she asked.

'Maybe you could set the table? Cutlery in the top drawer.' He gestured to the set of drawers opposite the stove. 'I thought we'd eat here if it's okay with you. We don't use the dining room much. It's a bit of a mess. Mitch has been using it to set up some stuff.'

'Fine by me.' Liz was grateful to be staying in this warm, comfortable room. It was strange how country kitchens all seemed to have a welcoming atmosphere. Judy's was the same. She and Alec practically lived there.

The chicken, served with roast potatoes and salad, was delicious. During the meal, Sam regaled her with more humorous tales of his exploits as a journalist, avoiding any further reference to his days as a war correspondent. It reinforced her opinion he was an interesting companion, easy to talk to, and had plenty of anecdotes of his attempts to juggle management of his acreage with his role at the newspaper. Liz barely needed to say anything.

This suited Liz. After hearing about Afghanistan, she was in the mood to be entertained. Sam seemed to understand this and kept the conversation flowing. It was almost with a feeling of regret she saw the time. 'I should be getting home,' she said. 'Thanks for a lovely evening, and thanks for…' She couldn't say it, and she knew the images he'd spoken of would haunt her dreams.

'Glad I could be of some help.' He gave her an awkward hug, then released her suddenly as if regretting what he had done. He cleared his throat. 'I enjoyed tonight. Perhaps we can do it again sometime?'

This was the man who refused to help save her shop, but to her surprise, Liz found herself agreeing. She'd enjoyed the evening, too. Sam Walker was good company, restful to be with and he didn't appear to want anything more from her, to have any hidden agenda. She drove home in the firm belief she'd found a friend.

Twenty-three

When he awoke next morning, Sam was restless. He'd found Liz Pender good company. He'd been surprised when she asked about Afghanistan and had been reluctant to go into details. But she seemed anxious to know, so he'd given her a potted version. No one who hadn't been there could possibly imagine what it had been like. Brought up on tales of his father's time in Vietnam, Sam had thought it might be glamourous to be a war correspondent so had leapt at the opportunity. It was far from glamourous.

He'd made some good mates there, both with the other correspondents and a couple of the army bods but couldn't wait to get back home. It had cured him of ever venturing into a war zone again.

He thought back to last night, to the feeling of Liz's body in his arms, her soft curves fitting against him. He'd been tempted to kiss her, but had drawn away, conscious she was still vulnerable, still grieving for her husband.

Mitch was still in Canberra trying to persuade Brooke to visit Granite Springs, to at least give it a try. As far as Sam knew, his son hadn't yet given Chris a definite answer, but the owner of CAT wouldn't wait for ever.

Sam took his morning coffee outside to sit on one of the chairs he'd set on the veranda, where he and Liz had sat the previous evening, where he'd relived the horrors of his time in Afghanistan. It was years since he'd thought about those days and weeks when he didn't know if he'd live to see another day. Even war correspondents weren't immune.

Like many of the army personnel he'd come across, he too had nightmares for years afterwards. It was only now, in this peaceful spot, he'd been able to consign it to the past and move forward. But last night had brought it all back.

He wondered how Liz was feeling this morning. Had he brought up demons for her, too? It was the last thing he wanted to do. She was a lovely woman, her vulnerability only making her more attractive. Would she ever be ready for another relationship? At least he now felt they were friends. Friends! That's what Ann Baird had said when he invited her to dinner. He'd been attracted to Ann, enjoyed her company, but there had been no great sense of loss when he discovered she and Chris Thomas were together.

Liz was different. Sam knew that even after such a short acquaintance, his feelings for Liz Pender went deeper than friendship, far deeper. At least she seemed to have got over her annoyance at his refusal to use The Advertiser to promote their cause; there was nothing he could do to stop the development in Main Street.

A horrible thought occurred to him. She couldn't be using him – pretending friendship in the hope of changing his mind? No. He shook his head. He'd lay bets she was as honest as the day was long. And loyal, too. Her grief was genuine. She hadn't asked him to talk about Afghanistan with some hidden agenda. She'd truly wanted to know, regardless how much it hurt. And it had hurt. He could see that.

Sam took a deep breath and gazed out at the sheep peacefully grazing in the paddock. He'd need to make up his mind soon what he was going to do with this twenty acres. He liked the idea of having animals on it. He enjoyed watching Alec Thomson's sheep. But if he kept his own flock – or a herd of alpacas like Col Ford, or goats, like Owen Larsen, there would be the fuss of looking after them. Col was retired. He had all the time in the world. But Owen worked at the university. How did he manage? It was all too difficult. He'd meant what he said to Liz about wanting to spend all his time here, but that couldn't happen for many years to come. Meantime, he had to earn a living *and* manage this property. It was going to be a juggling act, whatever he chose to do with it.

His phone rang.

'Hi, Sam.' Owen's cheerful voice banished Sam's reflections.

'Owen, good to hear from you.' Sam tried to figure out what Owen might want on a Sunday morning without success.

There was silence on the other end of the phone then Owen spoke again. 'I wanted to ask a favour.'

'Oh, yes?' It was usually Sam who was asking for favours, had been throughout his career, asking for people's time, their opinion, sometimes even their life story.

'It's like this. The music festival. It's getting closer and a few of the young guys are getting a bit nervous about it. They don't have any experience of performing in front of strangers. Daft, really, as it's what they're studying for, but there it is. So, Fran and I are having a group over for a bit of a jam session this afternoon. We thought we'd invite a few people, put on a bit of a spread – beer, sausages – you know the sort of thing. Would you be up for it? Around three? Sorry it's such short notice.'

'Sounds good. I'd love to come.' It would get him out of this house which suddenly seemed very empty.

When he hung up, Sam drained his coffee and went back inside. Maybe he'd get the chance to have a yarn to Owen about keeping goats. It seemed they might take less looking after than alpacas, though what did he know? But he rather liked the idea. He had an inkling they'd eat anything, so would at least keep the grass and weeds down and reduce the fire hazard. Alec's sheep were doing a good job, but he'd be taking them back one of these days.

*

When Sam drove up to Owen and Fran's home, he was surprised to see a large number of cars parked by the fence surrounding the house. He parked his Range Rover beside a blue ute, avoiding a group of older vehicles which looked as if they had been abandoned. Probably belonging to students, he thought, remembering his own student days and the old bomb he'd been so proud of at the time. If the sounds coming from the backyard were any indication, the music had already begun.

There were already quite a few people jostling for spots on the lawn where Owen, helped by Col Ford, was setting out fold-up chairs. It was clear some people had brought their own, something it hadn't occurred to Sam to do. He was still a novice in this country living thing.

Suddenly, it seemed everyone had found a place to sit. Sam hurriedly dropped into a vacant chair at the end of a row and settled back to enjoy the performance.

'Welcome, everyone,' Owen said, standing between the audience and the performers. 'I'm grateful you were all able to come to help us out. My students…' he waved a hand to the groups behind him, '…are grateful, too. This is the first public performance for many of them, so I hope you'll be kind. I remember my own first gig. I was shit scared. Sorry!' he added, seeing Fran glare at him.

Everyone laughed.

'Anyway, we hope you enjoy this taste of what you'll hear at the music festival next month. And if you haven't already bought your tickets, you can see Fran afterwards.'

There was another bout of laughter, in the midst of which Sam caught sight of a familiar redhead on the other side of the audience. His heart leapt. It was Liz. Liz Pender was here, too. He knew Granite Springs was a small community, but what were the chances? Pretty good, it appeared.

*

Liz had been surprised to receive a call from Peta inviting her to join a group of people out at Fran and Owen Larsen's that afternoon. She'd met Fran several times. She was a good customer and she knew her from the choir. But they'd never become friends. And she didn't know Owen at all outside of the choir.

She was feeling vulnerable after the previous evening. Sam's revelations about Afghanistan had affected her more than she'd realised at the time. She hadn't got much sleep, and that which she had was disturbed by nightmares of a desert filled with men wielding knives and guns and the sound of screams. The worst was when she saw Dan. He was sitting in an army truck and she knew it was going to explode. She tried to warn him, but, when she opened her mouth, no sound came out. Then there was an explosion. She wakened from that one in a cold sweat and took ages to get back to sleep. Even the comforting presence of Marmaduke lying in the crook of her knees failed to have its usual soothing effect.

So, Peta's call, while not exactly welcome, came as a reprieve from her own thoughts which, today, revolved around Dan and what he must have suffered. She'd been on the point of calling his old army friend – one who'd come back alive – when Peta called. She wasn't sure what she wanted to say to Glen after all those years of silence, perhaps ask for reassurance Dan's death had been sudden, that she'd been told the truth about what happened. Or perhaps confirmation of Sam's account of life over there. Maybe she could even persuade him to give her more information. She was sure Sam hadn't given her the whole picture.

Anyway, she'd agreed to Peta's cajoling and here she was sitting on a canvas chair on a Sunday afternoon listening to a group of students who were… surprisingly good. She applauded with all the others when the concert finally came to an end. If this was a taste of the supporting acts at the music festival, she'd certainly be buying a ticket and she'd always been a fan of Trent Bridges. He was the only country music singer among the posters of pop stars which had graced her teenage bedroom wall.

'I'm just going to duck inside to help with the refreshments,' Peta whispered in her ear. 'I think someone wants to speak with you.' She grinned.

'Who? Oh!' Liz turned quickly to see Sam Walker standing behind her. 'I didn't know you'd be here.' She blushed, remembering another part of her dream, one in which he featured. That one hadn't taken place in Afghanistan.

'I didn't expect to see you either. But, as I'm learning, the Granite Springs community is a small one. Owen only rang me this morning.'

'Peta rang me then, too. She…' Liz looked towards the house into which her friend had already disappeared.

They smiled awkwardly at each other, then both spoke at once.

'Did you…'

'I…'

They laughed, the awkwardness disappearing.

'You go first,' Liz said.

'How are you today? Did you get any sleep last night?'

'Not a lot. I was tortured by nightmares. I kept waking up. Even Marmaduke's furry presence failed to comfort me.'

'Sorry.' Sam stared down at his feet.

'Not your fault. I did ask, and it was good to hear it, but… now I can't get the images out of my head.' She shook her head as if it would help dismiss them.

There was silence, apart from the noise of others chattering and the clink of glasses around them.

'Sounds like the refreshments are being served. Can I get you something?'

All Liz wanted to do was to be alone with her thoughts, but a glass of wine would be welcome. It might help to blunt the memories which Sam's presence had conjured up. 'Thanks. Wine would be good.'

'Coming up.'

While he was fetching her drink, Liz looked around. No one was paying any attention to her, busy either chattering to their friends or congratulating the students. Spying a bench at the far end of the veranda, she headed towards it, sinking gratefully onto the soft cushioned seat.

She was feeling calmer by the time Sam appeared carrying two glasses of wine and a plate containing two sausages wrapped in slices of white bread and oozing with tomato sauce.

'Thought you might want something to eat, too. If not, I'll have them both. May I join you?'

'Thanks, but I don't think I could eat anything. Do sit down.' She moved along the bench to make space for him. While she had wanted to be alone, she knew Sam's presence wouldn't be intrusive. She'd changed her opinion of him. He was no longer the enemy. He had become a friend.

Twenty-four

Mitch's car was sitting outside the fence surrounding the house when Sam returned home. The event at the Larsen's had proved more enjoyable than Sam anticipated. And meeting Liz again had been a bonus. After their dinner together, he'd been eager to see her again, but unsure how soon to contact her. While he wanted to pursue a relationship, he didn't want to scare her off. She'd been on her own for twenty years, and he was sure it wasn't for lack of offers. She was an attractive woman and, even here in Granite Springs, he was sure there were plenty of men who would seek her out.

Sam respected the fact she'd been open with him about her husband, but how could he compete with the memory of a war hero? But they'd had a pleasant chat over a glass of wine, and he felt they'd become closer. Sam was still thinking about Liz when he walked into the kitchen.

Mitch was sitting at the table with a can of beer.

'You got back early.'

'Wasn't much point in staying.'

'How did it go with Brooke?'

Mitch tightened his fingers around the beer can. 'Could have been worse. She did agree to come to Granite Springs. It was the mention of the music festival that got to her. She's a fan of Cecy Wright.' He grimaced. 'But she refused to stay here. She says she'd prefer a motel.'

'Oh!' Not a good sign, but at least she was willing to come, and Sam couldn't hide the sense of relief he wouldn't have to suffer her presence in the house.

'I said I'd organise accommodation for her.'

'And Abi? She's coming too?'

'Of course. She may be a bit young for the festival. Maybe I can do something with her while Brooke's there.'

'Mmm.' It didn't make much sense if the point of the exercise was to get the pair of them back together, but Sam knew better than to try to reason with Mitch. He was sure his son could work it out for himself, though he hadn't been doing too well so far.

'I've booked a room for them at *The Springs*. Wanted to show Brooke Granite Springs isn't the hick town she imagines.' Mitch took a last swig of beer, then crushed the can. 'Do you think I'm doing the right thing, Dad?' He gave Sam a pleading look. 'I can't tell what Brooke's thinking is on this.'

'Did you tell her about CAT's offer?'

'Yeah. It did seem to impress her – for all of one second.' He chuckled. 'She didn't think a company like that would be interested in what she called "the stuff I play around with".'

'Well, it's a start.'

'Do you think so?'

Sam was startled how insecure Mitch was when it came to his wife. The woman really had him by the short and curlies. But he loved her, and we all did things for love that we might never do for any other reason.

'How was *your* weekend?' Mitch seemed unwilling to provide more details of his conversation with Brooke or his time with her and Abi.

'Good. I had a surprise invitation to the Larsens'. Some of Owen's students were putting on a bit of a concert – a practice for the festival. They were pretty good.'

There was no reply. Sam could see Mitch wasn't listening. He didn't really want to know about his dad's weekend. Sam sighed. He really hoped Brooke's visit to Granite Springs would work some magic. He was tired of seeing Mitch's sad face around the house and he'd appreciate having the place to himself again. He loved his son and wanted to see him happy again, but not at the expense of Sam's own peace of mind.

'How was Abi?' He tried again.

'Good.' Mitch's mouth curled up in an affectionate smile. '*She* was happy to see me. I miss her, Dad. So much.'

'And Brooke?'

'I miss her, too, of course. But she's so difficult to talk to these days. It's as if nothing I do can please her. I told her about those young couples you mentioned and the barbecue your friend's organising for us. She just turned up her nose and made some remark about country bumpkins and how she had no intention of becoming one.'

'I've met Neil and Sally and they certainly can't be described as country bumpkins. She may change her mind when she meets them. Judy said Neil has a daughter, though I think she's a bit older than Abi.'

'Will she be there? Abi would like that.' Mitch brightened.

'I'm not sure. She lives with her mother.'

'Oh!' Mitch's shoulders sagged. 'Another broken marriage. It's the kids who suffer.'

'Yours isn't broken.'

'Not yet, but…'

'Buck up, Mitch. What you need is a night out. Let me shout you a meal. I'll give The Riverside a call to see if I can book a table,' he said, referring to the best restaurant in town which was owned by Jo Ford and her son, Rob.

'The flash place by the river?' Mitch seemed to rouse himself somewhat.

'It is and it's every bit as good as any you'll find in the city – Canberra or Sydney, or even Melbourne,' he added, knowing the Victorian city was renowned for its restaurants.

*

It was fortunate Sam had thought to reserve a table because the restaurant was crowded.

'I didn't think there were this many people in Granite Springs,' Mitch said, gazing around in surprise.

'Ha ha,' replied Sam, waving to Jo and Col who were seated at a table in the far corner of the restaurant.

A tall man with spiky red hair, a mass of freckles flecking his pale skin, showed Sam and Mitch to their table. 'I hope you enjoy your evening with us,' he said, handing them menus.

Mitch was impressed. 'I didn't believe you, but you're right, we could be in a first-class restaurant in Canberra. Does the food live up to first impressions?'

'Just wait.' Sam smiled, pleased to see Mitch's reaction. If only Brooke could see Granite Springs in this light, too. 'What do you fancy?' he asked, his eyes scanning the menu before deciding on a wagyu steak with potato, portobello mushrooms and green beans. 'I'm having the wagyu steak.'

'I'll have the same.' Mitch put down his menu.

When a waiter appeared, Sam placed their order, including a bottle of cabernet sauvignon. He would only have one glass as he was driving but he could see his son was in the mood for more. In one corner of his mind, he wondered if Mitch might have a drinking problem, before dismissing it. He was merely going through a bad patch. Sam remembered how his own drinking had escalated when his marriage was in trouble. He just hoped Mitch could salvage his.

Sam and Mitch made desultory conversation while they ate. They had ordered coffee having both decided against dessert, when a group of people stopped at their table.

'Don't often see you here,' Alec Thompson said, shaking Sam's hand. 'This must be your son.'

'Alec. Good to see you – and the family. Yes, this is Mitch. Mitch, this is Alec Thomson, the owner of the sheep you see in my paddock. And his wife, Judy, and Neil and Sally, the young couple I mentioned.'

'We're taking the opportunity to get out as much as we can before the bub arrives,' Sally said with a smile, patting her burgeoning baby bump.

'And we've had some good news. Neil's Daisy'll be here next weekend. She didn't want to miss the music festival. Did you know Owen Larsen has managed to get *The Puggles* to come? Though Daisy's a tad old for them. She's more into Cecy Wright.' Neil rolled his eyes.

'Abi loves *The Puggles*,' Mitch said, speaking for the first time. 'But I thought the festival was for grownups.'

'Granite Springs is such a family focussed community, it would be difficult to have an event like this which didn't cater for all age groups. I hear there will be a few other activities for the younger ones too – a jumping castle and a couple of rides,' Alec said.

'Looks like I need to have another word with Owen,' Sam said, annoyed he'd missed reporting on this aspect of the event. But he could still include a few paragraphs about it in the next edition of The Advertiser. 'Thanks for letting me know, Alec.'

'I think it's a bit of a last-minute thing. I only heard from my brother yesterday. He's in Rotary and they've been co-opted to help with refreshments. The usual sausage sizzle thing, you know. I think there'll be other food stalls, too. It's a big deal for the town. A lot hangs on its success.'

'We should be going and let you enjoy your coffee,' Judy said as a waiter appeared with their coffees. 'Good to meet you, Mitch, and looking forward to seeing you and your wife and daughter at our place next weekend.'

Mitch looked at Sam when they'd left. 'So, those are the people you told me about. They seem nice, not...'

'Not too countrified?' Sam chuckled. 'Even Brooke couldn't accuse them of being country bumpkins.'

Mitch reddened and picked up his coffee cup.

'Thanks, Dad. You were right about the food, too,' Mitch said as they drove home.

Sam had been right about the wine, too. Mitch had managed to consume most of it. And it had been a serendipity to have met Alec and his family. Granite Springs continued to surprise Sam with how small the community really was – and how close-knit.

As Mitch dozed off, no doubt the result of the wine, Sam's thoughts turned to Liz Pender. He wondered when he could arrange to see her again, if she planned to attend any of the events at the festival next week, and how he could arrange to accompany her if he had Mitch and Brooke with him, not to mention Abi. Though, now there were to be the children's events, his offer to look after Abi might be redundant. Then it occurred to him. The Riverside. Of course. He'd invite her to dinner at The Riverside. He looked at Mitch whose head was now lolling against the car window. He'd enjoy Liz's company more than his son's.

Twenty-five

Liz hadn't given up on the idea of talking with Glen Adams. She knew Dan's old army mate still lived in Canberra, though he'd left the army and taken a civilian position in the defence force, seemingly unable to let go completely. She hadn't seen him since Dan's funeral when he'd been a bit of a mess. She'd assumed this was the result of what he'd seen over there. Post-traumatic stress seemed to affect a lot of returning soldiers. Maybe even Dan would have been a victim of it if he'd returned. But she'd have given anything, put up with anything, to have him back with her.

Her mother had been surprised she was making another trip to Canberra so soon – on the excuse of checking up on her dad. Her comment that she seemed to have found the road to Canberra was said with more than a hint of irony. But Liz was determined to follow through with her plan. She had arranged to meet Glen in the city on Sunday morning, avoiding the church service at which her parents would no doubt want her company, and would catch up with her sister in the afternoon. It wouldn't leave much time with her mum and dad, but it would save the also inevitable recriminations about her life choices.

This time, she drove over early on Sunday morning, her mind flitting between memories of Dan and thoughts of Sam. So far, everything she discovered served to reinforce her view that Sam was a special sort of person. If he reminded her of anyone, it was Dan. Though the two were unlike in so many ways, they both had an innate honesty, a sense of integrity and a refusal to compromise their principles. With Dan, it had led him to join the army and to volunteer for deployment. With Sam it was his determination to keep The Advertiser out of local politics and, while she still hoped to change his mind about that, she had to admire his resolve.

As she drove, Liz wondered where this friendship might lead. It was a long time since she'd dated. There hadn't been anyone since Dan. As she told Judy – and Peta – she hadn't wanted anyone. She was happy with her life, content to spend the rest of it on her own. Then she'd met Sam Walker and there was something about the man that had got under her skin.

It wasn't the fact he was attractive – though that was undeniable – or that he was good company – he was that, too. It was more, something about the way he was always positive, even when things weren't going his way. Last night he'd shared his concern about his son's marriage, his opinion of his daughter-in-law, his desire to see more of his granddaughter and his disillusionment with Canberra journalism. But despite this, he was able to laugh at himself, at his own annoyances. Not many men could do that.

At first, she'd tried to tell herself it was the novelty of having a man interested in her, the fact they kept bumping into each other, even though her initial reaction had been one of anger. But she soon knew it was more than that. Men had been interested in her before and it had been easy to dismiss them. Sam Walker wasn't so easy to dismiss. She hugged the knowledge to herself as she drove into Canberra, the sky rosy from the rising sun, the avenue of trees failing to have their usual negative effect on her.

She arrived at her parents' in time for a late breakfast, causing her mother to fuss and her father to greet her with his usual hug. She was pleased to see he was managing to move around more easily this time.

As she expected, her mother expressed annoyance when Liz said she wouldn't be attending church with them. 'What do you want to see him for?' she asked, when Liz told her who she was meeting. 'I've heard he's gone downhill since leaving the army. There have been rumours...'

Liz didn't want to hear the rumours. Canberra abounded in them, much like Granite Springs.

'We'll see you for lunch?' her mother asked as they prepared to leave. 'Your sister won't be here today.'

'I'll be back. I'm seeing Ailsa and the boys this afternoon.'

'I don't know why she can't come here,' Sheila complained.

'The boys are dropping round to do some work in the yard, and Ailsa needs to be there to show them what needs done.' That was the explanation Ailsa had given her, but Liz suspected it was an excuse to avoid the interrogation she'd get from her mother if she arrived without Bob yet again.

'I suppose Bob can't do it.' Her mother sniffed.

Liz didn't reply. Sometimes that was the best response to her mother.

*

The café where Glen had agreed they meet was in a side street in Belconnen. Liz found it without difficulty. She ordered a cappuccino and selected a table from which she could easily see the door. She waited nervously, wondering if she'd made a mistake in arranging to see Glen. It had all been so long ago.

Each time the door opened, she jumped. She checked her watch. He was late. What if he didn't come? Then a tall, balding man shambled into the café. She peered at him. He looked vaguely familiar, but… He ordered at the counter, walked towards her and took the seat opposite.

'Hello, Liz.'

'Glen. Thanks for coming.' Was this wreck of a man really the same Glen Adams who'd been the life and soul of the party when he and Dan were at Duntroon together?

'Didn't recognise me, huh?'

Liz blushed. 'You've changed.'

'You haven't, Liz. Still the lovely girl you always were.' He coughed.

A waiter served his coffee. He took a long swallow and sighed. 'I come here a lot. They know me.'

Liz sipped her cappuccino, wondering how to begin.

'You wanted to ask me something? It's been a long time, Liz. I heard you'd left Canberra.'

'I do, it has, and I did.' She clasped her cup in both hands and leant across the table. 'I need to ask you about Dan, about what it was like. I know it was twenty years ago, but something occurred recently. I met someone who'd been in Afghanistan, who tried to tell me what it was like over there. I don't think he told me everything.' Liz could feel her stomach churning and her legs trembling, but she had to know.

His eyes narrowed. His brow creased. 'You don't want to know.'

'I do. I need to know.'

Glen stared into space, his eyes glazing over. 'It was really hell on earth. It was kill or be killed and sometimes… One of the problems we had was there was no way of knowing who were Taliban and who weren't. One time one of the guys made friends with a young boy on an airdrop, then saw the same kid slit another kid's throat on patrol a week later. Seemed there was no "enemy" and no real goal. Many of the local people had no idea why we were there. They believed we were demons. Everyone was just trying their damndest to survive. As I said, hell on earth.'

Liz stared at him, her mouth suddenly dry. She shuddered. She thought she was going to be sick. Her hands gripped the edge of the table. She forced herself to ask another question. 'I need to know how Dan died. Was it true what they said; he was in a truck, there was an explosion? Was it sudden? Would he have known? Were you there? Did you see?' Her voice trembled.

Glen turned ashen. He stared into his cup, then, 'It was sudden, but…'

Liz's eyes widened with fear. Her hand tightened on her cup.

'Dan shouldn't have been there, in that truck.'

'What?' Liz asked, unable to believe what she was hearing.

'It should have been me. I wanted to tell you at the time – as soon as I got back. But I was too much of a coward.' He looked down. 'I regret it every day of my life.'

Liz felt herself crumble. Dan hadn't needed to die. Glenn was still speaking, but there was a buzzing in Liz's ears. She tried to concentrate.

'I was hungover. A few of us had tied it on the previous night. When it was time for us to go out on patrol, I was a mess. Dan had stayed sober. He was trying to reach you, but the connection wasn't great. Anyway, when he saw the state I was in he volunteered to take my place. You know what he was like – a good mate. Then, when it happened, I… I wanted to die myself.'

Liz looked at him, at this man who had been responsible for Dan's death – or at least who should have been killed in his place. But she couldn't find any anger, just a great sadness for what might have been – and for the guilt he was carrying, would always carry. It didn't make it any better that Dan had been killed out of a misplaced sense of loyalty, but it made sense. She did know what Dan had been like. It was so typical of him to have wanted to protect his mate from a disciplinary charge.

'I'm sorry, Liz. If I could do anything to change things, I would. I shouldn't have come.' He stood up and walked away.

Liz stared after him, stunned by what he'd said. Then the anger set in. How dare he come here, tell her this, then walk off leaving her to process the fact her husband needn't have died. Of course, he might have died at any other time, but... A tear trickled down her cheek. *Poor Dan.*

When she left the café, Liz sat in the car for a time, trying to come to terms with what she'd heard. It didn't change anything. Dan was still dead, but now she knew he had died trying to protect someone else. Eventually, she wiped her eyes and drove back home to face her parents, vowing to keep Glen's revelation to herself.

She managed to hold it together over lunch, smiling politely at her father's attempts at jokes and her mother's interminable stories about her charity committees.

'I should get round to Ailsa's now,' she said when the meal was over, and she'd helped her mother wash up – Sheila had always refused to have a dishwasher. 'I'll just pop in to say goodbye to Dad.'

'Give your sister our love and tell her we don't see nearly enough of her and the boys these days,' Liz's dad said, giving her a hug. 'It's been good to see you again so soon. We might make it to Granite Springs next.'

'That would be lovely,' Liz said, hoping it wouldn't happen too soon. There was only so much of her mother she could take.

*

'How was lunch?' Ailsa asked.

The pair were seated on Ailsa's back veranda with glasses of wine. They were watching Liz's nephews digging up a line of pavers in preparation for the vegetable garden Ailsa wanted to establish. The boys had greeted Liz with hugs, surprising her with how grown-up they'd become. They weren't really boys any longer, but they always would be to her.

'Oh, you know. The usual.' Liz didn't want to talk about her parents or the lunch.

'And your meeting… with Dan's old mate. How was it?'

Liz hesitated, unsure how much to reveal. But this was Ailsa. They'd never kept secrets from each other. 'Surprising.'

'How so?'

'He told me…' Liz proceeded to relate what Glen had said, finishing with, 'And then he just left.'

'Wow! How do you feel?'

'I'm not sure. Shocked. Stunned. But it doesn't change anything, does it?'

'I guess not, but… How could he have kept quiet about it for so long?'

'I suppose no one asked him what actually happened.'

'But wouldn't someone have known… that Dan shouldn't have been there?'

'I expect everything was such a shambles. They either didn't know or didn't care.'

'Mmm. What will you do now?'

'Do? Nothing. What can I do? But I'm satisfied Dan's death was sudden. They didn't lie to me about that.'

'Why did you decide to talk with Glen? Why now – after twenty years?'

Liz bit her lip. She looked at her sister, knowing if she lied about this, Ailsa would know. She'd never been able to fool her. 'I've met someone.'

'About time!' Ailsa beamed.

'Not like that.' Though maybe it was. 'He was there, in Afghanistan. He described what it was like. It made me think, want to know more about what Dan experienced, how he died, to try for closure.'

'Oh, Liz!' Ailsa put an arm around Liz's shoulder and gave her a squeeze. 'And did it? It wasn't what you expected.'

'No, it wasn't. It made me sad and angry at the same time. Glen's had to live with this burden all this time. He said he wanted to die, and I believe him. He's suffered, is still suffering. He's a shadow of his former self. He didn't get off scot free, either.'

'But he's alive.'

'Mmm.' Liz wondered if being alive was more of a burden than anything else for Glen.

'But tell me about this farmer you've met. I told you there must be at least one.'

'He's not a farmer.' Sam's twenty acres couldn't be classed as a farm. 'He's the editor of the local paper, used to be a journalist. That's how he came to be in Afghanistan.'

'A journalist, huh? What's his name?'

'Sam Walker.'

'Sam Walker? My God, Liz. Don't you know who he is? He's a well-known war correspondent. Then he became a political journalist. He used to appear regularly on television on the Inside Your Government programme. Don't you keep up with the news now you're living in the country?'

'I don't watch a lot of television and I'd never heard of him.'

'He's famous – or was. He disappeared from the box – and Canberra – last year. I wondered what happened to him. And he's very dishy. You're a dark horse. You and Sam Walker. Well, well!'

Twenty-six

Ailsa's words about Sam Walker stuck in Liz's mind. It was her own fault. She'd told her sister she'd met someone. What else did she expect Ailsa to think? But it wasn't that simple. Liz was still trying to work out how she felt about the possibility of having a man in her life after so long.

She sighed as she drove along. Maybe she was fussing about nothing. Maybe Sam Walker wasn't interested in her. But she knew, even as the thought entered her mind, she was wrong. He was interested. A woman knew these things. And wasn't it why she'd gone to see Glen this morning? One of the reasons, at least. And she'd got more than she bargained for. Damn! She hit the steering wheel with her fist. Why had she been so determined to know?

Unbidden, tears coursed down her cheeks. She brushed them away with the back of her hand. She wouldn't think of it, of Dan cheerfully getting into the truck in Glen's place to ride to his death. She turned on the radio to drown her thoughts and drove the rest of the way listening to a boring radio quiz program, interspersed with news headlines.

By the time she reached home, Liz was feeling better. But she was still glad to have Marmaduke's company. The cat greeted her with a loud yowl of complaint at having been left alone for so long. Even though she'd made sure there was plenty for him to eat and drink, and the cat flap meant he could come and go as he pleased, her pet hated being left alone.

She was home later than she intended, having dropped in to farewell her parents before leaving Canberra. Of course, her mother had insisted on making her something to eat and quizzing her on the state of Ailsa's marriage, about which Liz still had no idea. Her sister was very close-lipped about anything to do with her relationship.

Exhausted, she fixed herself a mug of hot chocolate and fell into bed, allowing Marmaduke to curl up beside her as recompense for what he saw as her neglect.

She didn't check the messages on her phone till morning. When she did, she pressed to hear a now familiar voice.

'Hi, Liz. It's Sam, Sam Walker. Sorry I've missed you. I called to invite you to dinner again. I really enjoyed last time. How does The Riverside sound? I've provisionally booked a table for Wednesday. Hope you don't think I'm being presumptuous. Give me a ring to let me know if this suits – or perhaps I'll see you at choir on Tuesday.'

Oh! Liz stared at her phone, trying to stifle the butterflies in her stomach. Ailsa had been right. Liz hadn't felt this way since... since Dan. But was it being unfaithful to him for her to feel this way about another man?

As if she were in the room, Liz could hear her sister's voice. *'It's been twenty years, Liz. How much longer do you want to be alone? It's not what Dan would have wanted.'*

And, while Liz would have argued they had no way of knowing what Dan would have wanted, she knew her sister was right.

*

Liz smiled at herself in the mirror as Marmaduke paraded around her emitting loud purrs of appreciation. She'd splashed out and bought a new outfit for her date with Sam, sneaking out to Eve Tait's boutique during a quiet moment in the bookshop. The black dress with the V neckline set off her red hair and pale skin just as Eve said it did, but was it too much for a Wednesday night dinner in Granite Springs?

Marmaduke gave a loud meow as if to assure her it wasn't.

Liz sprayed on her favourite perfume – Dan had loved the scent of Obsession on her, saying it reminded him of their wedding night. Should she have changed it? Too late now. And she loved it too. It was part of who she was. She picked up her bag and went to the car.

Liz loved The Riverside. She remembered when it opened, how delighted everyone was to have a top-rate restaurant right here in Granite Springs. And how proud Jo Ford – she had been Jo Slater back then – and her son were to see their dream become a reality. Some people's dreams did come true.

Pushing open the large glass door, Liz breathed in the familiar aroma of garlic and spices to see Sam waiting for her. He put a hand on her shoulder and gave her a peck on the cheek sending a tingle right down to her toes.

'Ready for your table, now?' the waiter asked.

'Thanks.' Sam took Liz by the elbow.

She smiled at the waiter as he led them to a table close to the window. 'Thanks, Rob,' she said.

'You must come here a lot,' Sam said as they took their seats.

'I have been here a fair bit over the years. It's a lovely restaurant. And I like to support other local businesses.'

Once they had ordered – steak for Sam and salmon for Liz – the conversation stalled. Then they both spoke at once.

'You didn't…'

'Have you…'

They laughed, breaking the ice. This had happened before.

'You first,' Sam said.

'You didn't tell me you were a TV personality.'

'Oh that.' Sam winced and the tips of his ears turned red. 'It was nothing. Who told you?'

'My sister. I went over to Canberra on Sunday.' She frowned, remembering the other part of her trip.

'Something wrong?'

Liz shook her head. 'Not really.' She gazed down at her hands which were clasped tightly on the table. 'I met an old mate of Dan's.'

'It upset you?'

Liz nodded then, unable to stop herself added, 'They were in the army together, in Afghanistan. He said…' her voice broke, '…he said Dan took his place that day, the day he was killed.'

'Oh, Liz!' Sam's hand reached across the table to cover hers. He didn't say any more, He didn't need to. The gesture was enough. His touch comforted her.

'Thanks. I thought I'd managed to put it behind me. Obviously not.' She took a deep breath. 'I'll be okay. I'm not going to fall apart on you again and ruin another lovely evening. What were you going to say?'

'I was going to ask if you were planning to go to the music festival on the weekend. Sounds like it's going to be a good bash. Those students of Owen's certainly know their stuff and he has some big names coming. I hear they're now going to cater for the youngsters as well, making it a true family occasion.'

'I hadn't heard about that.'

'Owen has managed to organise for *The Puggles* to come. I spoke with him yesterday and it seems they were students of his when he was in Sydney. My daughter-in-law and granddaughter are coming for the weekend. Abi's very excited. There will be other activities for the kids, too.'

'Sounds wonderful. I do intend to go to a few of the sessions, on Saturday evening and maybe Sunday. We're expecting an influx of visitors to the town for the event so I'm hoping to be busy all day Saturday.'

'Perhaps we can catch up there.'

Their meals arrived at that point, along with the wine Sam had ordered. Their conversation ceased as he tasted it and their glasses were filled. 'To us,' he said, raising his glass.

Liz raised hers in return but wasn't exactly sure what he meant. Was there an 'us' or was it too soon?

'So, the festival?' he asked, when they were alone again.

'I'm sure we'll bump into each other. Won't you be busy with your family?'

'Part of the time, but I'm hoping it will be a chance for Mitch and Brooke to sort out their differences, to realise what they mean to each other, decide to make a fresh start. I don't want to get in the way. Maybe Saturday evening?' His eyes held the pleading expression Liz found hard to resist.

'Okay, if you're sure.'

'I am.' He heaved a sigh of relief. 'I suspect we'll all spend the day together and, hopefully, Mitch will spend the evening with Brooke and Abi. I think he wants to bring them here for dinner. We ate here the other night. He was impressed.'

'He still intends to stay in Granite Springs?'

'If he can persuade Brooke to move here. If not, I'm not sure what he plans to do.'

Liz tried to concentrate on her meal. Another unhappy couple. It made her think again about Ailsa. Her sister had refused to discuss her marriage, saying everything was fine. But Liz suspected it was all a front. Not for the first time, she wondered if her and Dan's marriage would have survived if he had returned. She'd heard of so many military marriages which hadn't stood the test of time. Theirs had been a fairytale love affair. They were still in the halcyon days of their romance when he'd gone overseas never to return. Maybe it was better to have only memories than to have had it all fall apart with arguments and recriminations.

'Penny for them?'

'Not worth it. I was just thinking about how many unhappy marriages there are. Perhaps Dan and I had the best of it. I only have happy memories. Our relationship didn't have time to get stale or fall apart.'

'It doesn't happen to everyone. There are lots of examples of happy marriages right here in Granite Springs. Your friend, Judy, and her husband are prime examples.'

'That's true.' Liz mentally enumerated the happy marriages she knew in town. There were a lot. 'Okay, you're right,' she said.

'Phew. For a minute I thought you were going to condemn all relationships. I believe any relationship needs work. My own marriage failed because I wasn't around. It was my fault. I admit it. I was young and foolish and valued my career more than my marriage. I've learned my lesson. I'd never make the same mistake again.' He grinned, his eyes crinkling.

Liz felt he was telling her something, something she needed to hear, but wasn't quite ready to acknowledge.

When they walked out of the restaurant, the night air seemed to wrap itself around them, the full moon giving the river a silvery glow. 'It's still early. Fancy a walk?' Sam asked.

Liz gazed up at the clear night sky filled with stars. It was too early to go home. 'Okay.'

Sam threw an arm around her shoulders as they made their way to the pathway along the side of the river. She shivered slightly, whether from cold or his touch, she wasn't sure. His hand tightened its grip and she allowed herself to move closer.

It was pleasant, walking along like this, a sensation Liz had all but forgotten. She felt warm, secure, wanted, even loved? No, that was ridiculous, She and Sam barely knew each other. And yet... 'How are your feature articles coming along?' she asked, to break the silence and the mood.

'Going well. Yours will feature in Friday's edition, then next week we'll be covering Pavarotti's. I'm interviewing the newsagent next week. He seems to be a character.'

'Roy? He is.'

They wandered along, Sam chatting about what he was discovering about the history of Main Street, till they reached the spot where the bridge crossed the river. They stopped. Liz assumed they'd turn back, but instead Sam turned towards her, put a finger under her chin and tipped her face up to his.

'You're a beautiful woman, Liz Pender. I'd like to kiss you. May I?'

Liz was stunned. She didn't think men asked permission for a kiss these days. Certainly, Dan never had. But it was nice, a gentlemanly thing to do. Sam was waiting for an answer and suddenly, Liz realised she wanted him to kiss her more than she'd wanted anything for a long time.

She could barely see as he bent his head, blocking out the moonlight. She felt his breath on her cheeks and their lips met.

Twenty-seven

'Everyone ready?' Sam called out, jingling the keys of the Range Rover and checking his watch. Mitch had collected Brooke and Abi from *The Springs* and all four of them had breakfasted together at Sam's. It was intended to give Brooke a taste of what life could be like in the country, but she didn't appear to be impressed. Abi, on the other hand, was thrilled to be 'in the real outback' and loved seeing the sheep.

They all piled into the car, Brooke fussing as to whether Abi was appropriately dressed and if they had enough water.

'There'll be plenty there,' Sam said, trying not to become annoyed. Did he really want Mitch to patch things up and to have Brooke as part of his family for the rest of his life? Then he looked at Abi, at her sweet little face, and at Mitch, trying hard to please her, and knew he just wanted them to be happy.

The showground was filling up when they arrived, reminding Sam of the country show. At least he had no responsibilities today. All he had to do was enjoy himself.

The day passed quickly. First, they all went to the main stage area where *The Puggles* were playing, and joined the crowd of other families as the children were entertained and sang along to their favourite tunes. Then he took Abi into the children's area, watching her on the rides while Mitch and Brooke watched Cecy Wright perform and, hopefully, spent quality time together. The singer was due to perform again in the evening, as was Trent Bridges so Sam could watch her then, if he so wished and if Liz wanted to. He thought he remembered

139

Liz saying Bridges was one of her teenage heartthrobs. Sam's heart leapt at the thought of spending another evening with Liz. The kiss they shared on Wednesday was something special. It had been difficult not to take things further. But he was aware that with this woman, he needed to tread carefully for fear of scaring her off. Still, she hadn't refused his kiss and her response, the way she'd melted into his arms, had given him hope. He felt a small thrill in anticipation of a repeat performance that evening when the musical performance was over.

They got together again for lunch, then Brooke said she'd had enough and would like to go back to the motel and have a rest.

'Can I come back with you, Grandpa, and see the sheep again?' Abi asked. 'I'm not tired.'

'Sure, sweetheart. Mitch?' Sam raised an eyebrow.

Mitch glanced at Brooke who refused to meet his eyes. 'I'll join you, Dad. We're still on for dinner, Brooke? I've booked a table for six, so we don't stay past Abi's bedtime.'

'I suppose.' Brooke yawned. But Sam thought he saw a weakening of her resolve. He hoped he was right.

*

The music festival was in full swing when Sam and Liz reached the showground in the evening. He'd arranged to pick her up, so they arrived together. It was just as well. If he'd thought it busy earlier, tonight the crowd had doubled, everyone eager to hear both Trent Bridges and Cecy Wright. On their way into the main arena, they found themselves buffeted by other festival goers, all determined to secure the best spots close to their idols.

Liz laughed as Sam put his arm around her to protect her from the crush. He loved the way she felt. She wasn't one of those skinny women, concerned about her weight like his ex and daughter-in-law. He loved her curves, the way her body moved against his, imagining what it would be like to hold her even closer.

They pushed their way through the crowd and finally managed to find seats not too far from the stage. 'This is perfect,' Liz said, gazing around. 'I'm glad we found seats. There are people standing at the back.'

The evening began, the audience yelling out the well-known lyrics to accompany the artists and applauding loudly at the end of each song. Owen's students performed between the two main artists and were well received, too.

It was late when the final act concluded. Liz's head had dropped onto Sam's shoulder.

'You must be tired,' he said. 'You've had a busy day.'

'Yes. It was the busiest Saturday I've had in the shop – a lot of visitors to the town. But I wouldn't have missed this for the world. Thanks for being with me. It wouldn't have been nearly as much fun on my own.'

Sam squeezed her hand and they started to leave, only to discover the crowd was just as thick as it had been on the way in.

They were almost at the car, picking their way across the uneven surface, when Liz stumbled. Sam lost his grip on her hand, and she fell to the ground.

'Liz!' Sam bent down to help her up, cursing himself for not taking enough care. 'Are you all right?'

'Yes, I…' She tried to rise, then sank down again. 'Sorry, it's my ankle. I can't seem to stand on it.'

'Maybe it's broken. We need to get it seen to.'

'No, I'll be all right.' Liz tried to stand on it again then gave a yelp of pain. 'Sorry.'

'I'm taking you to Emergency. No arguments.' Sam picked her up in his arms and carefully made his way to the car, marvelling at how soft her skin was and how natural it felt to hold her like this.

Liz stopped protesting and soon she was tucked into the back seat of his car heading towards Granite Springs Base Hospital.

Fortunately, it was a quiet night in the emergency department. They only had a short wait before a nurse called Liz's name and she was wheeled out of the waiting room – she'd been provided with a wheelchair when they arrived.

'Shall I…?' Sam asked, rising to his feet.

Liz shook her head, so he sat back down again, forced to wait impatiently for her return.

It seemed to take ages, but Liz finally emerged, hobbling on a pair of crutches, her ankle wrapped in a bandage.

Sam rose again. 'Is it...?'

'It's not broken. The doctor said I've only sprained it – a mild sprain, he called it. I need to take care and see my GP in two or three weeks.' She grimaced. 'I'm not sure how I'm going to cope, but I suppose I'll manage.'

'Are you still in a lot of pain?'

'The bandage helps, and he's given me painkillers to take later to help me sleep.'

Sam wanted to do something for her but felt helpless. 'Let me take you home and help you get settled down,' he said.

At Liz's house, Sam carried her inside, despite her protestations that she could manage on her own. Once inside, they were greeted by Marmaduke who, sensing something was wrong with his mistress, managed to get underfoot and almost caused Sam to drop Liz.

'Damn cat!' he said, trying to avoid any mishap.

'Poor Marmaduke,' Liz said, managing a grin. 'You know something's up, don't you? I'll be fine, now,' she said to Sam.

'I'm not sure you will. Why don't I make you a hot drink? I can wait with you while you drink it and make sure you're okay. I feel responsible for your ankle.'

'Thanks.' Liz looked up at him with a smile. 'A hot drink would be lovely. But you're not responsible. I should have been looking where I was going instead of gazing up at the stars. The sky was so beautiful tonight, so romantic.'

Her words took Sam by surprise. This was exactly what he'd been thinking.

Sam settled Liz on the sofa with her ankle elevated and went into the kitchen to fix them both hot chocolate. Following her instructions, he found mugs and chocolate in the cupboard and soon returned with the two drinks.

Marmaduke gave a baleful glare as Sam joined Liz on the sofa, and leapt down from where he'd been lying on her lap.

'Oh dear,' Liz said. 'I think Marmaduke's jealous.' She chuckled then winced as her ankle moved slightly.

'Should you take those painkillers now?' Sam asked.

'I think perhaps I should. I hope I can get a good night's sleep.' Liz sighed. 'It's a good job tomorrow's Sunday. I can stay here all day. But I need to open the shop on Monday as usual.'

'I don't think that's a good idea.' Sam was worried about her. Surely it would be better for her to stay home for a few days at least?

'I'll be fine. I can sit behind the counter with my foot up like this.' She pointed to the injured extremity.

'Hmm.'

Liz obediently swallowed her medication. Then, when they'd finished their drinks, she said, 'I think they're beginning to work. I can barely keep my eyes open. I can probably make it to the bedroom.'

'Let me.' Sam picked her up again and carried her through into a bedroom which was as unlike his own as could be. His was stark and what designers called minimalist, while Liz's reflected her taste with its white plantation shutters and brightly coloured bed linen. The whole room was a tribute to the woman who owned it and it smelt of the unique fragrance he'd noticed she always wore.

Sam placed her gently on the bed but wasn't able to extricate himself easily from her arms around his neck. As he carefully moved her hands, their faces were so close he could see the hazel flecks in her eyes. Unable to resist, Sam brushed a strand of hair from her face. He planted a kiss on her forehead, his lips travelling down across her eyelids to her mouth. As her arms reached up to draw him closer, Sam pulled her into an embrace, then tucked a cover over her, whispering, 'Sleep tight,' before he left.

Twenty-eight

Liz awoke, surprised to discover she was still fully dressed, then she remembered. She'd tripped and fallen, hurt her ankle. She pulled back the cover to see her damaged ankle. She tried to flex it, but it was too tightly bound. However, the pain seemed to have gone. Amazing what a good night's sleep would do. She struggled to sit up and gazed around the room, seeing the crutches leaning against the bedside table. She smiled. Sam was a dear man. He'd thought of everything.

Pushing herself to the edge of the bed, Liz managed to lower her legs to the floor and grab hold of the crutches. Then she hobbled into the ensuite.

It was sometime later when she slowly made her way into the kitchen, wondering where Marmaduke was hiding. She normally awoke to find him lying on her bed.

The aroma of coffee greeted her and there standing by the window was Sam Walker. Marmaduke was lying outstretched at his feet.

'You... you stayed here all night?'

'I didn't think you should be alone. I slept on the sofa.'

'Oh!' Liz's first thought was that she must look a fright. She had washed her face but hadn't taken time to brush her hair and was still dressed in the outfit she'd worn to the music festival. It seemed to have taken place so long ago. Was it only last night? She ineffectually patted her hair.

'You look lovely as you are,' Sam said, as if reading her mind.

'Oh!' she said again. What did you say when you found a man in your kitchen on a Sunday morning?

'I've made coffee. Why don't you take a seat? I can make breakfast, too, if you'd like some.'

As if in a dream, Liz sat down at the kitchen table. Marmaduke immediately leapt onto her lap and started kneading her. Her hand automatically began to stroke him. 'Thanks. Toast would be good.'

'I can do better than that. I see you have eggs. I'm a dab hand at scrambled eggs. Yes or no?'

'Yes, please.' Liz realised she was hungry. It was a long time since she'd eaten.

She sat, sipping her coffee and watching while Sam cooked breakfast. It was strange to see a man in her kitchen, but somehow Sam didn't look out of place. He'd shed the jacket he was wearing the night before and rolled up his shirt sleeves to display tanned forearms. His hair was dishevelled – he hadn't brushed or combed his either. It made him seem more approachable, more… Liz felt a flash of desire as he turned towards her, his eyes twinkling in amusement. How could she ever have thought him arrogant? She shivered, remembering their embrace, and how he'd pulled away before it could become too intense. He was a good man. He understood she wasn't ready for more – not yet.

'I hope you slept well.'

'I did. How about you?' She didn't think her narrow sofa would have been very comfortable for a man of his size.

'I think I dozed off close to dawn.' He chuckled and dragged a hand through his hair before turning his attention back to the eggs.

'That was delicious. Thank you,' Liz said, swallowing the last mouthful of toast and scrambled egg. She needed to have a shower and change, then… probably spend the day in bed or on the sofa, she thought.

'I'm afraid I can't stick around. I have… I've arranged to take Mitch and his family to a barbecue at Wooleton. We – Mitch and I – are hoping that meeting some young people will help persuade Brooke of the benefits of a move to Granite Springs. Neil and Sally are around their age and Neil has a daughter, too. I can pop round later to see if you need anything.' Sam stood awkwardly, shifting from one foot to the other.

Liz almost laughed at his discomfort. 'No worries. I wouldn't expect you to spend your Sunday here. I can call Peta if I need anything. But you're welcome to drop round later if you want,' she added, seeing his crushed expression.

When he had gone, farewelling her with a kiss – on the cheek this time – Liz slowly made her way back to the bedroom for a shower and pulled on a kaftan which she rarely wore. Then she called Peta.

In less than half an hour, Peta was at the door. 'I didn't bring Lily today,' she said, when Liz hobbled to the door on her crutches. 'Shouldn't you be lying down?'

'I will, but I can't lie around doing nothing. This'll teach me to be more careful.'

'Just as well Sam Walker was with you. Did you say he stayed all night?' Peta's eyebrows rose.

'On the sofa. It was all very correct.'

'He's a good man.'

'He is.' Liz smiled, remembering the way he'd made her feel, and his concern for her wellbeing. 'I was wrong about him.'

'You were at the music festival together. Are you two…?'

Liz blushed. 'I think we may be. Oh, Peta…'

By this time they had reached the living room and Liz collapsed on the sofa, Marmaduke immediately taking up the spot on her lap.

Peta sat opposite. 'You can tell me. I won't say a word.'

'I have feelings for him. I never thought I would, not after Dan. But somehow Sam has managed to get under my skin. It's just like that Magda woman said. He held out his hand … and I took it.' She blushed again. 'But, I'm not sure…'

'About what?'

'Dan.' Liz twisted her fingers together. 'Would I be betraying Dan if Sam and I…'

'Liz!' Peta's voice held a note of surprise. 'Dan's dead. He died twenty years ago. How can you even think that?'

'I… he… Perhaps you're right.' Liz wanted to believe her but made a vow to herself. As soon as she was able, she'd go back to Canberra. She'd visit the cemetery, go to Dan's grave. Last time, she'd felt his presence so strongly. People might think her mad, but she needed to know he approved of her moving on with her life.

Twenty-nine

It was difficult for Sam to leave Liz. She looked so helpless, with her foot trussed up in a tight bandage, but she appeared cheerful enough and seemed happy to see him go. All he wanted to do was pick her up and take her back to the bedroom. But he didn't want to rush things. What they had together was too important to spoil. He was determined to be patient, knowing the time would come when she was ready to take the next step. He trembled in anticipation of what lay ahead.

But that was in the future, and today he needed to focus on his family. Mitch was relying on him to help smooth the path for Brooke here in Granite Springs, and Sam knew the Thompson clan would do their best to help.

'Dad.' Mitch greeted him looking as if he had slept on a sofa, too. His shirt was hanging out and his hair was a mess.

'Rough night?' he asked without thinking. Then he remembered. 'How did dinner go?'

'It was good. You were right. Brooke was impressed with The Riverside and Abi loved the special colouring sheet they gave her. Chris Thomas was there too with his partner, so I was able to introduce Brooke to him and he told her how impressed he was with my ideas. I think it took her by surprise. She's been so used to hearing me put down. She... I...' He looked down at his feet.

The penny dropped for Sam. 'You didn't sleep here last night either, did you?'

'How did you know? You just got home. Where were *you*?'

'It's a long story, but I spent the night on a sofa half my size. I guess you didn't?'

'Not exactly.' Mitch pulled on one ear. 'Abi was exhausted after her busy day, so we went back to the motel to put her to bed. We talked over a few drinks and one thing led to another. But this morning Brooke was back to her old self. I don't know, Dad.' He shook his head.

'Women! We poor men will never understand them, son. But we can't help but love them and we can't live without them.'

'So, where did *you* spend the night?' Mitch asked, when they were sitting on the veranda with their second cups of coffee.

'You know I went back to the music festival? I took Liz Pender. She owns the bookshop in town. I've seen her a few times lately.' He cleared his throat. 'We were on our way to the car park at the end of the evening when she took a tumble. Ended up in Emergency with a sprained ankle. I couldn't leave her on her own, so…'

'You did the gentlemanly thing.' Mitch chuckled. 'That's so like you, Dad. Another man would have taken advantage of her weakness, but not you.' He chuckled again.

'She's a respectable widow, Mitch. And I have a position to uphold in the community.'

'Spare me, Dad.' Mitch looked across the paddock at the grazing sheep. 'Tell me more about this place we're going to for lunch. Abi is excited at the prospect of visiting a real farm. She's decided this acreage is only a pretend one.'

'Her and most of the farmers around here.' Sam laughed. 'But it's real enough for me. I just need to decide what I'm going to do with it.'

'You don't regret it, do you? Buying an acreage, I mean.'

'Absolutely not! I love it here. Where else could I find a peaceful spot like this?' He waved an arm to encompass the pasture stretching almost as far as they could see.

'It's a bit too quiet for me. I think it would be for Brooke, too. She likes to have people around her. That's why…' He bit his lip.

'What you need is a shower, then to get changed. I do, too. Then we can get going. When did you arrange to pick Brooke up?'

'Eleven.'

'Better get a move on, then.'

*

It was a perfect day to visit Wooleton. Sam arrived first and was already sitting on the wide veranda with a beer when Mitch drove up. Brooke stepped out of the car and gazed up at the house, but Sam couldn't work out from her expression what she was thinking. Abi was different. She saw the dogs and immediately bent down to pat the nearest one.

'That's Blackie.' Daisy joined her, eager to show off her superior knowledge and make friends with the younger girl. 'I'm Daisy. What's your name?'

At least the children were prepared to be friends, Sam thought, stepping down from the veranda to greet Mitch and Brooke.

'You've already met my son,' he said to Alec and Judy who followed him. 'This is his wife, Brooke, and the little one with Daisy is Abi.'

'Welcome to Wooleton,' Judy said, with her usual friendly smile. 'Come up and meet Neil and Sally. Neil's our nephew, and they live here on the property. As you can see, we're soon to have an addition to the family.' She gestured towards Sally.

The rest of the visit passed smoothly with Brooke and Sally finding plenty to chat about. Neil was interested in what Mitch proposed to do at CAT, leaving Sam to talk with Alec and Judy.

'I had a call from Liz this morning,' Judy said, in a lull in their conversation. 'She told me how helpful you'd been. What a thing to happen. I hear the festival was a success, too.'

'Isn't it still going?' Alec asked. 'A weekend event, I heard.'

'You're right. But one day was enough for us. I think today's events are more focused on the younger generation. How was Liz when you spoke with her?' Sam asked, remembering how she looked when he left her and wishing again he could have stayed.

'She sounded pretty cheerful. Peta was going to pop round to keep her company, though Liz has never been one who needs other people around. I've always told her she's too self-sufficient, that she needs to let other people in.' She gave Sam a meaningful look. 'She's been on her own a long time, too long. I think…'

'Leave it, Jude,' Alec interrupted. 'Sam doesn't want to hear your views on Liz. And she's told you often enough to let her be, that she's happy with her life as it is.'

Judy subsided, but not before glaring at her husband.

All too soon, it was time to leave. A quick glance at Brooke told Sam she had enjoyed the visit, giving him cause for hope. There was no doubt Abi had enjoyed herself. She and Daisy had quickly made friends, the older girl happy to take charge and, when Neil took them both off to see some late-born lambs and to feed the hens, she was in heaven.

'See you, Dad,' Mitch said when they left.

Sam hoped it wouldn't be too soon, though he thought Brooke planned to drive back to Canberra before dark.

As Sam drove the short distance home alone, his mind went to Liz. He wondered how she was and decided to make the trip into town to check on her.

Thirty

Three weeks passed before Liz was fit enough to drive to Canberra again. Although she'd made it to the shop each day, she'd missed the meetings of the protest group committee, but Peta kept her informed and had reported there was no progress. During the three weeks, she and Sam met on a regular basis for drinks or dinner. In the first week, he'd arrived at her house every evening, either prepared to cook or bringing a takeaway meal for them both. As she had become more mobile, he'd driven her out to his acreage, where she met Mitch and learned about his plans to move his family to Granite Springs. Mitch was hoping to buy one of the new homes Danny Slater was building on the outskirts of town. But it wasn't clear if his wife had agreed to the move.

And, while they'd exchanged kisses and warm embraces, Sam had been the consummate gentleman. She was pleased he seemed to realise she needed time before they took their relationship to the next level.

In Canberra, Liz spent the morning visiting all the places that meant something to her and Dan. They'd always hold memories for her, but she knew it was time to say farewell. She'd held on to them long enough and allowed those memories to spoil her infrequent trips to the capital.

Finally, she drove to the cemetery. At Dan's graveside, Liz dropped to her knees, tucking her legs under her. With tears in her eyes, she spoke to her dead husband.

'Dan, I don't know if you can hear me or not, but I think – I hope

– that you can. Last time I was here, I felt you wanted to tell me something. This time, I have something to tell you, to ask you. I've been true to your memory for all of twenty years. I never thought I could meet anyone who'd touch my heart again. But I have. I think you'd like Sam. He's kind, gentle, principled – all the things you were, the qualities I admired in you. I still love you. I always will. Nothing and no one can change that. But I love Sam, too. In a different way. He was in Afghanistan too. He knows what you went through and has tried to help me understand. I was angry when I spoke with Glen – angry with him and angry with you, too. But knowing you, I was aware you couldn't do anything else. You had to help your mate. I just wish it hadn't ended the way it did. You'll always be my first love, my hero.' She sniffed and wiped her eyes. 'What I need to ask is this. I need your permission to be with Sam. He's been patient with me, knowing I'm still grieving for you. But as both Ailsa and Judy keep telling me – you'd probably tell me to listen to them if you were here – I need to move on. But before I can, I need to ask if it's okay with you. I realise it's a stupid thing to ask. You may not even be there – wherever that is. But if you can send a sign of some sort…'

Liz closed her eyes and listened. There was only silence broken by the sound of birds. She opened them again and as she did, the sun came out from behind a cloud, blinding her with its brightness. It was as if Dan was answering her.

*

Liz had arranged to meet Ailsa in the café in the Art Gallery. Oddly, it was one she and Dan had never visited together but had always been a favourite catch-up spot for the two sisters. Liz ordered an iced coffee and went across to join her sister at a table by the window looking out onto Lake Burley Griffin.

'How's your ankle?' Ailsa asked as soon as Liz sat down.

'Better. It's taken longer than I thought. But I'm ninety-nine percent back to normal.'

'What brings you to Canberra today? And why so mysterious about it?'

Liz fidgeted in her seat. 'I didn't want Mum to know. You know what she's like, she'd have fussed, wanted to put on a meal. I had things to do.'

'What things?'

'I needed to visit Dan's grave, I wanted to talk to him. I haven't gone mad,' she said, seeing her sister's expression. 'When I go there, I sense his presence. I know it sounds stupid, but I do.'

'Okay, so you wanted to talk to Dan. What about?' Ailsa looked skeptical.

Liz drew imaginary lines on the table with her thumb before replying. 'Since I hurt my ankle, I've been seeing more of Sam Walker – a lot more. I really like him, Ailsa.' She smiled across at her sister.

'Well, it's about time. I like the sound of him. Have you...?' Ailsa asked.

'No!' Liz blushed. She hated how prone she was to blushes. It had been that way ever since she was a child. While other kids could easily lie to their parents, for Liz, the red blotches staining her cheeks almost obliterating the freckles, was a sure giveaway. 'But...' she stirred her iced coffee, unwilling to meet her sister's eyes, '...I want to, and I think he does, too.' Liz remembered how his breath caught each time he pulled away and knew it was only his fear of her rejection that kept him from forcing the issue.

'What's stopping you?'

'It's Dan.' Liz looked up to meet Ailsa's eyes, seeing them filled with amazement.

'Dan? Dan's been dead for twenty years, Liz.'

'I know.' Liz remembered how Peta had told her that too. 'But... Anyway...' she stirred her coffee again, '...I wanted to ask his permission to get involved with Sam.' She looked at her sister, daring her to say anything.

'And?'

'The sun came out.' Liz glowed, remembering how she'd felt at what she was sure was a sign from her husband.

'That's it? The sun came out and you think...? My God, Liz. What's happened to you? You've always been so pragmatic. You even refused to have your fortune told at the fairground when we were teenagers. We all lined up, even though we knew it was phony, but you never would.'

'I know. But this was different. I can't explain it.'

'So, what you're saying is, you now feel it's okay to make love with Sam because your dead husband has given you permission?' She shook her head.

Said aloud in Ailsa's voice, it did sound mad, but... 'I guess so,' Liz replied.

*

Carpe diem. The words Ailsa whispered into her ear when she hugged her goodbye swirled around in Liz's head as she drove home to Granite Springs. It was all very well for her sister to urge her to seize the day, but Liz wasn't about to take the initiative in moving her relationship with Sam to the next step. The impetus would have to come from him. Liz was old-fashioned in that respect. She sighed. It might never happen. But there was the lighting of the Christmas tree lights to look forward to later tonight.

For Liz it was one of the highlights of the year. She loved how the whole square lit up and everyone cheered. In previous years she'd gone alone, or with Judy and Alec. Last year, Peta and Frank had joined her with Lily. It had been special to see the spectacle through the eyes of a nine-year-old.

But this year, it would be different. Sam had arranged to pick her up and they planned to walk to the town square together. It was odd to have the lighting of the tree on a Sunday evening, but the town council in their wisdom had made the decision to change the day.

She remembered the excitement two years ago when a group of Owen's students had begun to play immediately after the lights came on, a first in what proved to become a tradition at the lighting of the tree. Members of the crowd had begun to dance, including the old couple who were Magda and George Turnbull. It was there she'd first seen Magda, Liz realised.

What was it the old woman had told her again? Something about holding out her hand, finding happiness where she least expected it and... there was something else. But she couldn't remember. It didn't matter. It was a load of old rubbish. But she had met Sam, hadn't she?

And their first meeting hadn't been propitious. Back then, she'd never have imagined… She smiled to herself, wishing she could drive faster.

It was close to four o'clock when she arrived home, just time to have a shower and change before Sam arrived to pick her up. But before she took care of herself, she devoted time to giving Marmaduke a cuddle and filling his food and water bowls. The animal was displeased at having been left alone all day and followed her around once she set him down again, rubbing himself against her ankles and generally getting in the way.

Showered and dressed in a bright pink sundress – intended to confound those who said redheads couldn't wear pink – Liz waited nervously for Sam to arrive. She took several deep breaths, wondering if he'd be able to sense any difference in her. She felt different. It was as if she'd been given the key to her future, a future she'd never dreamt possible.

By the time Sam arrived, Liz could scarcely breathe. But he didn't appear to notice any difference in her.

'You're looking as lovely as always,' he said, giving her the usual hug and kiss on the cheek, before reaching down to scratch Marmaduke's ears. 'Ready to go?'

'Sure.' Liz smiled. What was she worrying about? It was just another evening, one in which they'd watch the lights go on, have dinner, then kiss and go their separate ways. She took a deep breath. 'Let's go.'

Thirty-one

Sam couldn't pinpoint what it was that was different about Liz tonight. There seemed to be a suppressed excitement about her, a glow that didn't have anything to do with the tree lighting they were about to enjoy. She had been fine the night before.

Sam took Liz's hand in his as they walked along, following groups of others intent on reaching the town square in time for one of the main events of the year. It heralded the lead-up to Christmas. There were few who would miss it.

As they reached the outskirts of the crowd, Sam nodded to several acquaintances and waved to Jo and Col Ford in the distance.

'There's Peta and Frank,' Liz said, pointing to her friends who were close to the tree.

'Do you want to join them?'

'No.' Liz shook her head. 'They must have got here much earlier. Lily would have nagged them to come so she could have a good view.'

Suddenly there was a shout, and the tree was lit up by a blinding array of lights. The crowd erupted in loud approval as once again the centre of Granite Springs rung with the sound of Christmas carols played by Owen's students.

Liz's grip on Sam's arm tightened and she turned her face up to his, her eyes beaming with delight. 'Isn't it wonderful? It's the same every year, but I never tire of it. It's so magical.'

The music changed and, as the crowd started to disperse, several couples began to dance. 'Shall we?' Sam asked and, without waiting for a reply, swung Liz into his arms to join the other dancers.

Sam smiled down at Liz. He loved to see her so excited. She was like a little girl, her eyes twinkling, her mouth curved into a smile, her hair blowing in the breeze. The dress she was wearing showed off her curves and made him want to carry her away.

They danced as long as the music played, Liz's body blending with his as if she belonged in his arms. When the group finally packed up their instruments, Sam looked around to realise they were the only couple still in the square. 'Hungry?' he asked, reluctantly releasing Liz.

'Yes,' she laughed. 'Wow! That was wonderful. I can't remember when I last danced. I thought my dancing days were over.'

'Not at all.' Sam vowed they'd dance again. It was such a wonderful excuse to hold Liz in his arms. 'Pavarotti's?'

'Lovely.' Liz still appeared to be infused with the euphoria he'd noticed earlier, and which had only intensified with the music and the dancing.

Over the past few weeks, Pavarotti's had become a favourite spot for them to eat. Sam had discovered Liz shared his love of Italian food and the meals at Pavarotti's were spectacular.

He waited until they'd finished eating and were at the coffee stage before asking, 'Did something happen today?'

'Why do you ask?'

'You seem different, more…' Sam didn't know how to describe the change he'd noticed in her. It was as if she'd cast off something that was weighing her down.

'I went to Canberra. I spoke to Dan.'

Sam felt his stomach churn. She talked to a dead man? 'Your husband?'

Liz ran a finger around the rim of her cup, then raised her eyes to meet his. 'I wanted to ask him… I enjoy being with you, Sam. I have feelings for you. Our relationship… There hasn't been anyone in my life since Dan and… I wasn't sure what… I didn't want to be unfaithful to him, so… I went to ask his permission.'

Sam swallowed. Did Liz mean what he thought she did? 'And…?' he asked huskily.

'The sun came out.' She beamed, her eyes glistening with tears.

The sun came out? What the hell did that mean?

'It was a sign,' she said, seeing his puzzled expression. 'Oh, I don't normally believe all that fey stuff, but this time… If you'd been there and seen it, you'd know what I mean. I truly believe it was Dan trying to tell me it was okay for me to move on.'

'Right.' There didn't seem to be anything else to say.

But when they left the restaurant and were on their way back to Liz's home, Sam forgot his surprise. Instead, he rejoiced in the feel of Liz's soft body against his as they strolled along the deserted street arm-in-arm, stopping only to admire the brightly lit Christmas tree by the war memorial.

'Won't you come in?' Liz looked up at him when they stopped at her front gate. 'Another coffee?'

'Thanks.'

As soon as they walked through the door, they were greeted by a ball of fur. Marmaduke was glad to see his person home again and rubbed himself around their ankles.

'Steady on,' Sam said, his arm around Liz's shoulders.

'Did you miss me?' Liz squatted down to fondle the cat, leaving Sam's arms empty.

He'd thought… Well, perhaps he'd been wrong, he decided as she continued to fuss over the cat. 'You mentioned coffee?'

*

Liz stood up. When they walked through the door, her intention to take their relationship to the next level made her feel awkward. Thank goodness for Marmaduke. It was easy to hide her embarrassment in talking to her pet. Then Sam reminded her of the invitation to coffee. What had possessed her? The last thing she wanted was another cup of coffee.

'Mmm.' They moved into the kitchen, Marmaduke following, purring contentedly. Liz opened the fridge and, seeing a bottle of champagne left over from some earlier celebration, picked it up instead. 'Coffee or champagne?' she asked, brandishing the bottle.

'Champagne, I think. But first…' Sam took the bottle from her, placed it carefully on the benchtop and took her in his arms. 'I've been wanting to do this all evening,' he murmured into her hair. Then his lips were on hers.

Liz felt herself melt into his embrace. She was aware of her heart beating madly. Her legs felt weak. Was this…?

Sam's phone rang, killing their passion. 'Damn!' he said. But the interruption had cooled the hot flash of desire that flared between them. He took the phone from his pocket and glanced at it. 'I need to take this. It's Mitch.'

Liz went to the loo while Sam answered his phone. She gazed at herself in the mirror, seeing a woman she barely recognised. Her eyes were bright, her cheeks red, and her lips swollen from Sam's kiss. She held onto the edge of the sink and took several deep breaths. If the phone hadn't interrupted them, would they have…? Liz sluiced her face with cold water, drew a comb through her tousled hair and went back to the kitchen.

'Is there a problem?' she asked, seeing Sam standing motionless, the phone still in his hand.

'It's Mitch. There's been an accident. I need to go.'

'Of course.' Liz was thrust into action. She went to Sam and hugged him – a passionless hug. 'Is there anything I can do?'

'No.' Sam shook his head. He seemed to be in a daze. 'He was on his way back from Canberra. He's in Base Hospital. He says it's not serious, but…'

'You need to be with him. Are you sure you're okay to drive?'

'What?' Sam gazed at her, his eyes clouded. For a moment he said nothing, then he pulled himself together. His face cleared. 'I'm fine. I'll call you. I'm sorry.'

'I am, too.' Liz stretched up to plant a brief kiss on his lips, a very different kiss from the one which was interrupted. 'Take care. I hope he's not too badly injured.'

After saying goodbye to Sam and watching his car disappear, Liz returned to the kitchen. She looked at the bottle of champagne sitting on the benchtop, and sadly returned it to the fridge. So much for moving her and Sam's relationship forward. Fate had decided otherwise. *Maybe it was for the best*, she thought as she fixed herself a cup of chamomile tea. She needed something to calm her and help her sleep.

She took the tea through to the living room and curled up on the sofa, Marmaduke immediately leaping onto her lap and starting to purr.

'Just you and me again, Marmaduke,' Liz said sadly. The night which had held such promise had been rudely interrupted. It was almost laughable. After all her soul-searching, her conversation with her dead husband, fate had taken a hand. She finished her tea, rose, stretched and, after making sure Marmaduke had plenty of water, went to bed to dream of being in Sam's arms with nothing to interrupt them.

Thirty-two

Sam parked at the hospital with a sense of *déjà vu*. It seemed no time since he had taken Liz there after the music festival. Now it was Mitch who needed his help.

The emergency department was packed with people in various states of pain. He went to the desk. 'Mitchell Walker. I believe he's been brought in. I'm his father.'

'Just a minute.' The woman hit a few keys on her computer. 'He came in about half an hour ago. He's with the doctor now. You can go through to see him.' She pointed to a door along from her desk.

'Thanks.' Taking a deep breath, Sam pushed open the door.

On the other side, he found himself in a large room filled with cubicles divided by curtains. He walked along nervously, peering into each cubicle until he saw Mitch.

'Hi, Dad.' Mitch was lying on the narrow hospital bed propped up with pillows. He had a plaster on his forehead and one arm was in a sling. His face was very white.

'How are you, son? What happened?'

'I'm okay, Dad. The car came off the road at the bridge just outside town. The paramedics said I was lucky it wasn't any worse. Good job the airbag worked. Another driver stopped and called the ambulance, and here I am.'

Glad it wasn't any worse, Sam collapsed into a chair by the bed. 'You're very pale. Your arm?'

'Broken. I'll be out of action for a few weeks. Should be right by Christmas.'

Sam frowned.

'I hadn't been drinking, Dad.'

'Of course not.' But that had been Sam's first thought. He heaved a sigh of relief. No drunk driving charge to worry about. It seemed Mitch had learned his lesson.

A nurse popped his head into the cubicle. 'Mr Walker.'

Both men turned.

The nurse smiled. 'Mr Mitchell Walker. I presume that's you,' he said to Mitch with a grin. 'I've spoken to the doctor and you're good to go. Remember to take care, keep your arm elevated and ice it regularly. You should see your GP in around three weeks.' He handed Mitch a packet containing several tablets. 'Take one of those when you get home. It will help you sleep. You can take another tomorrow if you're in pain.'

'I can go home?'

'I presume this gentleman is able to take you.' The nurse smiled at Sam.

'He's my dad.'

Sam was never more glad of anything, than that he was here to take care of Mitch, to take him home.

As the pair walked out to where the Range Rover was parked, Sam thought about how much had happened that night. The tree lighting ceremony seemed to have been so long ago, yet it was only a few hours since he and Liz had been dancing in the town square, since he'd had such hopes for the evening, hopes which had been quashed by Mitch's accident.

'I need to let Brooke know,' Mitch said as soon as he was settled in the car. 'I promised to call her when I got back. She'll be worried.'

Sam glanced at his son, trying to gauge his feelings. Mitch had spent the weekend with his wife and daughter in Canberra, had been doing so for the past few weeks. Sam knew there had been some talk about her moving to Granite Springs but, as far as he was aware, nothing had yet been decided between them.

'Why not wait till we get home?' he suggested.

'Okay.' Mitch grimaced with pain, leant his head back and closed his eyes. Sam frowned. The poor guy. What a thing to happen, just when he was starting to work for Chris Thomas, too. Mitch had finally taken up the position Chris offered a week earlier, optimistic he could persuade Brooke to make the move to Granite Springs.

Sam had to rouse Mitch when they reached his home. When they walked into the house, Mitch headed for his bedroom, while Sam went to the kitchen. After all that had happened, he needed a drink.

As he sipped the ten-year-old malt whisky, he could hear Mitch's voice in the bedroom. He was calling Brooke. Sam wondered what her reaction would be when she heard about the accident. This led him to wonder about Mitch's car. Mitch hadn't mentioned it, probably too traumatised. But it would have to be taken care of. He'd ask him in the morning.

The events of the day were beginning to catch up with Sam, his eyes starting to sting, when the sound of Mitch's voice stopped. On his way to bed, Sam popped his head into Mitch's room. 'How did Brooke take it?' he asked.

'She's coming to see me tomorrow and bringing Abi. Can they stay here for a few days, Dad?'

Sam's eyes widened. This was the last thing he'd expected. 'That'll be fine, son,' he said, his thoughts whirling. His daughter-in-law under his roof? She must be really worried about Mitch – and it was a sign there was hope for their marriage after all.

Once he was alone, Sam took out his phone. He needed to call Liz, tell her what had happened.

'Sam. Oh, I'm so glad to hear from you. How's Mitch?'

'He'll live. He was lucky, only a few cuts and bruises and a broken arm. It'll slow him down a bit.'

'Oh, I'm glad. And how are you? It must have been a shock.'

'I'm good, too. I'm sorry we were interrupted and I had to leave. I'd hoped…' His voice trailed off. Had he read her wrong?

'I had, too,' she said in a voice so quiet Sam had to strain his ears to hear her.

His heart leapt. 'There'll be other times.'

'There will.'

Sam could picture her, smiling into the phone. He wished he'd Facetimed her, been able to see her face. He gripped his phone tighter as if it would bring Liz closer.

'There's the performance on Saturday – the Messiah. You'll be there – and the practice on Tuesday?'

Sam had all but forgotten. How could he have? The choristers had been practicing for weeks until Owen was satisfied with them. It was to be the highlight of the year for the choir, a tradition that seemingly had been going on for years in Granite Springs. 'Of course. I wouldn't dare miss it.'

'I'll keep the champagne on ice,' Liz said, before ringing off.

Thirty-three

Liz ended the call and clasped the phone to her breast, trying to suppress her disappointment. This was to have been their night. It had started so well. She'd felt she was floating in Sam's arms as they danced to the old sentimental melodies. Then there had been dinner when she'd told him about her conversation with Dan. She hoped he'd understood what she was telling him. She didn't want to spell it out, only to be rejected.

Things seemed to be moving in the right direction when Sam took her into his arms. Then his phone rang, and he had to dash off. She understood, of course she did, but couldn't help a niggle of annoyance that Mitch's accident had ruined their evening.

Had she been too forward in taking the champagne out of the fridge – and in mentioning it again on the phone? Liz bit her lip. She was so out of practice. Maybe she should forget the whole idea of a relationship with Sam Walker. She'd been perfectly happy on her own until he came on the scene. She could be again. But... Liz sighed, remembering how it had felt in his arms, how feelings she'd thought dead for ever had resurfaced. It was hard to deny their existence.

Before going to sleep, she picked up Dan's photo from her bedside table and kissed it. 'Am I doing the right thing?' she asked him, before replacing it. 'Oh, Dan, why did you have to leave me?' She closed her eyes and burrowed into the pillow.

*

Next morning, Liz awoke in a more positive frame of mind. A call from Sam to report on Mitch's progress and apologise again for his abrupt departure helped brighten her day. Any temptation to linger over thoughts of him evaporated when her phone pinged with a message.

Remember. Meeting tonight. See you there. Peta

Liz's focus immediately shifted. The protest committee meeting tonight was an important one. They were at a loss as to why the planning committee hadn't replied to their submission other than to say it had been received. Tonight's meeting had been arranged to work out what their next steps should be. It was getting close to Christmas and, like everything else in Australia, the council would close down for weeks while everyone celebrated and took holidays. She quickly typed her reply.

I'll be there. Liz

Once she arrived at work, Liz had no time to think about either Sam or the meeting. She received the delivery of several boxes of books and, between customers, spent the morning unpacking and entering details into her database. It was lunchtime before she drew breath.

'Hello.'

Liz looked up to see a friendly face. 'Judy! What are you doing in town today?'

'We needed a new attachment for one of the water troughs, so I volunteered to pick it up. Alec and Neil are busy drenching. I thought you might like some lunch.' She waved two paper bags.

Liz suddenly realised she was hungry. She hadn't packed a lunch today intending to pop over to The Bean Sprout Café to pick up something. 'Wonderful,' she said, recognising The Bean Sprout logo on the bags. 'I was meaning to get something myself, but I've been too busy. Come through the back.'

Once the two women were settled in the tiny back shop area with cups of peppermint tea and the special Bean Sprout sandwiches filled with avocado, feta, mushrooms, olives, hummus and greens, Liz sighed. 'This is perfect, Judy. How did you guess?'

'I know what you're like. You don't take enough care of yourself. And I wanted to have a chat, to catch up with you after the weekend. You mentioned you planned a trip to Canberra, to Dan's grave, and I saw you and Sam dancing at the tree lighting ceremony. What gives?'

Liz sighed again and sipped her tea before replying. 'I went to Canberra yesterday and I did speak with Dan. He...' She decided not to tell Judy about the sign she believed Dan had given her. She didn't want her friend to ridicule her. She knew how she'd react if the boot was on the other foot, but it had been a special moment. 'I found closure,' she said instead. 'Then I came back to Granite Springs and went with Sam to the tree lighting where you saw us. End of story.'

Judy raised her eyebrows in disbelief. 'That's it?'

'We had dinner, then Sam had a call. His son was in an accident and he had to rush to the hospital.'

'Oh, no! The poor man. Is Mitch badly hurt?'

'It seems not. Sam said a broken arm and a few scratches. But it'll mean he's stuck there, unable to drive.'

'He's still staying with Sam?'

'Yes. There's some talk of his wife joining him and their buying one of Danny Slater's homes in his newest development, but nothing definite.'

'Hmm. Well, at least Danny's developments aren't an eyesore. He manages to blend them into the landscape. Is your friend, Peta, still working with him?'

'Yes, she is.' Liz was glad Judy had changed the subject. 'She's still designing the interiors. Her business has really taken off. To think when she began, people said there would be no work for an interior designer in Granite Springs. How wrong they were.'

'Speaking of Peta. Are you still involved in the protest group Frank Beattie set up? There doesn't appear to have been much movement on the development front.'

'I'm going to a meeting tonight. We have no idea what's going on and just hope it's not all happening behind closed doors and we'll suddenly hear it's been approved.'

'They wouldn't do that, would they? Look, Alec's brother used to be on the council. He'd still have contacts there. Why don't I ask Ken if he knows what's going on?'

'That would be good.'

'I'll see if I can contact him before tonight. I'll let you know. Now, I have some good news.'

'Always happy to hear good news.'

'It's about Daisy – Neil's daughter. She's been begging her mother to let her live with Neil and Sally but, although she's allowed her to come up more frequently for weekends, she's refused to let her move here.' Judy leant forward, her face beaming. 'She's finally given in. I think her new fellow may have something to do with it. Daisy's moving here after Christmas and will start at Granite Springs Primary in the new year.'

'You must be delighted.'

'We're over the moon. It's been so lovely to have Neil and Sally so close. And we're excited about the new baby. To have Daisy here, too, will be the icing on the cake. She's ten now.'

'The same age as Lily, Peta's granddaughter.'

'And she and Sam's granddaughter got on well. I think Daisy enjoyed playing big sister, practicing for when Sally's baby arrives.'

'Mmm.' Liz didn't want to discuss Sam anymore, in case she gave away her feelings. Though she suspected Judy already guessed. 'Tell me about the sheep,' she said instead, knowing Judy could talk for ever about their flock.

'Don't forget to talk to Ken,' Liz said, when Judy rose to leave. 'I'm interested to know what he can find out.'

'Will do. I'll call you.' Judy hugged Liz and left.

*

'Liz has something to tell us.' Frank fixed Liz with his gaze as the room fell silent. They were all sitting in the back room at The Bean Sprout Café, the one normally used for cooking classes or children's parties.

Liz squirmed. She hated being pushed into the limelight like this, but the news in Judy's call before she left home had been a surprise, one she had to share with the other committee members. 'I have a friend who's related to Ken Thompson,' she began, looking around the group. 'He's one of the good guys.'

Everyone nodded. Ken had been a well-known and well-respected local realter for many years and been on the council for a number of them before retiring.

Liz cleared her throat. 'He told my friend it was stuck in the planning committee. It seems there are a few members of the committee who are in the pocket of the developers – his words, not mine – and are agitating to have it passed. But there are others who want our submission to be considered.' She paused. 'He said that two of the committee have been unable to attend the latest meetings – one is overseas, and one is sick – and the others have pushed to delay their report. I know this doesn't help our cause any, but it does perhaps explain the delay.'

'Thanks, Liz.' Frank looked around the group. 'Anyone want to comment on what Liz has told us or add anything?'

There was a general shaking of heads, then Danny Slater asked what was on everyone's minds, 'Do you think we can get it settled by Christmas?'

'Why don't you ask your father?' the newsagent asked. 'He's the mayor. Surely, if anyone can hurry things along, he can.'

There was a lot of murmuring, before Danny replied, 'I wish I could, but Dad and I don't discuss council business. There's too much chance of being accused of a conflict of interests with the number of applications I submit to council.'

'Sounds fair,' Frank said. 'We shouldn't put Danny on the spot. We all know he and his father don't see eye-to-eye on this matter.'

'Time you stood for council yourself, Slater,' someone muttered.

Danny turned red.

The meeting continued going over the same ground again and again. Liz let her thoughts wander. She wondered what Sam was doing tonight. When they spoke this morning, he'd told her his daughter-in-law was arriving today with young Abi. She knew Brooke and he didn't always get on and wondered how they were managing and how Mitch was feeling. Hopefully, she'd find out at choir the following evening. She shivered in anticipation, despite the threat to her shop still hanging over her.

Thirty-four

When Sam got home from work on Monday night, Brooke had arrived. He was greeted by Abi running out to the car. 'We're here, Grandpa. I didn't have to go to school and Mum says I may not need to go back till after Christmas.'

'Are you pleased about that?'

'Yes and no.' Abi looked solemn. 'I like being here with Dad – and you – but I miss my friends and I was in the Christmas pageant and the choir. We were going to visit some old people and sing carols to them.'

'It's too bad if you miss those special events, but it's lovely to have you here.' He picked her up and gave her a hug. 'How's your dad?'

'Grumpy.' Abi slid out of his grasp and laughed. 'Mum's fussing over him and I don't think he likes it. Here she is now.'

Sam looked up to see Brooke emerge from the house, a frown on her face.

'I expected you home before now,' she said, her lips tight with disapproval. 'I've been making…'

'Steady on, Brooke. I'm glad you and Abi arrived safely. It's good to see you. I'm sure Mitch is pleased you're here, too. But there's no need to…' He broke off as she began to weep.

'I'm sorry, Sam.' She sniffed. 'When I heard Mitch had been in an accident I didn't… It made me realise how much I need him, how much *we* need him.' She hugged Abi who had run to her mother's side at the first sign of her tears. 'I'm so glad it's nothing more serious.

I've been on edge all day. I cooked a big meal, then when you weren't here, I… I'm sorry, I know this is your home and I'm only here on sufferance. I know I wasn't your ideal choice for Mitch, but I do love him.' She sniffed again.

'And he loves you, Brooke.' Sam was touched by her show of affection. 'Let's go inside and have dinner. I'm sure whatever you've cooked will be delicious.'

'Dad.' Mitch was seated at the kitchen table, his laptop open. 'Brooke and Abi are here.'

'So I see,' Sam said as the pair followed him in.

*

Sam tried, but was having difficulty in adjusting to not one but three extra people invading his privacy. He had become so used to living alone, it was hard to find Brooke practically taking over his kitchen after only one night's stay. And, while it was lovely to have the company of his granddaughter, the presence of the young child was wearing.

He shook his head as it began to ache from the loud chatter and arguments over breakfast. He must be getting old.

'You'll be home earlier tonight, Sam?' Brooke asked, as he downed his second cup of coffee.

It was a long time since he'd been subject to the sort of demand implicit in her question. It reminded him of Olga. What had his ex been saying to Brooke about him? Sam stifled the sharp reply which came to his lips. 'Not tonight, Brooke. I belong to the Granite Springs Choristers. It's our final practice before the performance of The Messiah on Saturday evening. I'll get a bite to eat in town and go straight there. You should come along on Saturday – Mitch and Abi, too.' He hoped the invitation would soften his refusal.

'What's The Messiah, Grandad?' Abi paused in spooning up her cornflakes. Where had they come from? Brooke must have gone shopping.

'It's a special piece of choral music composed a long time ago by a man called George Frideric Handel. It's often sung at Christmastime and it's performed every year in Granite Springs.

'Mmm. Would I like it?'

'Well, it's really for grown-ups, but I'd like to think you'd enjoy it.'

'Can we go, Mum?' she asked.

Maybe it wasn't all bad, having his family here, Sam thought. Abi was a delightful child. But he wondered how long Brooke intended to stay.

'What do you think, Mitch?' Brooke asked. 'Will you be up to it?'

'It's my arm that's broken, Brooke. I can move around. I just can't drive. I'd like to go. They're a good group. I went along with Dad one time,' he said. 'They were all a bit old for me, but Dad fits in well.'

'Thanks, Mitch.' Sam chuckled. He'd heard this before.

On his way into work, Sam thought about Liz. He'd see her tonight and remembered her comment about the champagne. Was it a promise? He'd fully intended to find out, but Brooke's arrival had put a spanner in the works. Now he had house guests, he felt obligated to go straight home after choir practice. It was almost as if he were a teenager again, afraid to stay out late lest he receive a punishment. He chuckled. How ridiculous. But Brooke had that effect on him. Sometimes he pitied Mitch.

Once in the office, he had no time to think. There was the next edition to plan, an interview with another of the local businesses to arrange and calls to field regarding a contentious article Jason had written about the local cricket club. It hadn't seemed contentious when Sam approved it. One never knew what members of the community would latch onto. *Another reason to avoid covering the prickly issue of the development proposal.*

Eventually, the day was over, his staff left, and Sam had the office to himself. He leant back in his chair, pleased with what he had achieved, not just today but since he arrived in Granite Springs. It had been a leap of faith to come here, to accept the position of editor of a small-town newspaper after the high-powered environments he was used to working in.

But, so far, it had proved a success. The paper was doing well, circulation had increased, as had revenue from advertising – all good signs. He was enjoying the slower pace of life in Granite Springs. He loved living on his acreage. And there was Liz Pender. What more could a man want?

Checking the time, he closed up and headed to the RSL for a quick bite before driving across town to the church.

*

Liz had an empty feeling in the pit of her stomach that had nothing to do with the evening's choir practice. She had changed the sheets on her bed and checked the champagne was still cooling in the fridge, all the while telling herself to stop worrying. But it had been twenty years – more – since she'd made love. She was forty-nine, not twenty-nine, and her body bore testament to the fact. What if Sam didn't find her extra curves attractive, what if she repelled him, what if she'd completely misjudged his intentions?

Liz quivered with excitement and an unfamiliar sense of anticipation as she rifled through her wardrobe in an attempt to find exactly the right outfit. Finally, she drew out a loose sundress. It was a lovely pale lemon colour, the hemline was strewn with fronds of green. She slipped it on and stood in front of the full-length mirror, turning this way and that, before deciding its flowing style managed to hide those extra kilos. Then she brushed her hair till it shone, applied a touch more makeup than usual, added an extra squirt of Obsession and smiled at her reflection. Her stomach lurched at the thought that, next time she stood here, Sam would be with her.

The choir was already forming when Liz arrived. For this final rehearsal they were meeting in the church where the formal performance would be held on Saturday. Although not a churchgoer, Liz loved the feel of the old building with its high arched ceiling and stone pillars. It gave one a sense of permanence. It had always been there and always would be.

There was no time for more than a quick wave to Sam before she took her place among the contraltos, smiling to Kay and Donna as she slipped into her place between them.

Then it was all about the music, and everything else faded from her mind as Owen led them through the oratorio for Saturday. They finished on a high as Owen beamed at the group.

'I think you're ready,' he said, 'but don't be over-confident. I'll see you all on Saturday. Best bibs and tuckers.'

They all laughed. There was no choice. They'd all be dressed alike, the men in black trousers, the women in black skirts, and all wearing red tops of one sort or another. It was their uniform for every performance.

There was the usual shuffling and muffled chat as everyone prepared to leave, excited about Saturday's performance, the end of the year for the choristers.

Liz looked around for Sam, the butterflies in her stomach which had stilled during the practice, now in full flight.

He was waiting just inside the door.

'Hello,' she said, suddenly shy.

'I saw you arrive, but it was too late to speak. Owen...'

Liz smiled. Owen might appear to be a laidback hippie, but he could be a hard taskmaster.

'It was good tonight. I felt uplifted,' Sam said.

'The Messiah can have that effect on people. Wait till Saturday. It's even better with an audience.'

'I need to talk with you.' Sam took Liz by the elbow and steered her out of the church and into the car park. It was a warm evening, the air filled with the loud mating call of the cicadas in nearby trees.

Sam looked and sounded serious.

Whatever Liz had been expecting, it wasn't this. Her stomach dropped. She knew she wasn't going to like what he had to say. 'How's Mitch?' she asked as they walked along.

'He's good.' But Sam seemed distracted.

Sam stood awkwardly by their cars. Liz had deliberately parked her little Mazda next to his Range Rover so they could easily leave together. He drew a hand through his hair. 'I'm sorry, Liz. I wanted tonight to be... special, but...'

But? Her heart sank. She thought of the clean sheets, the chilling champagne, then forced herself to listen.

'My daughter-in-law arrived yesterday with Abi. They... she seems to have taken over. I feel a stranger in my own home, stupid as it sounds. But I need to get back. It means we can't... I can't... It's not how I intended tonight to end. I'm sorry.'

Liz didn't know how to react. Had she been too forward? Was this Sam's way of telling her he didn't want a relationship? A blush rose to her cheeks and she was glad it was dark so he wouldn't be able to see.

All around, people were saying goodbye, cars were starting up. All she could do was gaze at him in dismay.

'Come here.' Sam pulled her towards him. She felt his breath on her cheek, then his lips on hers in a brief kiss before he took her by the shoulders. 'I haven't changed my mind. I still want the champagne you promised. I hope you'll keep it for us. I want to think of it waiting for me. Take care and sleep well. See you on Saturday. Maybe we can have dinner before the performance?'

'Of course,' she said. He kissed her again, then they parted, and she felt his eyes on her as she pressed the control and got into her car.

Liz bit her lip and tried to hide her disappointment as she waved to Sam and drove off. Was his reference to the champagne what she thought it was? Was he being honest with her? How long would his daughter-in law be staying? Did it mean they couldn't be together till she left? Her mind was filled with questions as she drove home to her empty house, only the thought of seeing him on Saturday preventing her from having a complete meltdown.

Thirty-five

By Saturday, Sam had made peace with himself and accepted Brooke's presence in the house. She cooked the meals and seemed content to leave Sam to his own devices. Mitch was doing work for CAT from home with his good hand and a perpetual smile played on his lips. Abi was hanging around her dad as if afraid to let him out of her sight.

It seemed to Sam that Mitch's accident had done what no amount of pleading or cajoling on Mitch's part had been able to do. Brooke and Abi were here in Granite Springs, and it looked as if any cracks in their marriage were healed – or in the process of being plastered over.

'We'll come to your performance, Dad,' Mitch said over breakfast. 'It'll be a late night for Abi. We thought we'd get a meal in town first. Do you want to join us?'

'I need to go into the office today and I'm not sure when I'll get away.' Sam didn't want to make any arrangement he might have to wriggle out of afterwards. He was planning to eat with Liz, then to spend time with her after the performance. He'd given a lot of thought to this and come up with a solution. 'Don't count on me. I'll see you at the church.'

'Will you be singing any tunes I know?' Abi asked. 'Like *The Puggles*.'

'No, sweetie. My music will be very different to *The Puggles*, and the audience won't be joining in.'

'Oh!' There was a note of disappointment in her voice.

'You'll enjoy it. There will be a lot of other people singing with me, and we'll be in a big church.'

Abi lost interest and slid down from her chair. Sam hoped she would enjoy the performance and not find it boring. He was looking forward to it. Last year he'd been part of the audience and had been impressed.

Mitch followed Sam to his car. 'Thanks, Dad.'

Sam was puzzled.

'For putting up with Brooke. She's not so bad, really.' He pushed his good hand through his hair. 'She's been great since she got here. She can't do enough for me. I think the accident scared her. She told me it made her realise how she'd feel if anything really bad happened to me.'

'I'm sorry it had to take an accident to make her see sense, son. But I'm glad the two of you seem to be getting things sorted between you. Is she rethinking her stance on moving?'

'We're going to have a look at some display homes in the new Slater development this afternoon.' Mitch grinned. 'She won't admit it, but I think she's excited.'

'That's good news.' Sam clapped Mitch on the shoulder. 'I need to get off now. Have a good day.'

Sam had a smile on his face as he drove into town to the newspaper office. From what Mitch said, it looked as if he could stop worrying about his son's marriage, and he'd be able to see his beloved granddaughter grow up right here. The only question now was how soon they'd be able to decide on a house and move in. Sam couldn't wait to have his home back again.

*

The day dragged for Sam, his anticipation of the evening, both the performance of The Messiah and seeing Liz again, taking over as he tried to focus his attention on the tasks on hand. He really needn't have come in today, but he didn't want to stay home with Brooke and Mitch. They needed time together alone as a family if they were going to patch things up.

Finally, it was time to pack up and meet Liz. He'd arranged for them to have an early dinner at the Thai Kitchen, knowing they'd be served quickly. He wasn't very hungry.

Liz was flustered when he picked her up at the bookshop. Sam kissed her on the cheek. 'You look amazing,' he said, admiring the white tunic top and wide matching pants she was wearing.

'I'll need to take Marmaduke home and change first. Is that all right?'

'You don't mind going to the Thai in your choir gear?' Sam thought of his own red shirt hanging in the car. He hadn't worked out where or when he'd change into it.

'Not at all, everyone knows we're performing tonight. You can follow me home and take one car from there. Okay with you?'

'Sure.' Sam felt a ray of hope. If they were going to travel to the church in his car then he'd need to bring Liz home again. Perhaps they'd get to open that champagne tonight after all.

At Liz's home, Marmaduke leapt out of his basket and straight to his empty bowls. He knew the routine. Liz filled his bowls and looked at her watch. 'Do I have time for a shower?'

'If you're quick.'

While Liz was in the shower, Sam fetched his special shirt from the car, prepared to change for the evening ahead. He had just taken off the blue striped one he was wearing when Liz came out of the ensuite wrapped in a towel, droplets of water on her eyelashes, her hair and face still damp. Sam thought he had never seen anything so beautiful.

'Come here,' he said huskily, holding out his arms.

They moved towards each other without hesitation. Liz's towel dropped to the floor. Suddenly, she was in his arms, her naked body against him, her skin against his bare chest. All thought of hunger was forgotten.

*

When Liz stepped out of the shower and wrapped herself in a towel, she was very aware of Sam's presence in the house. Her stomach churned at the thought that, in only a few hours, they might be here again, and then they might... She trembled with a mixture of nerves and excitement, the butterflies of Tuesday returning with a vengeance along with her fears Sam wouldn't find her mature body attractive.

What if his family had only been an excuse, what if he didn't really fancy her, what if he was repelled by her references to the champagne? No matter how much she tried to dismiss it, the anxiety was there, the little voice reminding her she was no longer the sexy young woman Dan had fallen in love with.

What she hadn't expected when she walked out of the ensuite, was to see him standing there in her bedroom, naked from the waist up, his red shirt in one hand. Her breath caught in her throat, she walked toward him like a magnet drawn, her hands rose to her mouth and the towel dropped to the floor at the same time as the red shirt was cast aside. Liz was in his arms before she knew what was happening. There was no time for thought, no time to wonder if this was right, no time for the anxiety to surface, no time for anything but the sensation of his skin against hers.

She was vaguely conscious of Sam lifting her onto the bed, of the crisp feel of the clean sheets on her back, of Sam's lips on hers, of his hands in her hair, their bodies entwining. She heard herself moan with pleasure, then time stood still.

Liz was filled with the sense of how right it was to be here in Sam's arms. How right it felt to be making love with this amazing and gentle man. It was as if she had been waiting for this for a long time, as if all her dreams had come true.

Liz sighed when they eventually pulled apart.

Sam wrapped an arm around her, kissed her bare shoulder. 'That was…'

'Incredible,' Liz said, 'and we didn't even drink the champagne.'

Sam chuckled. 'We missed dinner, too. I guess we should make a move if we don't want to incur Owen's wrath. I don't think he'd accept our excuse that…' He dropped a kiss on Liz's hair.

'You wouldn't dare tell him.' Liz was shocked, then laughed, realising he was joking.

*

There was a hum of excitement in the church as the choristers filed in to take their places in the choir loft. Liz was right. Even before they started to sing, Sam could feel the atmosphere was very different to what it had been during their practice. Owen took his place in front of the group as usual, bowed to the audience, then turned towards them and it began.

It was glorious. Sam couldn't believe he was part of this amazing experience as the music rose through the building, echoing through the nave and up to the rafters. Already feeling on top of the world after the intimate moments with Liz earlier, Sam was filled with such a wave of emotion he could have wept with joy.

Owen had put a lot into the preparation for the concert, and it was a triumph. The church was full and, as the music soared, so did Sam's mood. It was easy to forget all the worries about the paper, Mitch, the acreage, even the damned proposed development.

All too soon it was over, the audience breaking into thunderous applause. With a strange sense of emptiness mixed with euphoria, Sam turned with the other members of the choir to leave their places, as the audience, too, left the church.

Sam found his family waiting for him outside the door.

'Well done, Dad,' Mitch said, clapping Sam on the shoulder.

'It was really very good.' Brooke seemed surprised as well as impressed.

'Did you enjoy it, sweetheart?' Sam asked Abi.

Abi thought for a moment. 'I think I prefer *The Puggles*,' she said with a serious expression.

The three adults laughed.

'See you at home, Dad?' Mitch asked.

'Not for a while.' Sam glanced around to see Liz in a group of women. 'I'm having a meal in town with a friend. I may be late.' *Or not home at all.*

'Bye, then. And well done again, Dad. You were ripper!'

Sam watched proudly as his little family walked off.

'Ready?' He joined Liz who was chatting with two women. They both gave him an appraising glance, before drifting away to leave Sam and Liz together. 'It might be too late for the Thai Kitchen. How about we see if we can get a table at Pavarotti's?' Sam wanted to celebrate, and the Italian restaurant was a more fitting venue.

'I'm not very hungry, but Pavarotti's sounds good. Then…' There was a question mark in Liz's eyes.

'I'll stay in town if I may?'

She nodded, her face turning that delicious shade of pink it did when she was embarrassed.

Sam wanted to pick her up in his arms there and then and carry her off to bed again. But he managed to limit himself to a quick kiss on her lips.

At the restaurant they ordered pasta dishes with a bottle of pinot grigio and, despite assuring each other they weren't hungry, managed to polish them off and also to share a dish of tiramisu.

'Home?' Sam raised an eyebrow.

'I can't wait,' Liz said with a smile.

'That makes two of us.' He put his arm around her waist and led her to the car.

Thirty-six

Liz looked at the man lying beside her, unable to believe what had finally happened. After all her misgivings, all her fears, she and Sam had finally made love. She'd slept with a man who wasn't her husband, who wasn't Dan. And she didn't feel guilty. Instead, she felt... she stretched out in the bed... she felt wonderful.

'Good morning.' Sam opened his eyes and smiled blearily. Then he pulled Liz into his arms and kissed her soundly. 'I didn't dream last night.' He gently stroked a tendril of hair from her eyes.

Liz snuggled into him, amazed at how natural it felt to be with this man, this man who she'd first considered arrogant. He was anything but. He was kind, gentle, honest and... a marvellous lover.

Over breakfast they rehashed the previous evening's performance with Liz saying it was the best yet.

'What shall we do today?' Sam asked, when they had finished the scrambled eggs with mushrooms and bacon Liz had cooked.

'Today? Don't you have to go home? On Tuesday you said...' She remembered how disappointed she'd been when he rushed back to his family.

'No.' Sam leant his elbows on the table. 'Mitch and Brooke seem to be sorting things out. They were planning to look at some display homes yesterday. I'm hoping Mitch's accident has changed Brooke's mind and she's going to agree to the move. We can spend the day together. Of course, we could go back to bed...' his eyes twinkled, '... but it's a glorious day. Perhaps we should think of some outdoor pursuit? Any ideas?'

Liz thought about the plans she had for the day. 'I had intended to go into the shop to do some accounts and redo my Christmas display,' she said. 'I've been busy and haven't had time with the various Christmas events in town and…' The protest group, she thought, but didn't want to spoil the mood by mentioning it.

'Can I help?'

Liz chuckled. But there were several heavy boxes to shift. 'If you don't mind being put to work. I can make sandwiches for our lunch.'

'I have a better idea. Why don't we go for a drive when we're done at the shop? I'm sure there's at least one country pub which does a counter lunch, and it would be good to get out of town. I will need to get back home at some stage. I'll need fresh clothes for tomorrow. But I'd like to explore a bit of the countryside around Granite Springs. I haven't made time for that before now.'

'Sounds like a plan.'

At the bookshop, Liz put Sam to work emptying boxes and checking out their contents, while she took care of filling the gaps in her Christmas display made by eager customers. It had been a busy few weeks. The article in The Advertiser had brought in new customers and the influx of visitors to the town for the music festival had meant she had to re-order many of the more popular titles.

'I think that'll do.' Liz stood back to critically examine the new window display. She'd left it till last, wanting to make sure the one inside the shop was completed first. She replaced a couple of ornaments on the artificial Christmas tree in the centre of the shop as she walked past. Marmaduke had been up to his tricks again. He loved to pounce on the collection of packages lying at the bottom of the tree which would be distributed to the children's ward at the hospital on Christmas Eve, and his paws often dislodged the shiny balls.

When she looked around, Sam was standing watching her. He was leaning against a bookshelf, his ankles crossed and his arms folded, looking very much at home. Liz blushed. How long had he been watching her?

'You look so lovely reaching into the window. It's a terrific display. I can see why so many are attracted into the shop.'

All the more reason to work on its continued existence, thought Liz. But today wasn't the time for arguments, not when she was feeling so happy with Sam. She tucked away the potential annoyance, sure the time would come when they could discuss it like two sensible adults and when he'd change his mind.

*

'It's beautiful here.' Sam gestured to the paddocks stretching as far as the eyes could see, some filled with round bales of hay, some in which the farmers were still harvesting. 'Makes my place look very small in comparison.'

'You wouldn't want a larger lot, would you?'

'Absolutely not. My humble twenty acres is perfect for my needs. I've almost decided to take Owen's advice and buy a few goats once Alec takes his sheep back. Owen tells me they're fun to watch and don't need a lot of care. He says he could be willing to sell me a few of his to get me started.'

Liz chuckled. She could imagine sitting on Sam's veranda watching goats roam around the paddock.

'He told me about a pub not far from here,' Sam muttered, peering into the distance.

As if by magic, another small town appeared on the horizon and, as they drove along the narrow main street, they came to an old white painted stone building, the characteristic iron lacework on the veranda overlooking the street on one end. It seemed to be the only hotel in this one-horse town.

It was dimly lit inside, the only customers a few locals who ignored the newcomers.

Liz and Sam settled themselves at a table in an alcove and ordered the standard fare – pie with chips and salad – with a beer for Sam and a glass of white wine for Liz.

'This is nice,' she said, glad to be away from any scrutiny from friends or customers. It was a rare event. Anywhere Liz went in Granite Springs, she was sure to be recognised, and she wanted to enjoy their new-found intimacy in private.

Liz let out a sigh of pleasure as Sam covered her hand with his, their knees touching under the table. She'd thought she'd never feel this way again, safe, loved – even if the L word hadn't been mentioned. She knew Sam wasn't the sort of man to make love to a woman on a whim. His reluctance to rush her had proved that. She smiled.

'Something amusing you?'

'I'm feeling happy.'

Sam tightened his grip on her hands. 'I am, too. I can't tell you how much last night meant to me.' His eyes bored into hers.

Liz looked down, unsure how to respond to the emotion in his voice.

Fortunately, their meals arrived, and they were silent as they enjoyed the simple country food.

'What are you doing for Christmas?' Sam asked, when their plates had been removed and they were enjoying a second round of drinks.

Liz hesitated. She'd agreed to spend Christmas Day with her parents as she had done each of the past twenty years. It was always a sad day for her, one in which she missed Dan even more than usual. He had loved the festivities, making the day special with lots of gifts and jokes, and they'd always tried to outdo each other with numerous cards. Nothing could live up to those memories. But her mum and dad tried their best, and Ailsa and Bob would be there, along with her nephews. Liz had made up her mind this year would be different. This year she'd make more of an effort to join in the celebrations.

'I'll be going to Mum and Dad's, to Canberra.'

'Oh, pity.' Sam gave a pretend sigh. 'I'd hoped you might join us and help me cope with Brooke.' He grinned. 'How about Boxing Day?'

Damn! If only she'd known, but how could she have? Last year Peta had invited her for lunch on Boxing Day and expected her again this year. Then the day after, it was the annual barbecue at Wooleton. 'I'm afraid…'

'Don't tell me you're fully booked for the entire Christmas period?'

'Not quite, but people do have the habit of taking pity on us singles at this time of year.' She thought for a moment. 'I'm invited to lunch with Peta and Frank on Boxing Day. I'm sure they'd be happy for you to join us.' Happy? Liz knew Peta would be delighted to see her with Sam.

'Are you sure?'

'Very sure.' She could already hear Peta's squeals of delight.

'Good. I'm invited to Wooleton on the twenty-seventh. I suppose you are, too?'

'Their annual barbecue? Yes.'

'We could go together,' he suggested boldly, 'if...' he gave Liz a glance from under half-closed eyes, '...if you have dinner with us on the twenty-sixth and stay over – maybe for a couple of days?'

Liz's stomach began to do cartwheels. He wanted her to stay at his place – when his family were there? Meet them? In what capacity? 'I...' she stammered. 'Will your family still be there?'

'Mitch gets his plaster off on Christmas Eve, so they'll stay with me till after Christmas. Then?' Sam shrugged. 'Who knows? It will depend on Brooke, I expect. But whatever they decide, Brooke and Abi won't stay around my place, thank goodness.' He grasped Liz's hands again. 'I want them to meet you, get to know you properly. I know you've already met Mitch, but Brooke's a different matter.'

Liz felt awkward, almost the same way she'd felt at the prospect of going to meet Dan's parents all those years ago. But this time it wasn't parents she was to meet but a daughter-in-law and a granddaughter.

'It'll be fine,' Sam assured her, sensing her doubts. 'You have to meet them sometime, and Christmas is as good a time as any, when everyone's filled with festive cheer.'

Liz wasn't so sure about the festive cheer. It had managed to elude her most Christmases in the past. But, since last night, she had a feeling this year might be different. Could one man make such a difference to her life?

'Maybe,' she said, 'but I'll have to make arrangements for Marmaduke.' She pretended to sound doubtful, but she knew Peta and Lily would be happy to make sure he was fed and watered. She'd often offered, urging Liz to take a few days off, to take what she considered to be a much-needed holiday.

'I'll take that as a yes.' Sam grinned, and Liz felt a flare of hope for the future.

Thirty-seven

'As good as new.' Mitch flexed his wrist. 'I can drive again, Dad.'

Sam was glad to see his son's arm had mended. It was a good Christmas present for the young couple who appeared to have resolved their differences. 'What now, son?'

Mitch glanced at his wife who was sitting beside him on the sofa, while Abi played a game on her dad's iPad. 'We have some news, Dad.'

'Oh yes?' Sam had had a busy day at the paper. He was glad it was Christmas Eve and he could relax for the next week, having decided to close the office until the new year. He hoped what Mitch had to say was good news. He couldn't bear anything bad, especially at this time of year. He'd hoped to spend tonight with Liz, but she had gone to Canberra already, muttering something about a midnight carol service and resolving to be more considerate of her parents' wishes.

Mitch took Brooke's hand and smiled at her before turning to face Sam again. 'Remember we went to look at Danny Slater's display homes? We've talked a lot about them. Brooke fell in love with the one we went through, but it takes several months to build.'

Sam's stomach dropped. He knew what was coming. While pleased Mitch and Brooke now seemed to be on the same page, the thought of sharing his home with them for another six months or so was not the way he wanted to start the new year.

'We went back to talk with Danny today to put down a deposit and we were in luck. Danny had just decided to put several of the display homes on the market, including the one we liked. So, we don't need to wait to have one built. In fact, we can move in early January and pay rent till the sale goes through.'

'That's excellent news.' Sam felt a weight drop from his shoulders. 'So...?'

'It's been lovely of you to have us here,' Brooke said, 'but I'm looking forward to having our own place. This'll give us time to put our Canberra house on the market. We'll go home after Boxing Day to pack and talk to realtors. It means Abi can start school here and I can look for a job.'

'This deserves a celebration.' Sam rose to fetch a bottle of champagne and three glasses. When he got back, he saw Mitch and Brooke draw apart and grinned. Maybe his daughter-in-law wasn't so bad after all.

*

Christmas day dawned, promising to be hot and humid. Sam awoke to squeals of delight from Abi and reflected there were some advantages to having his family here for Christmas. In previous years they'd met for lunch in Canberra along with his ex. The meal had always been fraught with unspoken recriminations and he was always glad when it was over.

He'd missed out on the early morning excitement of experiencing Christmas through the eyes of a child. The sounds he was hearing reminded him of when Mitch was Abi's age and the boy had wakened his parents at the crack of dawn. Keen to be part of Abi's enjoyment, Sam rose quickly and pulled on a pair of shorts and a tee-shirt before heading through to the living room from where the sounds were coming.

He found Abi sitting by the large Christmas tree which he'd insisted on setting up. She was unwrapping the pile of gifts which had magically appeared under the tree overnight.

'Look what I got, Grandad,' she yelled as soon as he walked in. She had a Barbie doll in one hand and a book in the other. Mitch and Brooke were looking on indulgently.

'Merry Christmas, Dad,' Mitch said, rising to give Sam a hug, followed by Brooke. Abi was too busy with her gifts to move.

'Merry Christmas,' Sam replied. 'Looks like Santa found his way here,' he said to Abi who was tearing the paper off yet another parcel.

Eventually, Abi had opened all her presents and the adults had exchanged gifts, Sam appreciative of the thick volume by John Donne and wishing he'd been more imaginative in his gift to Mitch and Brooke. In retrospect, the wine voucher he'd hurriedly purchased on the internet seemed paltry and impersonal. However, Abi was delighted with the new bike he'd chosen for her, keen to show everyone how well she could ride it along the veranda while the adults ate a breakfast of fruit and waffles.

It was still early when breakfast was over, and Sam was hopeful of spending the rest of the day relaxing. But Mitch and Brooke had other ideas. They wanted to take him to see the house they were buying.

'We won't be able to get inside today,' Brooke said, suddenly much more friendly to her father-in-law, 'but you can see the outside, check out the neighbourhood and we can peek through the windows. Abi loves it, too, and there's a children's playground being constructed just a block away.'

Surprised at Brooke's sudden conversion to life in Granite Springs, Sam agreed. Then Abi persuaded Mitch and Brooke to take her along the lane with her new bike, leaving Sam to relax in peace. He picked up his phone to call Liz, desperate to hear her voice.

Thirty-eight

Liz awoke on Christmas morning in her old room in Canberra. It made her feel like a teenager again to awaken in her parents' house, even though the room had been remodelled and the walls no longer bore the posters which had been her pride and joy. There was something about being back here that took her back to her childhood.

She sighed and turned over, but she could hear her mother in the kitchen clattering dishes and knew it was time to get up if she didn't want to antagonise Sheila. Last night had been better than she expected, the service reminding her of the performance of The Messiah – and all that followed. She wished she was wakening with Sam this morning, but this had been her decision and her parents were pathetically pleased to have her with them. It was the least she could do, and the presence of Ailsa and her family would make today's celebrations easier to cope with.

'Merry Christmas, Lizzie,' her father greeted her with a kiss on the cheek and a warm hug.

'Merry Christmas, Dad.'

'Your mum's in the kitchen getting things ready for lunch. If you want breakfast, you'll have to get it for yourself.'

'No worries.' Liz went through, wished her mother a Merry Christmas and made herself tea and toast, before taking it out to the courtyard where it was quiet and she wasn't disturbing her mother who was elbow deep in preparations for lunch. She was enjoying what she regarded as the peace before the storm of Christmas lunch when her phone buzzed.

'Merry Christmas.' Sam's voice was so welcome, Liz almost wept.

'Merry Christmas to you, too.' Liz's fingers tightened on the phone, imagining Sam. Was he sitting on the veranda looking out across the paddock or in his study. She imagined him at his large wood desk, his laptop open in front of him, leaning back and gazing out the window. For a few moments she was transported from the Canberra suburb to the open spaces outside Granite Springs. Then reality returned. She was sitting at her parents' white-painted wrought iron table looking at her dad's carefully tended garden, and her mother was in the kitchen behind her, no doubt wondering who she was talking to.

'How was the carol service?'

It was amazing how the very sound of Sam's voice managed to comfort her. 'Not too bad. It made me think of The Messiah and…'

Sam chuckled. 'I thought of you last night, too. I wish you could have been here with me.'

'Me, too.' Liz couldn't stifle a sigh at the thought of being in Sam's arms.

'Mitch and Brooke had some news for me. They've bought one of Danny Slater's houses – one of the display homes – and can move in early in the year.'

Liz chuckled at the relief in Sam's voice. 'You must be pleased.'

'I am. It's made me think…' He paused. 'They plan on going back to Canberra on the twenty seventh. Now I'm going to have the place to myself again, why don't you arrange to stay until the new year? We both have time off. It seems mad to stay alone in our separate houses. What do you think?'

Liz hesitated, but only for a moment. There was Marmaduke to consider but Peta had been delighted to be asked to look after him for a couple of days after Boxing Day. She'd no doubt be thrilled if Liz asked her to continue for the rest of the week. 'Sounds like an excellent plan,' she said, butterflies already leaping around in her stomach at the thought of spending an entire week with Sam on his property away from town, away from everything and everybody.

It was a sharp return to reality to go back into the house and face her mother.

'Who were you speaking to?' Sheila asked as she walked in. 'Was it Ailsa? Did she…?'

'A friend from Granite Springs, Mum.' Liz wasn't ready to share Sam with her parents, not just yet. Though she knew she would have to tell them some time if the relationship continued, if it became serious.

'Hmm.'

'Can I do anything to help?' Liz looked around the kitchen in which the piles of vegetables and serving dishes seemed to have multiplied since she left.

By the time Ailsa arrived with Bob and the boys, Liz was at screaming pitch. She'd helped her mother with the vegetables and set the table, all the while trying to ignore Sheila's insistent reminders of 'what it used to be like when you were younger' and her hints that it was time Liz moved on with her life and found 'a nice man to take care of you'.

In the flurry of hugs and Christmas greetings, Ailsa managed to whisper, 'What about your man? Is he still in the picture?'

Liz merely nodded, hoping her sister would be able to contain her curiosity till they were alone.

The presence of her nephews was a blessing. It had been some time since Sheila and Doug had seen the boys, so there were the usual comments about how they'd changed, how grown-up they'd become, interspersed with questions – mostly from Sheila – about why they didn't visit more often. Liz thought it was enough to keep them away for at least another year, but Nathan and Patrick didn't seem to mind, taking it in good part and merely shrugging and laughing instead of replying.

Lunch ended up being quite a jolly affair. The boys managed to regale them with tales of university, encouraging both Bob and Doug to relive their own student days, much to Sheila's disgust and the amusement of Ailsa and Liz. Liz had often wondered why her mother was such a killjoy, but had got used to her manner over the years, knowing Sheila loved her, Ailsa and their father even if she didn't always show it.

It was when the meal was over and Liz and Ailsa were washing up in the kitchen, that Liz found herself being interrogated by her sister.

The boys had disappeared on afternoon activities of their own, Doug and Sheila had been persuaded to put their feet up in the living room while the sisters cleared up, and Bob had joined them with the excuse of reading a paper.

'Now, do tell,' Ailsa said, her hands in a sink full of soapy water. 'Gosh, I wish Mum and Dad would get a dishwasher. This is for the birds.' She swept a strand of hair out of her eyes with an elbow. 'This man of yours.' She gave Liz a calculating look.

'Sam's not mine,' Liz objected, carefully drying one of her mother's favourite platters and placing it back in the cupboard. 'He's a friend.' She felt her face redden at the lie and was glad Ailsa had turned back to the sink.

'So, what's happening with this *friend* of yours? When are we going to meet him?'

Meet him? Liz hadn't got that far in her thinking. It was difficult enough for her to meet Sam's family, hers was a different matter entirely. She could just imagine her mother's delight, how she would fawn over him, a newspaper editor, a former Canberra journalist. Sheila might even have heard of him, watched him on television. Both Sheila and Doug were avid television watchers and liked to keep up with local and national politics.

'I don't think…' Liz glanced at the door into the living room, hoping her mother couldn't hear the conversation. 'We're not at that stage yet.'

'Not yet, so that means you will be, that this is serious? You're sleeping with him?'

Liz almost dropped the plate she was holding. Trust her sister not to mince words. She knew there was no sense in denying it. Her face would give her away. She didn't answer.

'I guess that means you are. It's about time, Lizzie. You've been on your own too long. Dan wouldn't…'

Liz put her now empty hands over her ears. 'Enough, Ailsa.' She now regretted telling her sister about her trip to the cemetery.

'Okay, okay.' Ailsa put her soapy hands up in a defensive position. 'But don't blame me if Mum guesses something's up.'

A terrible thought occurred to Liz. 'You haven't, you didn't… Please tell me you haven't said anything to her.'

'Not yet,' Ailsa laughed. 'But don't leave it too long or I won't be able to keep shtum about it.' She chuckled. 'I think we're done here.' She gazed around the now tidy kitchen.

Liz folded the tea towel and hung it up, then the pair went to join Bob and their parents.

'What are you two looking so secretive about?' Liz's mother wanted to know when they walked in.

'Nothing.' Liz glared at her sister, daring her to say anything. 'I should be getting off soon,' she said.

'We should, too,' Ailsa said almost immediately. 'It's been lovely, as usual, Mum.' She hugged her mum and dad and she and Bob left with promises to host the parents on New Year's Day. 'You'll come, too, Liz?' Ailsa asked, with a wink.

'I'll see. I'm not sure what I'll be doing.' She had no intention of travelling to Canberra again in a week's time for a repeat performance of today at Ailsa's house. The thought of spending the next week with Sam was all that had kept her going through the day.

After Ailsa and Bob left, Sheila tried to persuade Liz to stay another night, but Liz was adamant, citing the need to get back to Marmaduke.

Once on the road back to Granite Springs, Liz heaved a sigh of relief. She'd done her duty for another year and managed to evade the worst of Ailsa's questions. Now all she wanted to do was get home, give Marmaduke a cuddle and speak to Sam on the phone.

Thirty-nine

Sam whistled to himself as he dressed on Boxing Day morning. Christmas Day had been good. It had been lovely to spend the day with his family, to see little Abi enjoying the day, and Mitch and Brooke with smiles on their faces. He was looking forward to their move to Granite Springs and to spending more time with them.

He revisited his call with Liz the previous night. She had recounted her Christmas Day, which did sound duller than his, and agreed to spend the next week with him. His heart leapt in anticipation of a whole week together. But first he had the lunch with her friends to get through.

He knew Frank from his frequent visits to the café, and he thought he'd been introduced to Peta. But it would be different to meet them with Liz, as her... partner? And Frank was the force behind the protest group. Sam hoped they'd steer clear of the topic over lunch but wasn't optimistic. He sighed, hoping it would be resolved soon in favour of the shopkeepers. The articles he'd published were testament to the value of retaining the line of shops in their current state. But he was still adamant The Advertiser couldn't become involved.

'Off to lunch with your bookshop lady, Dad?' Mitch asked with a wink, when Sam walked into the kitchen where he was enjoying a mug of coffee. Brooke was making a snack for Abi who was playing on her dad's iPad.

Brooke turned around. 'Who?'

Sam realised he hadn't mentioned Liz in Brooke's hearing. Mitch obviously hadn't either.

'Liz Pender is a friend of mine. She owns The Reading Corner.'

'You know the one, Brooke. It's where we bought the books for Abi,' Mitch said.

'Oh, the lady with the auburn hair. She's a friend of yours?' Brooke's eyes narrowed.

Sam drew in a breath. Brooke and his ex were close. They'd remained friends after the divorce. He could imagine them discussing him and Liz.

'A good friend. We've been seeing each other. The lunch is at the home of friends of hers. Frank owns The Bean Sprout Café and Peta is *Forrest Interiors,* the company which designed the interiors for the Slater homes.'

'The designs you love so much, honey,' Mitch said, in an attempt to forestall anything negative Brooke was about to say.

'Oh!'

'There's something else.' Sam shuffled his feet. 'I've invited Liz to dinner tonight. I'll do the cooking,' he added, wincing at the expression on Brooke's face. This wasn't going the way he'd hoped.

'There's no need, Sam.' Brooke's tone was frosty.

'I'm planning a barbecue, and I can throw a salad together.' He was tempted to remind her it was his house, his friend, but didn't want to destroy the rapport they'd managed to build up over the past few weeks.

'Sounds good, Dad,' Mitch said, still trying to keep the peace.

They were interrupted by Abi saying, 'I liked the book lady. She has a nice ginger cat,' before turning back to her dad's iPad.

The three adults looked at her in surprise. Then Sam started to laugh. At least Liz would have one supporter tonight. No, that wasn't fair. Mitch had met Liz and appeared to approve. It was only Brooke's attitude Sam was concerned about. Should he say she would be staying, spending the week with him? He glanced over at Brooke who was now pouring Abi a glass of milk. No, best to say nothing, he decided. They'd find out soon enough. Surely Brooke could work it out for herself. Where did the woman think he'd been on those nights he hadn't come home?

*

'Merry Christmas again!' Sam picked Liz up and twirled her around and around.

'Put me down, you silly man,' she objected, but there was a smile in her voice.

Sam gently lowered Liz till her feet touched the ground, then ran his fingers through her hair before taking her face in his hands and kissing her. 'I've missed you,' he murmured when they broke apart.

'We've time for a drink before we leave,' she said, leading him into the living room where a small artificial Christmas tree sat on top of a low bookcase. Marmaduke, lying by the window, raised his head when they walked in, then lowered it again and closed his eyes.

'Cheers.' Sam raised his glass to Liz's and took a sip of the sparkling wine. 'I have something for you.' He took a small package from his pocket. 'I thought of you as soon as I saw these.' He held his breath while she opened it to reveal a pair of earrings, each with a tiny ceramic stack of books designed to dangle from the wearer's ears.

'I love them! Thank you so much.' Liz reached up to kiss him, before removing the gold hoops from her ears to replace them with her new earrings. 'I have something for you, too.' She picked up a parcel from beside the tree and handed it to him. 'I hope you like it.'

Sam grinned. He could tell from the feel and weight of the gift it was a book. What else would Liz give him? He pulled off the wrapping.

'Just what I wanted.' Sam stroked the cover of the latest book by Chris Hammer, one of his favourite authors. 'How did you know?'

'I can't give away all my secrets,' she said with a grin, 'but I did notice where you were browsing last time you were in the shop.'

'Thanks.' With the book and its wrapping in one hand, Sam hugged Liz and gave her another kiss.

'Now, we'd better finish these drinks and make a move, or we'll arrive late and...'

'Understood.' Sam could imagine what Frank and Peta might read into their late arrival.

*

Frank's house was similar in style to Liz's, and like many others in Granite Springs where most of the homes had been built in the early part of the twentieth century or mimicked those which had. It was called federation style and the houses were very ornate with red brick facades, ridges of white mortar and impressive woodwork on the verandas. Inside, this one showed signs of a modern renovation.

'Impressive,' Sam said, entering the family-style kitchen which wouldn't have looked out of place in a restaurant.

'You can see Frank's hand in this, can't you?' Peta asked, nudging her husband.

When Sam had finished admiring the house, and Liz and their hosts exchanged Christmas gifts, they all settled down in the kitchen with drinks.

'It's good to see you two together,' Peta said, raising her glass to Sam and Liz.

'Peta!' Liz blushed.

'What? I'm just telling you what I think. As I've said before…'

'Peta!' It was Frank who spoke this time.

'Thanks for the book.' Lily sidled in to stand at Liz's elbow. 'I haven't read this author, but I've heard about her.'

'You're most welcome, Lily. I look forward to hearing how you like it.'

Lily's arrival prevented Peta from saying any more about how well-suited Sam and Liz were. Sam agreed with her but could see how it embarrassed Liz.

Lunch was a magnificent feast of poached salmon served with various salads. 'It's all Frank's doing,' Peta said when Sam complimented her on the meal. 'He's the cook. I just watch or follow his instructions.' She smiled at Frank.

'Grandma cooks too,' Lily told them, 'but I prefer it when Uncle Frank does it.'

'Your cat looks just like Marmaduke,' Sam said to Lily in a lull in the conversation.

'They're brothers,' Lily said proudly. 'We got Archie from an old lady who couldn't look after him anymore. I always wanted a cat and Uncle Frank organised it.'

Sam could see that, in Lily's mind, Frank could do no wrong. It was good to see how well he'd fitted into Peta and Lily's life. He thought back to Brooke's attitude when he'd mentioned Liz. He hoped by the time they got home, Brooke would have decided to accept her so they could all be a family, because he definitely intended Liz to be part of his life.

To Sam's relief, apart from some barbed comments from Frank, no one mentioned The Advertiser or the development, but he sensed it was still a hot item and one which would resurface after the Christmas season. He could only hope the council would see sense and find in the group's favour.

When Sam and Liz finally left, with promises to get together again soon, it was late afternoon.

'I like your friends,' he said, as they walked back to Liz's house.

'I thought you would. Will I like your daughter-in-law? I have to admit I'm a bit nervous about meeting Brooke. You've had some harsh words to say about her.'

Sam didn't know what to say. It was true he'd said some uncomplimentary things about Brooke when she was giving Mitch a hard time, but things had improved recently until... he remembered her expression when he told her Liz was coming to dinner. 'She... she's good friends with my ex,' he said.

'Does that mean she won't want to accept me?'

Sam's forehead creased. 'She may be... difficult, but I'm sure she'll come round when she meets you. How could anyone dislike you?'

'I have met her. She came into the shop with Mitch and Abi before Christmas.' Liz's brow furrowed. 'She appeared pleasant.' Then she smiled. 'Of course, she didn't know then...'

'And now she does. She was a bit stunned when I told her and Mitch you were coming to dinner. I think she expects me to stay celibate for the rest of my life, living on the memory of Olga and our marriage.' He pulled Liz to him again. 'But once we met, how could I resist you?'

Liz laughed.

When they reached her home, Sam made for his car, but Liz stopped him. 'I made a salad and have something for your family... for Christmas. It's not much, but...' she bit her lip.

'You didn't need to do that.'

'I did.'

They went inside where Liz picked up two parcels. Then she hesitated as if something had occurred to her. 'Can we stop off at the shop on the way? I have something there Brooke might like.'

Mystified, Sam agreed.

*

Liz wasn't sure what to expect when they reached Sam's home. All the way there in the car, her heart had been thumping madly. Sam's revelation about Brooke had done nothing to calm the worry she'd already been feeling at the thought of meeting his family. Even though she'd already met them in the bookshop, it was very different from being introduced to them as... what – Sam's lover?

All too soon, they were bumping over the cattle grid at the gate, and they'd arrived.

'This is Liz,' Sam said, when they entered the house to find all three of Sam's family in the kitchen.

Mitch came forward to give Liz a peck on the cheek, while Brooke stretched out a hand, her face devoid of emotion. Abi rushed up as Liz and Brooke shook hands. 'Did you bring your cat with you?' She gazed behind Liz as if expecting to see Marmaduke.

'No, sorry.' Liz laughed, glad of Abi's interruption to break the ice. 'He prefers to stay home when he's not in my bookshop. This is for you.' She handed Abi her present.

'Ooh, thanks.' Abi felt the package. 'It's a book!' She pulled off the wrapper.

'And this is for you both.' Liz handed Brooke the other parcel.

'Thanks.' Brooke made no effort to open it.

'And I thought you might like to have this. I noticed you looking at her books when you were in the shop. It's a proof copy. As a bookshop we get sent these prior to publication.' She reached into her bag and handed Brooke the copy of Lianne Moriarty's new release.

Brooke's face changed. She almost smiled as she took the book. 'Thank you,' she said, more warmly than before.

'Liz has made us a salad, too.' Sam held out the bowl he'd been carrying.

'I made one for us.' Brooke's frosty manner returned.

'Well, now we'll have two,' Sam said cheerfully, but Liz noticed his lips were taut.

'I think we all need a glass of wine.' Mitch stepped in to retrieve the situation, and soon the adults were all seated on the veranda with glasses of white wine, and the barbecue was heating up. Abi was engrossed in her new book.

With the wine, Brooke unbent sufficiently to politely answer Liz's questions about her and Mitch's move to Granite Springs and their new house. By the time Sam left them to barbecue the steaks, they were having an almost amiable discussion about their favourite authors.

'Can I have a cat in our new house, Mum?' Abi asked.

Dinner was over. During the meal, Abi had been peppering Liz with questions about Marmaduke which had obviously been leading up to this.

'Please,' she added, as there was no reply from either Brooke or Mitch.

'If your mum and dad agree, I'll buy you a cat for your birthday,' Sam said with a smile. 'But you need to learn how to look after it first.'

'I will… but my birthday's not till April,' she complained. 'That's ages away.' She looked at her parents for support.

'What your grandad says,' Mitch said with a grin. 'Perhaps Liz will allow you to visit with Marmaduke sometimes.'

Abi's attention moved to Liz. 'Will you?'

'Of course. As long as your parents agree.'

This seemed to satisfy the little girl who disappeared into the house.

The others stayed out on the veranda for some time longer, the two men discussing the pros and cons of Sam's decision to buy goats while the women sat back and listened, only contributing the odd word here and there.

When they all finally decided it was time to retire, Abi having been put to bed earlier, Liz was relieved. It had been a good evening, but she felt she'd been treading on eggshells where Brooke was concerned. She was unsure how the other woman felt about her – she seemed to blow hot and cold.

'How do you think it went?' she asked Sam when they were lying in bed together. She whispered lest her voice carried to the neighbouring room.

'I think you worry too much,' Sam said, kissing her forehead. 'Brooke will come round. She liked the book you gave her. She just needs time to adjust. I don't think it ever occurred to her I'd find someone else after Olga. As I think I said, they're close. They're very alike. She probably thinks she'd be letting Olga down to befriend you. Don't worry about it. You don't have to impress her. And she and Mitch will be gone in the morning. Then it'll just be you and me and twenty acres of open space with no one to bother us.

Liz smiled and snuggled against Sam's warm body. It sounded wonderful.

Forty

Christmas and Boxing Day were over. Sam couldn't believe what an amazing time it had been. The lunch with Liz's friends, Peta and Frank, then to have Liz there with his family, as part of their celebration, filled him with emotion. And today he and Liz had been invited to Judy and Alec's for a barbecue. His life had suddenly become busier. He was part of a couple.

The only fly in the ointment was the damned protest against the development. He knew Liz felt strongly about it, and he didn't blame her. But while he sympathised with their cause, he was adamant it wasn't in his remit to become involved. He was surprised the issue hadn't been resolved one way or another before now, but evidently the planning committee's decision had been delayed due to absenteeism and the decision was being held over till after the festive season.

'We're off now, Dad.' Mitch's voice brought Sam back to earth. 'Thanks for a great Christmas. Abi loved being here with you. And it was good to get to know Liz better. You serious about her?'

Sam flushed at the reversal of roles. He remembered asking Mitch the same question the first time he brought Brooke home to dinner. Now he knew how his son had felt. 'I like her a lot,' he said, 'but it's early days.' He knew he was trying to put Mitch off. More than anything, Sam wanted Liz to be a permanent part of his life, but he knew he had to move slowly. Their relationship had moved forward in the past weeks, but it was still in its infancy and could be overturned by the slightest thing.

Sam felt even more embarrassed as Liz appeared at his side. Had she heard the conversation? But if she had, she gave no indication, saying only, 'Have a good trip, Mitch. When do you get back?'

'We've booked the removalist in two weeks' time. That should give us time to pack up. Bye, Dad.' He gave Sam a hug.

'We're coming out to see you off.' Sam put an arm around Mitch's shoulder and the three made their way out to the car.

Brooke was standing waiting impatiently, while Abi was over by the fence talking to an indifferent sheep.

After more farewells and hugs, they finally set off, Sam and Liz waving till the car reached the gate.

Alone again, Sam and Liz turned to each other, both smiling. Sam took Liz's hand, and they went back into the house where he pulled her into his arms.

'I love my family, but I'm glad they've gone, and I have you to myself again,' he murmured into her hair. 'I can't wait till tonight.'

'I'm sorry I… last night, with them in the next room, I couldn't…'

'It's okay. I understand.' Sam had felt inhibited himself about making love in the room next to his son and daughter-in-law. He gave Liz a squeeze making her giggle. 'Now, I believe we have a barbecue to attend.'

*

Unlike lunch with Peta and Frank or their family dinner the previous evening, the barbecue at Wooleton was a big affair. It was a family tradition, started by Alec's father as a way of returning the hospitality of all his friends, combined with thanks to those he'd done business with the previous year.

At Wooleton, a large marquee had been erected in the home paddock. Judy, Sally and a woman Sam didn't know were organising groups of women Sam recognised as stalwarts of the CWA. They were filling long tables with what looked like enough salads to feed an army, while Alec and Neil, assisted by Alec's brother Ken, were manning the barbecue along with members of rotary. Sam recognised them from the music festival.

'Good to see you two,' Judy greeted them, hugging Liz and giving Sam a peck on the cheek. 'You can grab a beer or wine over there.' She gestured to the side of the marquee where more members of rotary were serving drinks. 'Food's self-serve and the steaks and sausages should be ready soon. Hopefully, we'll find time to talk once everyone is served. Until then, it's mayhem.' She disappeared to join Sally who was helping carry food to the marquee.

'Looks like we're on our own,' Sam said. 'Why don't I get you a glass of wine and find us a quiet spot. It seems ages since we had time to ourselves.'

Liz was happy to go along with his suggestion and before long they were seated on a bench in the back garden of the house, away from all the hustle and bustle.

'This is the life,' Sam said, reaching one arm around Liz's shoulder, a beer in his other hand.

Liz sipped her wine, the glass damp with condensation, and leant into his chest. It was perfect. She felt she could stay there for ever. The clamour from the barbecue faded away. It was as if they were in a cocoon, in their own little world where no one and nothing could disturb them or bother them ever again.

*

The television was on low. Liz was making coffee, and Sam was relaxing on the sofa after dinner when he heard a familiar name. He pressed the control to increase the volume and focussed his attention on the announcer.

'… the Australian political correspondent has been detained without charge in China. Sources close to Mae Chan say she is suspected of spying for a foreign government. Our consular officials are attempting to discover more.'

There was a shot of a slight dark-haired woman wearing a smart trouser suit, before the camera veered away to a street scene.

Sam picked up the glass of whisky he'd poured earlier and downed it in one gulp. A flash of fear curled in his stomach. It could have been him! Mae was a former colleague. They'd often covered incidents together and when he'd decided to give it away, it had been Mae who'd been given his assignments.

'What's the matter?' Liz came in carrying two cups of coffee. She glanced at the television screen where the announcer was reporting on the devastation of bushfires in Western Australia and the risk of floods in North Queensland.

Sam turned the set off and slumped back in his seat, his face ashen. 'A former colleague has been detained in China.'

Liz joined him on the sofa, her face filled with concern. She placed the two cups on the coffee table and put a hand on Sam's shoulder. 'Did you know him well?'

Sam didn't speak for a few moments, then, 'Mae and I covered the same sorts of issues. When I came here, she took over. If I hadn't left, it could have been me.' He shook off Liz's hand, rose and poured himself another whisky, feeling her eyes following him. 'Sorry, Liz. This is a blow.' He walked back to join her, feeling chilled despite the warm evening.

'I'm sorry.'

They sat in silence. Liz drank her coffee, but Sam couldn't face his. He needed to think.

'You should go to bed,' he said at last. 'I'll stay here for a bit longer. I need to see what I can find out.'

'If you're sure.' Liz seemed loath to leave him.

'I'm sure. I'll get onto the internet. There must be more information there.' He gave Liz a hug and kissed her, but his mind was elsewhere.

Alone, Sam headed for his study and fired up his laptop, searching for Mae Chan's name and anything relating to an Australian journalist detained in China. There were numerous hits, and he read them all. But he learned little more than the fact she'd been on assignment following a story about another journalist who'd been detained, when two uniformed police arrived at the door of her hotel room and she was taken into custody. She was being held at a detention centre.

Sam stayed awake for most of the night, drinking whisky and striding up and down, his mind veering from one thing to another. Finally, close to dawn, he made up his mind what he was going to do. He crawled into bed beside Liz, holding her warm body for comfort as he fell into a troubled sleep.

Forty-one

Liz slid out of bed, fearful of wakening Sam. She hadn't heard him come to bed last night even though she'd lain awake for what seemed like hours. She could see how the news affected him, even wondered if this Mae Chan meant more to him than a colleague. Then she dismissed the idea. She was here in his house, in his bed, wasn't she? This woman was in China and while Liz was sorry she'd been detained, it was really nothing to do with them.

But, somehow, the niggle of worry wouldn't go away. Liz couldn't forget the expression on Sam's face when he told her the news. And he must have been up most of the night.

When she went into the kitchen, the half empty whisky bottle was sitting on the table along with an empty glass. Liz made coffee and opened her phone to see if she could find any news of the woman. There was only one news item which didn't provide any more information than Sam had the night before, but the story was trending on Twitter.

She sighed and tried to put it out of her mind as she filled the electric jug and popped a slice of bread into the toaster. Sam was sound asleep when she left him; she had no idea when he'd emerge. It was a glorious morning, the sun shining through the trees, casting shadows onto the veranda. Liz took her tea and toast outside to enjoy the day. She missed Marmaduke, imagining how he would love it here and would follow her to settle in a pool of sunshine at her feet. She let her head fall back, looked up at the wide expanse of blue sky and listened to the sound of the birds. She could live here quite happily. Then she shook her head with a smile. Sam hadn't asked her to move in with him. But the week until New Year stretched before them in tantalising technicolour. They'd promised themselves this time together.

Liz didn't know how long she sat there.

When she went back into the house, she could hear Sam on his computer in the study. Popping her head in, she asked, 'Breakfast?'

He swung round to face her, his forehead creased.

'What's the matter?' Liz moved to lay a hand on his shoulder. Looking at the screen, she could see he was checking out flights. Her heart sank.

'I need to go to Canberra today to see my old boss.'

Liz dropped her hand and took a step away. 'Why?'

Sam rose and took Liz by the shoulders, gazing into her eyes. 'I need to do something, to try to help Mae. I can't sit here when she's in such danger.'

'But... what can you do?'

'I want to ask if I can go to cover the story and perhaps...' He dragged a hand through his already dishevelled hair. 'I don't know, but I still have contacts there.'

Liz sank into a nearby chair. This was the last thing she'd expected. Maybe she'd been right about this woman, this Mae Chan. Maybe there *was* something between her and Sam – or had been.

Sam came over to join her, crouching down beside her chair and taking her hands in his. 'I know we planned to spend this time together, said it was our time. But that was before all this blew up. I can't stay here pretending it isn't happening. And breakfast sounds good. I just need to make a call.'

Liz pulled her hands away. 'It's not fair!' The words burst out. 'You said you were done with all that. You won't help us save the shops here in Granite Springs, but you're happy to race off to China to help this Mae woman.'

'It's not the same.' Sam's eyes held a wild expression Liz had never seen in them before. 'You have to trust me on this one, Liz. It's something I have to do.'

'I don't understand. Why can't you stay here, let someone else go?' Liz knew she was pleading but was too distressed to care. Just when things were going so well, this had to happen. How could something happening in China matter so much?

'I have to make a call,' Sam repeated, sounding distant and picking up his phone.

Liz slowly returned to the kitchen where she made coffee and fried up bacon and eggs. She turned on the radio to drown out Sam's voice as he chatted with his old boss.

'He'll see me this afternoon,' he said when he walked back in. 'Something smells good.' He sniffed appreciatively.

How could he sound so cheerful when he had just decided to ruin the time they planned to spend together, to choose to go to China where there was every likelihood he'd meet the same fate as his former colleague?

'Don't look so down.' Sam poured himself a cup of coffee and took a seat.

'I thought you'd finished with all that,' Liz said again.

'I did, too. But you must see I have to try to do what I can. You do understand, don't you, Liz?' He gave her a pleading look.

She didn't, only seeing their week together disappearing. 'I'll go home after breakfast.'

'No. You don't need to dash off.'

Breakfast was a sorry affair. Liz pushed her bacon and egg around the plate, only taking small mouthfuls. It tasted like cardboard. She thought she was going to be sick. Finally, she pushed it all to the side of her plate and tried to swallow a mouthful of coffee.

'Not hungry?'

How could he even ask? And how could he eat his own breakfast with this hanging over him?

'I'll have something later. I should go and let you get on. Oh!' She realised her car was sitting in her garage. They'd driven here in Sam's Range Rover.

'If you're determined to go home, I can drop you off on my way. Don't look so downcast. We still have the morning together. Why don't we go for a walk? The fresh air will do you good.'

Liz wanted to cry. She wanted to stamp her feet and tell him she knew what would do her good, and it wasn't fresh air. It was for him to change his mind. But she said nothing. He'd made up his mind, and she knew nothing she said now would change it. She'd learnt that about him.

Sam took Liz's hand as they walked along the lanes around the property. She was surprised to realise Sam's acreage was the only one of that size in the neighbourhood. It had been sold off from a larger property he told her, pointing to a large farmhouse in the distance. Despite her misgivings, Liz found it pleasant to wander slowly along the deserted lane with Sam, his hand squeezing hers from time to time. But she couldn't rid herself of the thought this might be the last time they were together like this.

'What will it be like – in China?' she asked, her heart in her mouth.

'Difficult, I expect. But I won't know until I get there. Australian-Chinese relations aren't the best right now. I'll need to keep my head down. But I'll be all right. Don't worry about me. I'll call you when I can.'

'Oh, Sam!' Liz was almost in tears, her imagination running wild.

By the time they returned to the house, Liz had accepted Sam was leaving, but she was still not happy about it. While she bustled about making ham and cheese sandwiches for lunch, he was packing ready for the trip he was sure his former boss would agree to. How she hoped he was wrong and would appear at her door that evening to say he wasn't permitted to go.

All too soon they were in town and Sam was opening the car door to let Liz out. He walked with her to the house, gave her one last hug and kiss and murmured, 'I'll miss you, Liz Pender. Take care.'

'*You* take care,' Liz said, stifling her tears.

Then he was back behind the steering wheel and driving off.

Liz watched the dark red Range Rover disappear down the street and turned to go into the house, the tears she could no longer stifle streaming down her cheeks.

Forty-two

Sam could see Liz was close to tears. He hated to leave her like this. He knew she was disappointed at his change of plans. He was too. But he had to do this. His lips tightened at the thought of what Mae might be going through. He'd read reports of other journalists who'd been detained, incarcerated for months, years, before being allowed home. It couldn't happen to Mae. It wouldn't, if he could do anything to prevent it. But what could he do?

He only knew he had to be there. There was certainly nothing he could do from this distance. But first, he had to convince Bradley Hammond to send him over as a correspondent.

As he drove along, Sam's determination strengthened. He put Granite Springs and all thoughts of Liz behind him and focussed on the meeting ahead. This ability to compartmentalise his life had served him well for years, and he discovered it was easy to recapture it. It was one of the things that had ruined his marriage. Olga had been unable to accept how he could suddenly change focus from his family to the job in hand, but it had served him well in danger spots such as the one he was planning to visit.

In Canberra, it was like turning back the clock, as Sam parked outside the office he'd left with such delight just over a year ago, planning never to return. He received a few odd glances as he made his way to Bradley's office and knocked on the open door.

'Come!' Bradley Hammond uttered his usual greeting, and Sam walked in.

'You're really set on this?' Bradley asked, when Sam had outlined the reasons for his request. 'It's a bit unusual.'

'I am. I'm ready to leave today if it can be arranged.' It was lucky he'd kept his passport up to date and his APEC business travel card was still valid, though he hadn't expected to ever use it again.

Bradley took off his dark-rimmed glasses and peered at Sam as if he could see into his mind. 'Well, it would have been your assignment, of course, if you hadn't chosen to bury yourself in a country newspaper.' He replaced his glasses and shook his head. 'But the paperwork's in place. We were going to send Will Jack.'

Sam snorted. He knew Will Jack's work. It was slipshod to say the least. He wouldn't do Mae justice. And he had none of Sam's contacts. 'So, it's agreed?'

Bradley sighed. 'Seems so. There's a seat on a plane to Beijing leaving Canberra at two-ten tomorrow afternoon. That should give you time to make the necessary arrangements this end and to book accommodation. Now I need to give Will the news he won't be going after all.'

'He'll probably be delighted. Thanks. I'll get the red tape sorted out today. I won't need accommodation. I can put up with a mate from the old days. He can do a bit of digging for me, too. I won't let you down.'

'See you don't. I'm not altogether happy about this. Make sure you don't end up in detention, too. I know how you can be when you get your teeth into a story.'

'Thanks.' Sam grinned. He was already feeling the adrenaline rush of a new story, the anticipation of going into a situation which could be dangerous. It was something he'd thought never to feel again. But he remembered what he'd promised Liz. This time he'd be careful.

*

Once home and reunited with Marmaduke, Liz was at a loose end. She'd always enjoyed the solitude of her house, the house she'd chosen with such care all those years ago, the house she loved. But now, it seemed to echo with her disappointment. She finally sat down in the sun-filled kitchen.

Sensing her mood, Marmaduke leapt onto her lap and started to purr, his paws kneading her gently in sympathy. But Liz couldn't settle. She kept thinking of Sam travelling to China, not knowing what he'd find there, putting himself into danger when there was no need. But he clearly thought there was, and he'd gone. Now she was here with a whole week to fill before her shop was due to open again.

Liz knew she could change her mind, open up anyway. But what would be the point? Most of the inhabitants of Granite Springs chose to leave at this time of year, preferring to escape the heat and spend the holiday on the coast or overseas.

Suddenly she stood up, dislodging Marmaduke who landed on the floor, protesting loudly. She would go into the shop, but not to open it. It was the perfect time to do a stocktake. Sorting out her books and invoices would keep her busy and prevent her thinking about what was happening to Sam and still the little voice asking why the fate of this former colleague meant so much to him.

*

Liz was on her knees, checking a recent delivery from one of the major publishers when there was a knock on the glass door. Much to his annoyance, she'd left Marmaduke at home and she had been enjoying the silence and the familiar odour of new books. This was her life, her love. She didn't need the disruption of a man.

She pushed back a strand of hair which had fallen into her eyes and peered at the door to see a familiar face peering back at her.

Peta pointed to the door handle and mouthed something.

Annoyance at being disturbed warred with pleasure at seeing Peta. Liz rose to her feet and went to the door.

'What are you doing here? Where's Sam? I thought you two were spending this week in hibernation out at his place.' Peta stepped through the open door.

Liz locked it firmly behind her and turned to face her friend.

'What's the matter?'

Liz pushed back her hair again, realising her cheeks were wet. She hadn't been aware of the tears she'd been shedding while busy checking her inventory.

'Where's Sam?' Peta asked again.

'In China, or on his way there.'

Peta's eyes widened. 'What's he doing there?'

Liz sighed, all of her worries resurfacing, her stomach churning. 'A former colleague – a female one – has been detained, and he has gone to cover the story and see what he can do to help. I've no idea what he thinks he can do.'

'Oh, you must mean Mae Chan. We saw it on the news last night. She's a good reporter. Frank said what a pity it was. I guessed Sam would know her. But when did he leave? Your house was empty when I went round to feed Marmaduke this morning.'

'He went to Canberra after lunch to talk with his old boss. I guess he's not in China yet.' Liz pushed back her hair which seemed to have developed a life of its own today. 'But there was no way of stopping him. It was as if he became a different person. He was so determined.'

'Poor you. You were going to spend this week together having a lovely time. How was it meeting the daughter-in-law?'

Surprised at the change in subject, Liz reflected. 'It was difficult. She seemed to unbend a little when I gave her a copy of Lianne Moriarty's new release but clammed up again afterwards. I don't think I'm going to be her favourite person. But it may not matter.'

'What do you mean?'

'It's dangerous for Sam to go to China. This Mae woman has been detained. What if…? Oh, Peta, I'm so scared. What if it happens again? What if Sam doesn't come back? I don't think I could bear it.'

'Come here, you need a hug.' Peta put her arms around Liz and hugged her. 'You've been letting your imagination work overtime. I'm sure Sam knows how to take care of himself. He wouldn't do anything to put himself in danger. He's been there before, hasn't he?'

Liz nodded. 'So he says. He said he has contacts there who can help. But I can't stop worrying.' She wiped away a tear. 'Sorry.'

'You're not helping matters, sitting here feeling sorry for yourself, you need to be with people.'

'I'm keeping busy. I'm no company when I feel like this. I'll be fine. And I have Marmaduke for company. I don't need anyone else.' Somewhere in the back of her mind, was a little voice telling Liz she should have known better than to get involved with another man. It always led to disappointment. She'd thought Sam was different, but she was wrong. At the first opportunity, off he went to play the hero. Why did she fall for another man who wanted to be a hero?

'I don't agree. Marmaduke's a cat. You need to have people around you.' She paused, then, 'I know. We've been invited out to Jo Ford's for lunch on New Year's Day. You can come along. Jo won't mind another body. It'll do you good.'

'I don't think…'

'No excuses. We'll pick you up at eleven. Now, don't stay here too long. And stop worrying. You're just making yourself sick.' Peta gave Liz another hug and left, the door closing behind her with a snap.

Liz locked it and watched her walk off. Peta was a good friend, but she didn't understand. Then Liz remembered how Peta had lost her daughter under dreadful circumstances. Perhaps she did understand, perhaps she understood only too well.

Peta had fled Sydney for Granite Springs, much like Liz had fled Canberra. The town had wrapped them both in its comforting arms. But if something happened to Sam, where was there for Liz to flee to? Now Granite Springs held memories of Sam Walker and the good times they'd spent there.

Liz pulled herself together. She was behaving as if Sam had died and was never coming back, when he was probably still in Canberra. Peta was right. She was letting her imagination run wild with what ifs. Where was the stoicism that had got her through Dan's absence and subsequent death? She had a sudden memory of what the old grey-haired woman had told her, the words she'd thought of as rubbish. Hadn't she said something about a silver lining and happiness, about things coming right in the end? With all her heart Liz hoped she was right, but she knew she was grasping at straws.

Forty-three

Sam had forgotten how cold it would be. When he exited the airport a blast of icy air hit him, and he was almost blinded by a flurry of snow. He pulled up the zip on the parka he'd hastily managed to purchase before leaving Canberra and added the mask everyone was wearing to protect themselves from the pollution. Even though he'd been here before – several times – it was a shock after the clean air of Granite Springs and, even though it was early afternoon, the sky was dark. For a moment he regretted his decision, then choked back the thought and took a deep breath. He was here to do a job.

Exhausted after the seventeen-hour flight, Sam waited for his ride. Rick Sherwood was an American he'd bumped into at a shindig in the American Embassy several years earlier. He'd become a good mate and a useful source. Sam wasn't sure exactly what Rick did in Beijing and had learned not to ask, but he seemed to have good contacts and an ability to find information others couldn't.

A small car eased its way into a tiny space in front of him, and Rick's familiar face peered out.

'Thanks, mate. Good to see you.' Sam pulled the door closed behind him, glad to be out of the weather.

'Sam.' Rick shook his hand. 'Didn't expect to see you here again. Bad luck about your colleague.'

'Yeah.' It was more than bad luck. 'I'm hoping you can help with some info.'

'Not easy.' Rick's lips tightened as he wound his way through the traffic to his home. He lived in a one-bedroomed service apartment close to the centre of the city which Sam had visited on occasion. It would be a tight squeeze and he'd have to bunk down on the sofa, but he'd been glad when Rick agreed to put him up, relieved from the hassle of booking accommodation since he had no idea how long he'd be here. His visa allowed him to stay for two months, but he hoped a few days or weeks would be sufficient. Liz would certainly worry if he was away any longer.

Sam closed his eyes and thought about the previous night, the night spent in Canberra. When he'd called Liz to tell her the news of his flight, he'd guessed she was close to tears again and was tempted to pack up and drive back to spend one more night with her. But common sense prevailed. They'd already said their farewells, and he had a lot to do before his flight. It was the same reason he hadn't contacted Mitch or arranged to stay with him and Brooke. Instead, he'd booked into a hotel and, after calling Liz, had spent the evening mugging up on current Chinese politics and the news story Bradley told him Mae was covering.

'We're here.'

Sam opened his eyes to find they'd parked in a dark underground car park. Rick led him into a lift which took them up to his apartment.

'You probably want to grab a bit of shut-eye,' Rick said. 'You can pull out a trundle.' He gestured to the bedroom. 'I have to go out again, but I'll be back later. We can go out for a bite to eat and I'll tell you what I've been able to find out.'

He disappeared, and Sam was left to fall onto the trundle bed and catch up on some much-needed sleep.

*

When Rick returned, Sam had been awake for only a few minutes and was still feeling disoriented. But he quickly rose when he heard the apartment door open.

'Thanks for this, Rick,' he said, drawing a hand over his hair to smooth it down. 'Can we talk?'

'Sure. Let me brew coffee first. I bet you could do with some.'

'Thanks,' Sam said again. Coffee was exactly what he did need.

'Now,' he said, when they were seated in Rick's postage stamp sized kitchen with cups of strong black coffee, 'about Mae.'

'Your colleague is in deep shit,' Rick said frowning. 'She managed to get some officials offside with her questions, didn't know where to draw the line.' He shook his head. 'I'm afraid they want to make an example of her as a warning to other foreign journalists.'

A cold shiver ran up Sam's spine. 'Where's she being held? Can I see her?'

Rick shook his head again. 'No chance. From what I've been able to discover, even your consular officials are having trouble arranging to meet with her. The timing's not good.'

'Oh!' Sam's heart plummeted. But he hadn't come here only to turn tail and go back home again. 'What can I do? There must be something.'

'Might be best to get in touch with your embassy in the first place. Do you have any contacts there?'

'I might have.' Sam wasn't sure if his former embassy contact was still in Beijing. It had been a few years. 'But if they are having trouble... is there any other way?'

'I wouldn't risk it, or you might end up joining her. I'll keep ferreting away to see what I can unearth. But it'll only be information, not a visiting card.'

Sam felt deflated. To have come all the way to Beijing to hear this.

*

Next day, the first item on Sam's agenda was a visit to the embassy. After a frugal breakfast accompanied by more coffee, he made his way to the Chaoyang District. As he stood looking up at the flat-roofed building flying the Australian flag, he remembered the last time he was here. He had been reporting on a trade agreement and had been welcomed by both Australian and Chinese officials. Sam's gut told him he wouldn't be so popular this time.

He was right.

Fortunately, Adam Young was still on the embassy staff, but he wasn't pleased to see Sam.

'I thought you'd given this up,' he said, when the two had shaken hands and Adam had shown Sam into a small meeting room. 'It's not a good time for you to be here. You know about your colleague?'

'That's why I'm here. What can you tell me about Mae's detention?'

'Not a lot. Our guys are trying to see her, to provide her with consular assistance. But so far… It's not good, Sam. You journalists are not the flavour of the month here at the moment.'

Sam felt his shoulders droop. This was what Rick had already told him. 'Is there anyone here I can talk to… the person who's trying to see her?' Sam could feel himself becoming more and more agitated.

'No. That's what I'm trying to tell you. You shouldn't be here. I shouldn't be talking to you.'

Sam found himself being ushered out. He stood in the street, hands in his pockets, wondering what to do next. Then he sighed and made his way back to Rick's, stopping on the way for a serving of noodles and minced pork in a small eating house. But it was difficult to enjoy his food when he had no idea what was happening to Mae.

Sam was determined to keep trying, to keep visiting the embassy until he found out more about where Mae was being held and how she was holding up.

Forty-four

On New Year's morning, Liz awoke from another troubled sleep to find Marmaduke curled up beside her. Sam's calls had done nothing to allay her fears. He had arrived in Beijing and was staying with a man he described as an old mate and former good source of information, whatever that might mean. It all sounded very cloak and dagger to Liz, reminiscent of the John le Carré novels Dan used to read and which she sometimes flicked through.

She hadn't stayed up to see the new year in last night, instead going to bed early and trying to sleep. The sound of fireworks wakened her at midnight, and she had found it difficult to get back to sleep. When she did manage to drop off, she was beset with the same nightmares she'd experienced after Dan's death, but this time, the face was Sam's. She knew it was ridiculous. Sam wasn't in a war zone. But common sense had nothing to do with it. Liz had no control over the images that disturbed her dreams.

On automation, she rose and pulled on her robe. Then she fed Marmaduke and made breakfast, taking her tea and toast topped with almond butter and banana out to the courtyard where the native birds were singing to welcome the new year, and the sweet scent of jasmine filled her nostrils.

Liz wished she hadn't agreed to go to Jo Ford's new year celebration today. But Peta hadn't been in the mood to take a refusal. And it might not be too bad. Jo was a kind lady, and she lived on an acreage not unlike Sam's. Liz wondered if she'd ever stay at Sam's again, before giving herself a shake and trying to think more positive thoughts.

She checked the news on her phone as she did every morning. There was nothing new about Mae Chan, whose detention seemed to have lost the attention of the media in favour of New Year celebrations across the world. She was still sitting there when her phone rang and Sam's number popped up. She greedily pressed to accept the Facetime call.

Liz's mood lifted when she saw his smiling face on the screen. What had she been worried about? Here was Sam, alive and well.

'Happy New Year!' he said with a grin. 'Did you stay up to welcome it in? Wish I'd been with you.'

'I do, too.' Liz wished she'd taken time to shower, apply makeup and comb her hair. She should have known he'd call. She heard from him most days, sometimes a call, mostly a text or an email. He was keeping his word about staying in touch. He was in a city. He wasn't in a war zone, He wasn't Dan. She had to keep reminding herself. 'I went to bed early,' she said. He didn't need to know about her troubled sleep.

They chatted for a few minutes about mundane matters, his daily visits to the embassy, the different sights in the streets and the dishes he'd been eating. Liz knew he thought it best to avoid discussing the real reason for his trip or anything related to Mae Chan's detention in case of being overheard. Finally, he asked, 'What are you doing today?'

'I'm going to Jo and Col Ford's with Peta and Frank. Peta thought I needed to be with people.' Liz knew her annoyance showed in her voice.

'They're good people. Have a nice time and give them my best.'

'I will. I…' It suddenly occurred to Liz Peta and Frank would be picking her up in less than an hour. 'I should probably take a shower and get dressed before they arrive.'

Sam chuckled. 'I like seeing you in your robe like this, I can pretend we've just got out of bed and I'm sitting there with you enjoying coffee in the sunshine. It's perishing here.' He shivered.

Liz smiled, but his words brought an ache to her throat. She wished he was here, too. China was so far away. 'Be careful,' she said, knowing she was repeating herself. She said it every time they spoke.

Liz sat looking at the blank screen. It had been good to see Sam, to speak to him, but the call had seemed so short. She put her phone down and went inside, Marmaduke, who'd been lying in a pool of sunshine at her feet, following her in.

*

Liz peered out the window as the car bumped up the driveway at Yarran, Jo and Col Ford's property. Those strange creatures must be the alpacas she'd heard about. Unlike Peta, she wasn't a frequent visitor here, and hadn't seen the animals before. She'd heard Sam talk about them, debating whether to have them or goats on his acreage.

There were several cars already parked by the fence line. Liz hadn't expected this. She'd thought they'd be the only guests. Well, perhaps it might be easier with a crowd; she'd be able to blend in and avoid conversation. Normally voluble in social gatherings, Liz felt unable to be her usual self. She would have preferred to stay home. But then, she'd have given in to her worries about Sam. She could tell from the creases around his eyes and the way his mouth tightened from time to time, that things weren't going well for him.

With a glass of wine in her hand, Liz gravitated towards the house, finding a cane chair on the veranda to collapse into, from where she could watch the groups of people form and reform. She enjoyed this sort of people-watching but didn't get much opportunity for it. She was usually one of those who moved from group to group. It was almost like a dance, she mused, watching them move to and fro as if to some predetermined pattern.

'May I join you?'

Startled, Liz looked up to see a mop of white hair above a smiling face. It was that Magda woman, the one who'd made the prediction which kept rattling around in her mind. Tempted to tell her she wanted to be alone, but knowing it would be rude, Liz nodded and gazed off into the distance. She hoped the woman only wanted to rest and didn't intend to start a conversation.

The two women sat in silence for some time, Liz's thoughts in a whirl.

Then Magda spoke. 'You're going through a difficult time. I can see a journey, but it's not you who is travelling. You're worried about someone close to you. There's no need. He knows what the dangers are and will avoid them. He will return safely and with a solution for you. I'm sorry I can't tell you any more. I have no control over what I see.' She gave a wry grin. 'It's a blessing and a curse, this gift of mine. It's not something I ever wanted, but I hope I sometimes manage to help tortured souls.'

Liz was lost for words. Tortured soul? Was that how Magda saw her? 'I don't think…' she began.

'No, you don't need to say anything. I can tell you're not a believer, but your belief or otherwise doesn't change what I see.' She rose. 'I'll leave you in peace now. Do try to keep the faith everything will work out in the end.'

Liz blinked. Had she imagined it? No, the elderly woman was picking her way across the grass to join one of the groups Liz had been watching.

When she saw people beginning to eat, Liz left her secluded spot to rejoin Peta who was chatting to Fran and Owen's daughter, Pia.

'Where did you get to?' Peta asked. 'I was looking for you.'

'I found a quiet spot. It helped me to sit there watching everyone. I'm here now.' She managed a smile. 'How are you, Pia?' she asked the young woman. 'Did I hear there is to be a wedding?'

Pia blushed, and the women began to discuss Pia's forthcoming wedding. It was to be held early February on Fran and Owen's property. The wedding talk helped dispel Liz's mood and she happily joined in, remembering her excitement as her own wedding day approached. Pia had had a difficult time before landing in Granite Springs pregnant, having been abandoned by her child's father. Tor was now growing up, and Pia had formed a relationship with a new vet in town, much to her dad's delight. 'He's hoping to obtain free veterinary care for his goats,' Fran said, chuckling.

The afternoon over, Liz rode home again with Peta, Frank and Lily. She remained quiet on the drive, the memory of Magda's words running through her mind. But this time, she didn't dismiss them as rubbish. This time, the old woman had been right about Liz going through a difficult time, she'd been right about someone close to her travelling. Please God she was right about him returning safely, too.

Forty-five

Sam had been in Beijing for several weeks now and had made little progress. As with every other trip he'd made here, it took him time to acclimatise, to become accustomed to the difference in temperature and culture, to the lack of personal space when he was out in public, to the curious stares from people around him, to the absence of queues, to the apparent lack of road rules making crossing the road a nightmare.

He missed Liz and the peace and relative conflict-free atmosphere of Granite Springs. Thank goodness Jason and Tim were managing to keep the paper going. It was lucky he had only planned slimmer editions at this time of year. Some days he wondered why he was here. Then he'd make another trip to the Australian Embassy and he'd remember. But the lack of progress was frustrating.

Adam had finally introduced him to a couple of his colleagues, and the embassy had been as helpful as it could with the officials agreeing to meet with him, even though they must regard him as just another journalist seeking a story. He'd known before he arrived that there was little chance of him seeing Mae, but he had to try. The most disheartening part was the lack of any news about her, where she was being held, or what any potential charges might be.

Outside the embassy he was met with blank looks when he tried to ask questions. But he had managed to speak with Mae Chan's lawyer. Though he wasn't sure how much the inscrutable Chinese legal practitioner had understood of what he'd told him about Mae's assignment and his own relationship with her.

But Rick had assured him all was not lost, and he was continuing to seek information and do what he could, so Sam was trying to be patient and managing to file reports back to Canberra.

This weekend was Chinese New Year and he'd reluctantly agreed when Rick insisted they join in the festivities, assuring him no one would be available to talk with him till it was over.

On the most important holiday in China, there were lots of celebrations to choose from. First, Rick led Sam to visit a temple fair, explaining these were originally related to the religious activities of the temples, but they had become shopping markets and entertainment events, with the religious activities having become less important.

Once there, Sam found they were part of a crowd of people, many wearing red – a sign of celebration and good luck. The Chinese also believed the colour scared away spirits of bad fortune. It brought to mind his red shirt for the choir. He'd just taken his shirt off, about to change into the red one, when Liz had appeared in just a towel. And the towel had fallen. And… He gave himself a shake.

Sam had never seen so many people in one place. At one point he almost lost Rick in the crush. Along with Rick, he watched dragon and lion dances, demonstrations of traditional arts and crafts and sampled delicious foods from the many stalls. But he found it difficult to join the mood of celebration all around him, with thoughts of Mae always uppermost in his mind.

There was a sea of red everywhere, not only in people's clothing. There were flags, banners, lines of hanging lanterns and flower displays, so bright they almost hurt Sam's eyes. This was a celebration such as he'd never experienced. Almost deafened by the noise from excited people and the firecrackers going off everywhere, Sam was glad when Rick suggested they try to find a quieter spot.

But he soon found quieter was only relative, as he and Rick squeezed into the corner of an eating house to sample a hot pot lunch which Rick assured him was another New Year tradition.

By the time evening arrived and they again joined the crowds watching a magnificent display of fireworks, Sam was ready to drop. But he manfully followed Rick until his companion finally decided to draw the day to a close. If this was an example of how the Chinese celebrated the first day of their new year, Sam couldn't imagine how they could last for two weeks.

'The first day is always the most crowded,' Rick said, when they were back in his small apartment, the door closed against the lights and noise. 'But it's so spectacular I wanted you to experience it.'

'Thanks. I'm glad I did, though I don't think I'd like to do it again in a hurry. While I loved the colour, the entertainment and the food, I think I must be getting too old for those sorts of crowds. I just want it all to be over so I can get back to finding out what's happening to Mae.'

'Patience,' Rick advised him. But Sam had all but run out of patience. He wanted to find Mae. To see her free again. To go back home. He thought longingly of his twenty acres, the empty paddocks with only a few sheep grazing there quietly. And Liz, waiting for him.

*

Revitalised from a sound night's sleep, Sam was feeling better when Rick joined him in the kitchen next morning.

'Sleep well?' Rick asked with a grin.

'Like a log. I thought I might go back to the embassy today.'

'I wouldn't bother. Like everyone else in Beijing, I expect they'll be taking a holiday. Better to do some sightseeing.'

'No, I think I'll stay here.' Sam wanted to write the experiences of the previous day while they were fresh in his mind. He could combine his impressions of the day with reflections on how New Year was celebrated in other countries across the world, citing examples from places he'd visited, perhaps even call on some local Granite Springs family traditions.

'Right. I have to go out. Catch up later. Maybe we can go out to eat tonight again.'

'Sounds good.'

Sam had completed his piece on the celebrations and was fixing himself some tea and puzzling what he could do next that he hadn't tried to do already, when Rick burst through the door, a crazy grin on his face and a wild expression in his eyes.

'We've done it!' he yelled. 'She's to be released!'

'What?'

'Mae Chan. The government have decided to release her as some sort of Chinese New Year gesture.'

'Is this for real? Do they often do this?'

'I haven't heard of it before. But I do know your government has been trying all sorts to get her released. I've greased a few palms, too. It's paid off.'

Sam gazed at Rick sceptically. Had his friend really had a hand in Mae's release? It was difficult to believe, but Rick led such an odd life Sam could believe anything of him. He didn't know why he was in China, what he did, if he even operated within the law, but this was incredible news.

Forty-six

Liz couldn't believe how long Sam had been gone. Even though she heard from him every day, spoke with him on a regular basis, it was surreal. He wasn't here. And she had no idea when he'd be back. It was easy to become downhearted, to think this would go on for ever. Then she would remember Magda and her prediction he'd return safely and her spirits would lift – for a few moments.

Last night had been the first choir meeting of the year and she'd missed seeing Sam across the room, remembering their post-choir visits to Pavarotti's for coffee or a glass of prosecco.

She shook her head. Worrying about Sam wasn't going to change anything and would only make her miserable. Tonight, there was to be another meeting of the protest group's committee. They'd had word the planning committee had already met and prepared its report for the next council meeting. They wanted to be ready to submit an appeal if the decision went against them.

She ate a quick meal of leftover chicken and salad before heading to The Bean Sprout Café where the meeting was being held.

Most of the others were already there when Liz arrived so she was able to slip into a seat without a fuss. She shook her head at Peta's raised eyebrows from across the room. She knew what her friend wanted to know – had there been any news of Sam's return?

With Sam gone, Peta's company had been a godsend. Although her friendship with Judy was more longstanding, and Judy knew Sam, it was to Peta she'd turned for comfort. She wasn't sure why. Maybe because Peta had lost someone close to her, too, maybe because she lived nearby, while Judy lived out of town. For whatever reason, Peta had proven to be her rock.

'We're all here, now. Let's get started.' Frank's voice silenced the chatter which had been going on around her. 'It's taken a long time, but I think we're getting closer to some sort of resolution. I believe Danny has some news for us. Danny.'

Danny Slater cleared his throat. 'It's not good. I managed to have a word with Dad today. He broke with his habit and showed me the agenda for the next council meeting. The development proposal is the major item of business. He said he hasn't seen the report but had no reason to believe it will go in our favour. We need to be prepared and have our appeal ready.'

There was a general murmur of despair. It wasn't what any of them wanted to hear. Liz felt her heart drop. What would be left for her in Granite Springs if she lost both Sam and her shop? It didn't bear thinking about. Meeting Sam had given her a new reason to live, but without him, without The Reading Corner, what would she do? She was too old to start again as she had when Dan died. She'd be fifty her next birthday.

Damn Sam, she thought. If he had agreed to support the group, they might not be in this situation and if he hadn't chosen to run off to China, he'd be right here with her. It wasn't fair. But it was easy to blame Sam. He was only acting according to his principles. Why did she always have to get involved with men with principles?

Liz was so caught up in her thoughts, she missed the rest of the discussion, coming to only when she heard Frank say, 'So we're agreed – Danny and I will draft out a format for the appeal for discussion at our next meeting which will be after the council meeting?' He looked around the small committee for agreement.

Liz joined in the assent. It seemed the only way to go. But she hoped Danny was wrong and the next meeting would be one of celebration. Hadn't Magda said there was happiness ahead? She grimaced. Now she was putting her faith in the predictions of the woman whose words she'd been so quick to dismiss. She must be really desperate.

As the others started to leave, Peta slipped to Liz's side. 'You look like you need some company. Frank will be tied up here with Danny for a bit. Come back with me for coffee and we can talk.'

About to refuse, Liz thought of the empty house that waited for her with only Marmaduke for company. 'Thanks,' she said.

*

Lily was asleep when Liz and Peta reached the Beatties' home. Peta paid the student who'd been minding Lily and saw her off, while Liz made herself comfortable in the kitchen.

'Now,' Peta said when she'd made them cups of camomile tea, both deciding it would be more calming than coffee, 'how are you coping? Sam's been gone a while now.'

'I didn't think it would be so long. He calls when he can, but I know it's difficult for him. He has to be careful. I want him to be careful. He sent through some photos of Chinese New Year. He and this friend of his went to some of the celebrations.'

'Still no news of his colleague? Her detention seems to have dropped off the news here.'

'He doesn't mention her. I don't think he can, in case…' She frowned. 'It's especially difficult not knowing what's going on. I know why he's there, but he can't mention anything about it to me. I sometimes feel like I'm in a bad movie.'

'I wish I could say something to help.' Peta gazed at her helplessly. 'It must be so hard for you.'

'Thanks.' Liz clutched her cup in both hands. 'It's enough you're here. You're a good friend, Peta. Sometimes I feel so alone. I never did before. There are times when I curse that I met Sam, that I've become dependent on him, on his presence. I've lived alone for twenty years, never needed anyone. Now, after only a few months, I feel bereft because he's gone.' She looked down into her cup, her eyes moistening. She hadn't cried so much since Dan died.

'But he's coming home.'

'I hope so. But you hear such terrible things – people like Mae Chan detained, other journalists having visas revoked, being prevented from leaving. 'Oh, Peta, what if…?'

'Sam will be fine,' Peta said, but Liz thought she heard a hint of doubt in her voice.

'You two still here?' Frank entered the kitchen and gave Peta a kiss on the cheek. 'How are things, Liz? Still no news of Sam coming back?'

'That's what we've been discussing, Frank. I've been trying to tell Liz all will be well,' Peta said.

'Of course it will. We can't do without the editor of our local paper,' Frank said, cheerfully, then, seeing Liz's strained expression added, 'He's not stupid, Liz. He's been there before. He's used to being in sticky situations. It's natural for you to worry, but I'm sure he'll come through it.'

'Thanks, Frank. Thanks, both of you.'

'You're not drinking herbal tea, are you?' He sniffed at the contents of Peta's cup. 'How about a glass of wine?' He reached into the fridge.

'No, thanks, Frank, I should be going.' Liz drained her cup.

Marmaduke rose from the sofa to greet Liz when she walked in, rubbing against her ankles just as Liz's phone rang.

'Sam!' she said, her voice filled with relief. She sank down on the sofa, grasping the phone as if it was a lifeline.

It was a bad line, with lots of crackles and echoes, but she could make out the few words that mattered.

'Liz, it's over. I'm coming home.'

Forty-seven

Sam leant back in the airline seat, glad it was finally over. He was left with a feeling of satisfaction very unlike how he'd felt returning home from his overseas trips in earlier years, from previous assignments. Though he couldn't know for sure, he might have been able to be of some assistance, might even have had a hand in saving Mae's life. Though it was more likely it had nothing to do with anything he, the embassy, or even Rick had done. It was all due to some quirk of fate, the decision of some unknown Chinese official.

Sam's mind wandered to Granite Springs and to Liz. He'd been able to stay in contact with her all the time he was away, but he hadn't been able to call as often as he wanted and communication was difficult, He hadn't been able to tell her much. He hoped she understood. While it had been hard leaving her, this was something he felt he needed to do. It could so easily have been him in Mae's place.

Liz was still concerned about the plan to tear down those Main Street shops. He sighed. He knew she wanted him to do something, to use The Advertiser to promote their cause, but he couldn't give up on the vow he'd made to himself.

Sam closed his eyes. He'd hoped the feature articles on the shops would satisfy her and her fellow protesters, but it didn't seem to have had any effect. Sure, people were interested in knowing the background of places they shopped every day, but that's where it stopped.

He was almost asleep when he opened his eyes with a start. That was it – the history of the shops. He went over in his mind the last few interviews he'd conducted. One of the guys had brought out photos of what the street had looked like in the early nineteen hundreds, and Sam had been surprised they'd stood so long ago. They were of historical significance and as such should be preserved and heritage listed.

He punched the air with delight. He'd found the answer, the way to satisfy Liz and her fellow protesters without compromising his principles. And he'd be doing the town a service, too. He couldn't wait to do more research and tell Liz his news. But why hadn't they thought of this before now? It was such an obvious solution.

The rest of the flight passed quickly. Unable to sleep, Sam used his iPad to research how to get a place listed on the state and national heritage registers. By the time the plane touched down in Canberra, Sam was equipped with the information he needed for the group to submit an application to the state historic preservation office, and on how the properties would be evaluated.

He couldn't wait to pass on the information to Frank Beattie and his committee. And, of course, this changed things for The Advertiser. While unwilling to engage the paper in local politics, submission of the row of shops for inclusion on the heritage register was a news item he'd be glad to publish.

Sam was anxious to get off the plane, to see Liz again. It had been too long. He fumed impatiently as the routine arrival procedures seemed to take longer than usual, but finally, he made his way along the aisle, out of the plane, across the tarmac and into the airport.

Liz was waiting for him. The sight of her smiling face was balm to his soul. Regardless of the crowds of people, he dropped his bag and threw his arms around her, the scent of her hair reminding him of what he'd been missing. He hugged her tightly till she pulled away, laughing.

'I'm pleased to see you, too, but...' She glanced around and gestured to the other travellers being greeted by friends and family. No one was paying any attention to them.

'You must be tired,' she said, once Sam had collected his luggage and they were leaving the airport, arm in arm. 'It may be presumptuous of me, but I've booked a hotel room. I thought you mightn't want to drive home right away.' She looked at him tentatively, as if afraid she might have been wrong.

Sam sighed with relief. Now the flight was over, now he was back with Liz, all he wanted to do was take her to bed then catch up with his sleep. 'What a wonderful idea. My car's here, somewhere.' He tried to remember where he left it, his mind clearing as they entered the multilevel car park enabling him to find the Range Rover.

'See you at the hotel,' Liz whispered, kissing him on the cheek and walking off to her own car.

*

Where was he? Sam's eyes slowly opened to discover he was in a brightly lit room, larger than the one he'd been living in for the past few weeks. It took him a few minutes to remember he was back in Australia, in Canberra, with Liz. And Mae was free. The relief was enormous.

He'd been so exhausted when he reached their hotel room, he'd fallen asleep before... He looked around the room to see Liz curled up in a chair by the window, reading.

'You're awake.' She smiled. He had never forgotten her smile. The memory of that smile was what had kept him sane all those weeks they were apart, that and their infrequent calls. 'You must be hungry.'

At her words, Sam realised he couldn't remember when he'd last eaten, discounting the airline food which he never enjoyed. But first... He opened his arms. Liz dropped her book and flew into them.

When they extricated themselves sometime later, having assuaged one type of hunger, Sam remembered Liz's earlier question, and his own response. 'Do you still want something to eat?'

Liz snuggled against him. 'Why don't we order room service? I don't think I have the energy to get ready to go out anywhere.'

'Good idea.' Another reason he loved her. Olga would have insisted on getting dressed up, going to a restaurant and spoiling the mood of this moment. He lay back on the bed watching with pleasure as Liz picked up the phone and ordered two meals. Then she fetched two miniature bottles of champagne from the fridge and two glasses from where they were stylishly displayed on the benchtop and came back to bed. A woman after his own heart.

'I'm so glad you're back safely,' Liz said, when they'd eaten the hotel food, drunk the champagne and were once again lying in each other's arms. 'I was so afraid. I couldn't have borne to have anything happen to you. Not after...' Her eyes moistened.

Sam put a finger under her chin, moved at this sign she cared so much for him. He'd hoped in time she would come to love him, but he'd always been afraid, worried he couldn't match up to her dead husband. Dan Pender had been a war hero. Sam was a mere journalist.

He looked into her eyes, unable to believe what he saw there.

'I wasn't in any danger,' he murmured, his lips close to hers.

'But you could have been. Mae Chan was reporting on another journalist and she was detained. You could have been, too. I've been reading about journalists being detained, many of them for months, years even. Then there are others not permitted to leave. No wonder I was worried.'

'Does that mean you care for me... a little?' He held his breath.

'Of course I do. I wouldn't be here if I didn't. At first I thought you and Mae...'

Sam smiled. 'No. Mae's a lovely woman, a good journalist, a colleague. But there was never anything between us. She's married. Her husband lectures at ANU. I did what I'd do for any of my former colleagues if I thought I could help. I felt guilty as it would have been my assignment if I'd stayed.' He was touched at the thought she'd been jealous of Mae. It emboldened him to say the words he'd been longing to say ever since they met.

Sam stroked Liz's cheek. 'I love you, Liz Pender. I want to spend the rest of my life with you. I promise I'll never leave you again... ever.'

Forty-eight

On the day of the long-awaited council meeting, Liz awoke to the sound of kookaburras, and to Marmaduke yowling outside the bedroom window. She stretched luxuriously and turned to the man beside her, filled with a sense of gratitude at the way her life had turned out.

The past two weeks had been wonderful, more than making up for the week she'd lost after Christmas. When Sam suggested she spend some time at the property, Liz had initially hesitated. But he'd soon managed to persuade her and Marmaduke to join him, and she was glad of the opportunity to spend quality time with him.

So, instead of the one week together they'd planned for after Christmas, she'd now been here for two and dreaded the thought of returning home.

'I don't want you to go,' Sam murmured, putting his arms around her and pulling her in for a kiss. 'I may keep you here for ever.'

Liz laughed and slipped out of his arms. 'I do still live in town, remember,' she said. 'I'm only here because...'

'I know, I know. I have to be grateful for small mercies. But you know I want you to make this your home.' Sam nuzzled her neck, sending shivers up and down her spine. 'I love having you here, and Marmaduke seems to like it, too.'

Liz was torn. She loved it here, too, and the prospect of returning to her house in town only reminded her of how empty it had felt when Sam was gone. 'Perhaps,' she said with a smile. 'Now, we really should go. My shop won't open itself.'

'Pick you up for the council meeting tonight?' Sam asked, as they were getting into their cars.

'Course. Wouldn't miss it.'

*

Since he returned to Granite Springs, Sam had been busy. He'd met first with Frank who'd initially dismissed his news.

'It won't work,' he said, his forehead creasing. 'Roy tried that. Seems we don't meet the criteria.'

'He was wrong.' Sam couldn't believe the old newsagent had led the group astray. But subsequent digging on his part uncovered a link between Roy and the developer who'd bribed the newsagent with promises of compensation if he agreed to give the group a false report.

While Frank worked on the submission to the New South Wales and National Heritage Registers, Sam produced a double page spread for The Advertiser. The article lauded the efforts of a small group of concerned community members who'd taken it upon themselves to dig into the earlier articles published by the paper. As a result, Sam wrote, the unique line of shops in Main Street were now awaiting confirmation as being deemed historically significant, thus putting paid to any attempt to have them demolished.

The town hall was packed, the article in The Advertiser having encouraged the community to turn out in force. Mayor Gordon Slater stood up and called for silence.

'It's pleasing to see so many interested members of the community here tonight,' he said. 'I must remind you that you are here as observers only and no comments or observations will be tolerated. As you know, the main item of business tonight is the report of the planning committee on the proposed development on Main Street.'

There was a general murmuring which evoked a glare from him.

'I now call upon Bill Jenkins, chair of the planning committee, to speak.'

A small balding man rose to his feet, shuffling a bundle of papers. 'Mr Mayor, ladies and gentlemen, the committee have considered this proposal very carefully and believe it to have some merit…'

There was a collective groan.

'However, in the light of information which has recently come to hand – I believe we have to thank a concerned group of residents and shopkeepers for it.' He glanced up to where Liz and Sam were seated alongside Frank and Peta. He cleared his throat. 'In the light of this information that the line of shops in question is currently being considered for inclusion in the New South Wales Historical Register, we have no option but to deny the development application at this stage.'

He sat down to a roar of applause.

Liz high-fived Frank, then Peta and hugged Sam. She barely heard the rest of the meeting proceedings, thrilled with the result of their efforts and delighted it was Sam who found their solution. He was a good man. She'd known that all along, she thought, conveniently forgetting her initial opinion of him.

'Congratulations, Sam. It's all your doing,' Peta said as they left the building. 'Coming for a celebratory drink? A few of us are going to the pub.'

Liz looked at Sam. 'I don't think so. I want to get home.'

'And where *is* home these days? I hear you've moved out of town. Is it a permanent move?'

Liz felt Sam tense beside her. She hesitated, then replied, 'Home is where Sam is, so I guess it is.' She smiled up at Sam, and it was as if the rest of the world disappeared.

Sam waited till they were back on the property. Then he produced a bottle of champagne. 'I think we have something to celebrate, don't you?'

'The council meeting result?' Liz asked, knowing in her heart it was more than that. She'd seen the expression in Sam's eyes when she'd made that comment to Peta. Although Sam had said he loved her in the hotel in Canberra, he hadn't mentioned it again. They'd both been so busy since then, but she'd be lying to herself if she said it hadn't crossed her mind – she'd thought of little else.

Now, Liz's heart was beating so loudly she thought Sam must hear it. She wanted this moment to last for ever. She looked into the eyes she'd come to love, the face that had become so familiar to her.

Sam hugged her and rained kisses on her forehead, eyelids and cheeks before his lips finally found hers. 'You will marry me, won't you?' he asked, when they came up for breath.

Marriage? She hadn't thought that far ahead. What would it mean to be married to this man, to wake up with him every morning, to live in his house on this peaceful acreage? 'I will,' she said, knowing all that it entailed. Not only the closeness and the peace she'd known in the past two weeks. She'd also be inheriting a stepson and granddaughter – and a step-daughter-in-law who might not approve of their relationship.

She thought back to what Magda had said. The older woman had been right. Sam had returned safely. The difficult times were over, and happiness was within her grasp. She was finally going to have the life she dreamt of.

The End

If you've enjoyed Liz's story, I'd really appreciate it if you could leave a review. A few words will suffice, no need for a lengthy review. It will mean a lot to me and help other readers find my books.

It is with some sadness that, with this book, I say farewell to Granite Springs – at least for now. I've become so attached to the town and its characters it's hard for me to move on.

But move on I must and in my next book I return to my native Scotland. A Mother's Story, which begins during WW2.

A lost child. A mother's grief. A daughter's journey. What is the chain that links three women's lives?

In Scotland, in1941, as World War 2 increases in ferocity, Rhona Begg goes against her parents' wishes and enlists in the ATS—a decision that brings with it heart-breaking consequences. After the war, weighed down with regret and grief, Rhona receives news that has the power to change her life.

On the other side of the world, in Australia, Nell Duncan worries about her husband who is fighting in the Far East. When she receives the dreaded news that he is missing in action, her world collapses. The end of the war brings changes to Nell's life, but her dream of bearing a child is no longer possible and she grieves for what might have been.

In 1971, when Joy Baker gives birth to her daughter, she begins the journey to discover her ancestry. What she finds shocks her to the core and propels her on a journey to the land of her birth.

Three women. Three mothers. Three lives connected forever.

From wartime Scotland to present day Australia, A Mother's Story is a sweeping family saga filled with emotion.

You can order here getbook.at/AMothersStory

From the Author

Dear Reader,

First, I'd like to thank you for choosing to read *The Life She Dreams*. I hope you've enjoyed Liz's story.

Having spent seven years teaching university and living in an Australian country town, and on an acreage, I've enjoyed writing a series with a rural setting and drawing on my experience of living in the country – with goats – and teaching in university. This is the ninth book in the series set in the fictional country town of Granite Springs and I'm thrilled by the response of you, my readers, to this series, how you tell me my characters are real people you'd love to have as friends. I feel they're my friends too, and they've become a part of my life.

If you'd like to stay up to date with my new releases and special offers you can sign up to my reader's group.

You can sign up here https://mailchi.mp/f5cbde96a5e6/maggiechristensensreadersgroup

I'll never share your email address, and you can unsubscribe at any time. You can also contact me via Facebook Twitter or by email. I love hearing from my readers and will always reply.

Thanks again.

MaggieC

Acknowledgements

As always, this book could not have been written without the help and advice of a number of people.

Firstly, my husband Jim for listening to my plotlines without complaint, for his patience and insights as I discuss my characters and storyline with him, for his patience and help with difficult passages and advice on my male dialogue, and for being there when I need him.

John Hudspith, editor extraordinaire for his ideas, suggestions, encouragement and attention to detail.

Jane Dixon-Smith for her patience and for working her magic on my beautiful cover and interior.

My thanks also to early readers of this book –Helen, Maggie and Louise, for their helpful comments and advice. Also to Annie of *Annie's books at Peregian* and Graeme of *The Bookshop at Caloundra* for their ongoing support.

And a special thanks to Stella Quinn for suggesting *The Puggles* for my children's music group. For those who don't know, Puggles are baby echidnas.

And to all of my readers. Your support and comments make it all worthwhile. I'm thrilled you enjoy my more mature characters and that the situations they find themselves in resonate with you.

About the Author

After a career in education, Maggie Christensen began writing contemporary women's fiction portraying mature women facing life-changing situations. Her travels inspire her writing, be it her trips to visit family in Scotland, in Oregon, USA or her home on Queensland's beautiful Sunshine Coast. Maggie writes of mature heroines coming to terms with changes in their lives and the heroes worthy of them. Her writing has been described by one reviewer as *like a nice warm cup of tea. It is warm, nourishing, comforting and embracing.*

From her native Glasgow, Scotland, Maggie was lured by the call 'Come and teach in the sun' to Australia, where she worked as a primary school teacher, university lecturer and in educational management. Now living with her husband of over thirty years on Queensland's Sunshine Coast, she loves walking on the deserted beach in the early mornings and having coffee by the river on weekends. Her days are spent surrounded by books, either reading or writing them – her idea of heaven!

Maggie can be found on Facebook, Twitter, Goodreads, Instagram or on her website.

https://www.facebook.com/maggiechristensenauthor
https://twitter.com/MaggieChriste33
https://www.goodreads.com/author/show/8120020.Maggie_Christensen
https://www.instagram.com/maggiechriste33/
http://maggiechristensenauthor.com/

www.ingramcontent.com/pod-product-compliance
Lightning Source LLC
Chambersburg PA
CBHW020134120726
47903CB00007B/2244